Charlene Touby

Charlene Touby

Sweet Olive Tree

Sweet Olive Tree

By

Charlene Touby

Winston-Salem
2016

Copyright 2016 by Charlene Touby

First print edition of Sweet Olive Tree published
February, 2016

Manufactured in the United States of America
ISBN 978-0-9730116-3-0

For all the amazing people in my life and especially for Laurel and Michael whose endless support and love help me start each day with hope.

—Charlene Touby

Introduction

The pale white moon majestically glided across the heavens, slowly turning pumpkin orange. As it floated inside the curved edge of the earth's shadow, the moon metamorphosed into a globe of eerie blood red, signaling the climax of the lunar eclipse. The moon illuminated the black heavens with searing light. The tribal drums boomed louder and louder, jarring the stillness of the night. One by one, the disciples jumped up, wildly dancing and chanting to the rhythm of the music. Cymbals started clinking softly and then reverberated into a crash of resonating sound. The blustery weather became a vortex of power, causing gnarled oak trees to bend frenetically. The dancers swirled faster and faster until they fell to the ground with exhaustion. A bolt of lightning cracked the dark sky, illuminating the earth with white tentacles of light. A torrent of rain swamped the ground, followed by the crash of thunder. Hailstones bounced and scattered in all directions as they pelted the ground with large balls of ice.

The flock of spectators sat speechless, mesmerized by the dazzling panorama their Loas shared with them. Dressed in white and dripping wet, the worshippers ran for cover to the old wooden church waiting for the storm to abate before walking outside again to a large wooden altar illuminated by candles. They seated themselves on the cold, wet ground and watched silently as Maman Sophia raised her arms up to the sky.

The worshippers chanted jubilantly, "Maman Sophia, we are all your children; we are here to celebrate the blood moon with you tonight."

Sophia's vibrant voice reached out to the assembly. "Papa Moses and I stand in front of our altar to welcome our family to the night of the blood moon," she said, while joining hands with her husband. She stood tall and regal in her long white gown, her silver hair falling to her shoulders, and her honey-colored skin glistening with perspiration as she enchanted the crowd with her glowing smile.

Papa Moses raised his dark sinewy arms and said in his booming baritone, "My children, we meet in love tonight. It is our custom to

1

gather together at the time of the first moon in January and renew our vows to worship our Voodoo religion and our Loas and spirits." He pointed to an old wooden church with a tall wooden cross behind the altar "This is where our masters required us to worship their religion."

The crowd parted and bowed as a small wizened woman made her way to the altar. Her white garments and the white turban she wore on her head accentuated her ebony skin. She walked erectly and spryly despite her age and frail body. Papa Joe and Maman Sophia bowed to her in unison.

"Welcome Queen Seri. It is an honor to have you celebrate the blood moon with us tonight."

Queen Seri responded in a strong voice accented with French, "I am happy to be here with you, *ma famille*, tonight. I just returned from Haiti and I could feel my Loas calling me to join you on this sacred night. I am happy to see so many worshippers who have gathered here on this January evening. The air is frosty and damp, but I feel the heat of your passion."

Queen Seri stood before the altar and smiled at the expectant faces of the joyful supplicants. "Our people exited the ship from Africa hungry and frightened. A priest welcomed them to the new land. They could not understand what the priest was saying. All they understood was that after being on a steamy, stinking boat for months, the holy water he sprinkled on them cooled them down. It was months before they understood what was going on around them. Every Sunday the priest summoned our people to this little church where he spoke to them in a strange tongue.

"In Africa our people had been worshiping our Gods and Loas for thousands of years. Their spirits accompanied them in their hearts to this new country and quietly they banded at night and worshipped together. The priests found out about our spirits and forbid the devotees from gathering in prayer.

"But our elders persevered and found ways to worship their gods and still remain alive. By uniting the saints of the white man with our African gods, Voodoo was born. When our people sat in church praying to the saints, they were also praying to our Loas."

Queen Seri turned to Papa Joe and said, "Please share with our children the mystique of our religion."

Papa Joe turned to the altar and proudly picked up a brightly decorated statue of Saint Barbara. "This is Santa Barbara, who is also

Chango. Chango helps us with the affairs of our family, health and prosperity." He continued, pointing to statues of Saint Anthony, Saint Lazarus and Our Lady of Charity. "We have joined all of these saints and made them as one with our Loas. We are proud to practice Voodoo. Tonight we reach out to our gods, our dead, and our Loas to be united as one with them."

Queen Seri stepped forward. "We must give our spirits food and drink so they will bless us. I can hear them calling out to me in the darkness and telling me of their great thirst and hunger."

Maman Sophia handed a large, plump white chicken to Papa Moses who quickly grabbed the chicken's head with one hand and deftly slit its throat with a machete. Papa Joe chanted loudly as he sprinkled the chicken's warm blood on the beautifully ornamented saints on the altar.

One by one, the worshippers came forward, their arms full of ripe oranges, bananas, red grapes, sweet potatoes, and black beans, which they carefully placed next to the blood spattered saints. Maman positioned bottles of dark rum on the altar. She began chanting as she opened the sweet liquor and generously doused the fragrant amber liquid on all of the saints. Her chanting became more intense as she placed an offering of a thick black cigar in front of each saint and then handed Queen Seri a bottle of the nectar of the gods and a large black cigar.

She beckoned the crowd to come forward as she began distributing rum and cigars to the worshippers who called out to her, waving their arms anxiously in the air to ensure they'd receive their share.

Maman cautioned the five hundred or so disciples, "Pray passionately and honor the gods and Loas so that they would bring luck and joy to everyone's life."

Papa Moses made his way to the altar. He held a huge black snake up in the air with both his hands as he chanted, "Bon Dieu, come to us tonight."

He gently kissed the serpent's head and draped it around his neck and bulky chest. He started to sing an African ballad with fervor in his voice, while the snake remained peacefully inert. He placed the snake around Queen Seri's neck and it slithered over her tiny body, winding itself around her waist like a huge black belt. She continued to drink her rum from the bottle with one hand and smoke her cigar with the other, as she spun around to the beat of the music.

3

Melody filled the night and the earth seemed to resonate with the sounds of eerie music. The enthused crowd began to undulate and drink with abandon. The smoke from the cigars created a hypnotic gray haze around the supplicants and the night pulsed with magic. The snake was passed lovingly from worshipper to worshipper as they whirled around. Their movements, the drums, the music, became more passionate. The congregation stomped on the ground, shouting loudly as they poured the thick sticky rum over themselves, their neighbors and everything around them. They sucked the smoke from cigars as they merrily drank.

The group collectively became more boisterous as they gyrated and spun, wantonly calling to their Loas to quickly come and ride them in possession of their minds and bodies. Parishioners dropped to the ground, their bodies limp as puppets when Loas seized them, causing them to shake, scream and writhe. Some pulled at their clothing and hair and still others lay motionless on the ground as if dead.

As the spirits rode them, the enchanted spoke and even screamed in tongues and in the language of the Loas. Some had strange visions and others heard messages from their departed loved ones. The lucky ones dreamed of a beautiful new world that awaited them.

Mama Sophia fell to the ground and smelled the scent of flowers from the sweet olive trees. This was the scent of Paris, her sweet godchild. She was given a mental image of Paris, but it was not of the happy carefree girl who had grown into a beautiful serene woman. No. This apparition of Paris was a lost soul, weeping alone, in pain. The vision was so clear that Mama Sophia could see large bruises on the creamy white skin above Paris' forehead, and on her cheek. She knew Paris was in great danger.

"Our Lady of Mercy, Legba, I beg of you keep Paris safe," she implored. The specter of Paris' pale face haunted her while she floated into another dimension.

Chapter 1

Paris was having a beautiful dream. She was on the steps of St. Louis Cathedral and Doyle was standing next to her whispering, "Paris Marie Viverette, will you marry me?"

"We are married," she murmured back softly.

She felt Doyle's arms around her, holding her body to his very tightly. He was kissing her passionately. The heat of his body permeated her whole being. She gasped in pleasure, when suddenly she felt his body turn cold. Her gasp of pleasure turned to a scream of pain as she realized his hands were squeezing her neck.

She screamed, "No! No, please stop!" Her body went limp as she felt a piercing pain across the side of her face as Doyle pummeled her viciously across her face with his fist.

"Paris!" she heard her husband call out as she felt Doyle painfully shaking her shoulders. "Stop screaming, have you gone mad?" he said angrily. "I have to be in court tomorrow! I need my sleep! Someone's life is in my hands, and my stupid wife is wailing like a banshee in the middle of the night!"

Paris opened her eyes and realized, to her amazement, that she was still screaming. When she stopped, she started to tremble in fear. Tears were streaming down her face. She felt her heart beating wildly in her chest and she heard the sound of Tou-Tou, her miniature white poodle, barking loudly in the background.

"Get out of this bedroom now, you lunatic!" Doyle shouted. "Go sleep in another room, and take your stupid dog with you." Anger spewed like acid from his mouth.

"I'm sorry," she pleaded between sobs. "Please, I'm sorry. Please don't make me sleep in another room. I promise you I won't bother you again."

Doyle angrily picked her up and as she struggled to free herself from his arms, she fell to the floor hitting her head on the sharp corner of the end table. He carried her to the bedroom at the end of the hall, where he dumped her on the floor. Without another word, he turned and left the room. Tou-Tou, a small bundle of white fury, barked wildly as he chased after him, nipping at his ankles and managing to move too quickly for Doyle to kick him.

Paris remained on the floor silently sobbing. Her body ached. Her head throbbed with relentless pain. The side of her face felt hot and swollen and she was shaking uncontrollably. She was a mess. Tou-Tou lay beside her licking her face.

She remained on the floor for what seemed eternity thinking, "When I wake up he will apologize for what he did to me. He is nervous about the trial. He would never deliberately hurt me. He loves me. I am his wife." She kept repeating this mantra until she finally fell into a fitful sleep on the cold floor.

*****

The loud ringing of the telephone woke her up. Momentarily Paris was confused, not remembering where she was. She got up with difficulty and walked across the room, reaching for the phone on the desk. She groggily mumbled, "Hello?"

"Paris," Doyle bellowed into the phone, "it's almost noon. Why are you still sleeping?" Before she had an opportunity to reply, he continued. "I want all of your clothes and possessions moved to the downstairs bedroom. Your snoring and snorting are annoying me. I need a good night's sleep so that my mind is clear in the morning. The murder case I am trying is very important to me. I need my rest."

"Yes Doyle," she answered meekly, "I'm sorry for being inconsiderate."

"Good, I'm glad you are being reasonable," he replied. "I'm going to a conference this weekend and should be back Monday night. We will go to dinner." He hung up before Paris could reply.

Paris slowly made her way to the bathroom where she vomited into the commode. She looked at herself in the mirror. The woman who stared back at her was a complete stranger. Her image in the mirror appeared distorted, purple and swollen. She had long black hair, which was matted and tangled with blood. Her eyes were two small blue slits in her swollen red face. She seemed a parody of her real self.

She washed her face and rinsed her mouth with cold water, her eyes studiously avoiding the lady in the mirror. She grabbed a towel, wet it with warm water and tried to wipe off blood from the side of her head. As she wiped that blood away fresh blood started to ooze from her wound. She stopped trying to clean the gash, threw the towel with disgust on the bathroom floor and walked out of the room.

Paris made her way to the kitchen, telling herself that everything would be better. "Doyle will apologize when he sees me. He would never hurt me; he must have been out of his mind with worry about his case."

Paris poured fresh water in Tou-Tou's automatic water dispenser and filled his bowl with fresh dog food. She poured herself a glass of orange juice and while painfully trying to drink, her shaking hands spilled the juice over her blue silk chemise. Tou-Tou wagged his white furry tail and happily ran out his doggy door to play in the backyard.

The security phone rang. The guard requested permission to allow in the "Happy Maids," three young Spanish girls who cleaned her house bi-weekly.

Within minutes of his call the doorbell rang and the preppy girls dressed in pink uniforms cried in unison, "*Ola!*"

Paris sorrowfully drank in their appearance and cheerfulness as the maids walked in the door. They were young and fresh-looking, and they looked happy. Lola, spoke English and she translated instructions to the other two girls who only spoke Spanish. All three girls studiously avoided looking at her face and the dried blood coating her hair.

Finally Lola said timidly, "Senora you are hurt. I take you to hospital?"

Paris replied angrily, "I'm fine!"

"Alright *senora*, I just want to help you."

Paris ignored Lola's words and took the girls to her bedroom closet where her clothes, shoes and handbags were stored. In a quivering voice, she managed to tell Lola that she wanted her belongings moved to the downstairs bedroom. They started the moving process directly. Paris hurriedly left the room, sparing herself the pain of watching her belongings moved out of her bedroom.

She went to the nursery adjacent to the master bedroom and sat on the rocking chair next to a beautiful white cradle. The cradle had been handmade for her older sister Suzette by Papa Moses. As an infant, she also slept in the handsome white cradle lined with fine white satin.

She picked up a fluffy white lamb from the crib and wrapped her arms around the toy. Paris started to rock back and forth in a hypnotic motion. She gazed at the cheerful room, staring with distain at the cheerful rainbow painted on the pink and blue walls.

"My babies!" she sobbed, screaming: "Four dead babies in six years!" She walked to the carved white dresser, angrily pulled out all the pink-and-blue baby clothes in the drawers and threw them wildly on the floor. "God! Where are my babies?" she shrieked.

Lola, hearing the cries, came running into the room to see if Paris was hurt, Tou-Tou chasing behind her.

"Lola," Paris groggily said, "I am fine. Please finish your work. There is nothing you can do to help me."

Paris went back to the rocking chair and sat down. Her head throbbed in pain, Tou-Tou jumped onto her lap to comfort her, his pink tongue licking her face.

Lola looked at Paris' pale swollen face with the fresh blood running down the side of her head said to her, "Please *senora*, I help you…"

Paris slowly replied, "Lola thank you for offering your help. I am fine, please go away."

Lola ignored her, and bought a hand towel wet with warm water and soap.

She started to gently wash the blood off Paris face, and Paris screamed, "Don't touch me! Just get out of my house!"

Lola quickly walked out of the room shocked and hurt. She and the other girls left the house immediately. Paris closed her eyes and thought of happier times, like the day she first met Doyle.

Chapter 2

Paris loved Easter in New Orleans. All of New Orleans celebrated with brightly colored flower wreaths on their doors. The stores in the French Quarter were dressed up in Easter decorations of colored eggs and beribboned bunnies. The sweet olive trees had started to bloom and the scent of their flowers drifted through the city.

She had chosen a simple white silk wrap dress to wear to church. The dress was modest but still it accentuated her small waist and long, tanned legs. Paris wore a white lace hat trimmed with blue flowers and ribbons, contrasting her long black hair. The dress and hat made her feel a part of Easter.

She was in very high spirits as she walked to mass. She loved the majesty of St. Louis Cathedral. The azaleas in the square in front of the church appeared to be a lush pink carpet of blossoms. Paris felt the cathedral was the heart of the quarter. When she walked in the church she lit a candle for her sister Suzette and kneeled in front of the station for Our Lady of Prompt Succor.

"Please," she whispered, "watch over my sister in heaven."

Paris walked down the side of the church, admiring the beautiful stained glass windows illuminated by the sun. They illustrated the life of St. Louis, formally Louis IX of France. She seated herself as close to the altar as possible and her eyes feasted on its beauty as she listened to the grandiose sound of the organ music and inhaled the scent of the masses of white lilies and ruby red roses that adorned the splendor of the church, mixed with the wafting smell of incense. Paris was a history aficionado and took pride in her extensive knowledge of New Orleans' past.

The large altar was adorned with beautifully carved wooden Baroque-style smaller altars, constructed in Belgium and shipped to New Orleans piece by piece. They majestically graced the center of the cathedral. A great, painted dome-shaped mural of St. Louis leading the seventh crusade in the years of 1248 AD to 1254 AD hung above the altar next to other murals depicting scenes from the Bible which were vividly painted and glittered as if they were dipped in gold. The Romanesque tabernacle, the priests dressed in gold-trimmed vestments of white and red, and the sweet smells uplifted Paris and gave her a sense of well-being and peace.

When mass ended, she made her way to the entrance of the church and down the steps when someone stepped on the heel of her white shoe. She stumbled on the steps and her hat went flying with the wind. As she rushed after it, she saw a tall dark-headed young man retrieve it from the street.

He shook off the dust from her hat, and handed it back to her, saying gallantly, "A pretty hat, for a very pretty lady."

She found herself blushing as she replied, "Thank you so much for chasing my hat."

He looked at her with the most unusual blue eyes she had ever seen. They were so intense that they looked like dark blue sapphires.

"My name is Doyle O'Connor. What's your name?"

"Paris Viverette," she replied, extending her hand to shake his.

They smiled at each other and an electric current seemed to pass through the handshake. As they gazed at each other big, warm raindrops descended upon them. Doyle took her hand and led her across the square to La Madeleine Café where dozens of other rain-spattered people had come for shelter.

In his deep voice, Doyle declared, "We will never get a table; look at all the people who are ahead of us."

They stood together chatting and watching as dozens of people pushed their way into the café. After exhausting fifteen minutes of small talk about the mass and the weather, Doyle finally eschewed his courage.

"Paris, I feel awkward asking, I know we just met," he said stammering slightly, "but it's Easter and I hate to eat alone. Will you have lunch with me? If you would prefer to eat at a different restaurant that's fine, we can eat wherever you like." He paused for a moment. "That is if you have no other plans."

Paris stared quietly at him, absorbing the magnetism of his rugged features and his strong, well-muscled body, thinking to herself, "This is one good-looking man. He takes my breath away."

"Doyle, I do have plans for lunch." She saw a look of disappointment on his face. She quickly continued, "I'm having lunch with two of my girlfriends at The Dock on Bourbon Street. We're going to sit on the balcony and watch the Easter parade as we eat our lunch. You're welcome to join us."

"That sounds great," he said enthusiastically. "I have been so busy studying that I've missed many interesting happenings in New Orleans. I didn't even know about any Easter parade in the quarter."

They chatted like old friends as they stood in the café, waiting for the rain to stop. The two of them were sandwiched in a small space with numerous other people who were also trying to stay dry.

The feel of Doyle's warm body pressed against her was pleasantly comfortable. He smelled of clean soap and sandalwood. The rain outside and the feel of his body made her feel very sensual. Paris found herself unconsciously molding her body to his. She wished she could kiss his full lips as she breathed in his scent. She was smiling at what he was saying as, in her imagination, he was gently exploring her breasts. She was brought out of her reverie by Doyle tugging at her hand.

"The rain has stopped. We can go now."

Paris replied throatily, "Good. I'm so glad it finally stopped."

They began walking towards Bourbon Street and Paris realized that the man standing next to her was a complete stranger, whom she knew nothing about. It was unlike her to invite someone whom she did not know to lunch with her and her friends. The wild attraction she was feeling for this unknown man was even more bizarre. He was stirring feelings in her that she had seldom experienced before. She laughed to herself, musing that perhaps he carried a *gris-gris* bag in his pocket that some Voodoo queen conjured for him, making him instantly irresistible to every female he met.

"What's so funny?" Doyle asked, looking at her quizzically.

"I was trying to think how to introduce you to my friends," she replied giggling. "I could say that I found you in my Easter basket, even though you are a little bit too big for an Easter basket."

They both were happily laughing as they entered the restaurant. They walked up the stairs to the balcony and Paris said to Jon, the maître d', "Table for four please, I have a reservation."

Jon replied smiling, "I have your reservation. Follow me Miss Paris." He led them to a table directly on the terrace facing Bourbon Street. "It is good seeing you again Miss Paris. Will your friends be joining you soon?"

"Yes," she replied, reaching into her purse and placing a folded bill in his hand. "They will be here shortly, but you can bring the menus now."

He obliged, and Doyle looked mildly amused.

11

"I had no idea I was dining with a celebrity."

Paris smiled and looked up at him. "This is a very small town. My family has lived here for generations. We eat here quite frequently. That's why Jon knows me."

Doyle looked up as Paris gestured to two girls heading in their direction. When they were in their seats, Paris introduced Doyle to her friends.

"This is Daisy Lynn Parker," she said, nodding to a tanned, short-haired blonde. "And this is Shirree Anne Viverette, my cousin. Ladies, this is Doyle O'Connor. I met him at the cathedral after mass. Doyle rescued my hat so I invited him to lunch with us."

Doyle glanced between Paris and Shirree. "Paris, you and Shirree look like twins!" Doyle exclaimed with surprise.

Doyle's reaction was typical of a stranger meeting the girls for the first time. They were three months apart in age. Both had long dark hair, the same build, and were about the same height. However, their eyes were different: Paris had purple-blue eyes and Shirree's eyes were amber.

Shirree laughed, "People always say that. We aren't sisters, but we are double cousins!" she said merrily in her throaty voice.

"What are double cousins? I have never heard that expression before."

Shirree explained, "My mother and Paris' mother are sisters, and our fathers are brothers. What makes it more complicated is the fact that both our fathers and mothers married their second cousins."

"That sounds complicated, but it does explain why you gals look so much alike. Your voices are similar too. Do you share the same interests?" he asked.

"Our personalities are totally different," Shirree giggled, "I am the wild child, always going in different directions, very adventurous. Paris is the proper one, much more cautious and very logical."

Paris sat listening to Shirree, a smile on her face. She thought to herself, "I am cautious, practical and logical. However, I think I am in the process of changing. I met a strange man and within minutes I had fantasies of ravaging him—in front of the cathedral no less! I must be in heat, like some wild beast."

The waiter came over and took their drink order and Doyle asked, "What do you guys recommend for lunch?"

Without hesitation the three girls decided upon crab cakes, a fried oyster loaf, boiled red potatoes, and a salad of Creole tomatoes with Vidalia onions. They also ordered a bottle of dry white wine to accompany their lunch.

Astonished at their quick reply, Doyle said simply, "Sounds good to me," and handed the waiter his menu. He looked at Daisy and asked, "So are you a cousin too?"

Daisy had a completely different look about her: big brown eyes and honey-colored hair.

"No. I'm not even a southern belle. I'm from Long Island, New York. But I do love the food in Louisiana." Daisy spoke rapidly, "My father is a cardiologist. We migrated to New Orleans five years ago when he became the head of the cardiology department at Tulane."

"Where are you from Doyle?" queried Daisy.

"I say I'm from Miami, but really my family lived in many places when I was growing up because my father was in the Navy. I was born in Boston. Currently, I have a scholarship to Tulane and I am in law school. So here I am in New Orleans."

"We all attend Tulane," Paris said. "Daisy is majoring in business administration, Shirree—when she is not majoring in mischief—is majoring in interior design. And I'm a music major."

The food arrived. Doyle's eyes took in the steaming French bread, the Creole tomatoes and Vidalia onions covered with olive oil and balsamic vinegar, sprinkled with coarse freshly ground black pepper.

"This looks great!" Doyle exclaimed.

As the food continued to roll out the friends were assaulted by fine aromas and pretty platters. The *pièce de resistance* was a huge platter of golden fried onions. The crisp, chilled white wine added the right accent to the meal. Everyone at the table eagerly began eating and there was no sound other than the passing of food around the table. After they finished their food, they sat companionably sipping their wine.

The trumpeting of the hot rhythm band began as the group marched smartly in front of the parade.

"Great music," commented Paris.

A beautiful lady stood in an open carriage drawn by two ponies. She was dressed in a long silk flowered dress topped off with a large-brimmed, white straw hat covered with colored flowers. She was throwing stuffed animals, long strings of colored beads and packages of candy as she passed by. She waved to the crowd of adults and children who lined up on both sides of Bourbon Street.

They were wildly raising their arms to catch the presents and shouting, "Throw me something madam!"

Children squealed in delight as they caught the stuffed animals, candy and beads. Processions of beautiful women of all ages followed in open convertible cars and open carriages. They all stood up and tossed dozens of gifts to the crowd, which roared in pleasure. The music of other jazz musicians marching with the ladies echoed through the street.

"Some of the ladies marching today are exotic dancers, some are strippers, and others are socialites," Daisy explained. They all belong to a social club that marches every Easter. First, they have a luncheon and then a contest to judge the most original hat. The winner gets the honor of having her hat preserved in the Easter Hat Hall of Fame."

"It is an honor to march with these ladies," Daisy continued, "They are truly amazing. What an interesting group of women; all ages, all colors and from all different lifestyles.

"To the ladies of New Orleans!" she declared, raising her glass.

They all clicked glasses and chorused, "To New Orleans, the most interesting city in the world!"

When the parade ended they divided the check between them and left a hefty tip.

Paris turned to Doyle: "We're going to Pat O'Brian's for a drink. Would you like to join us?"

"I'd really like to go with you, but I have a lot of studying to do. I had a great time this afternoon. It is not often that I have the luck to be with three good-looking ladies. Thanks for asking me to join you. But I can walk you to Pat O'Brian's—it's on my way."

They walked down the street to Pat O'Brien's. Shirree and Daisy walking ahead of the couple. Doyle and Paris walked hand-in-hand talking about the great music that the bands had played.

At the entrance to Pat O'Brien's, Doyle turned to Paris. "I would like to take you for dinner on Friday night. That is, if you don't have other plans."

"That would be great. I'd like to have dinner with you."

"I'll call you Wednesday night to make plans."

She reached in her purse and took out a small white card with her name and phone number engraved in gold letters. She handed it to him. "I will look forward to our dinner," she replied smiling at him.

Doyle turned to Shirree and Daisy and thanked them again for a fun afternoon, and as he walked down the street, he turned and waved to them.

The girls entered through the carriage entrance of Pat O'Brien's, walking over the dark slate floors and passing the crossed muskets, which represented all the countries that once occupied and flew their flags over the state of Louisiana.

Paris looked at her friends and asked, "Which bar do you want to go to? The main bar, the piano bar, the patio bar, or the bourbon street bar?"

Daisy spoke up first. "The outside patio bar is my favorite. I love to look at the flaming fountain."

Shirree said, "Great, we can watch the sunset on the patio and enjoy the beautiful weather."

A maître d' came over to seat them and they requested to be seated at a table close to the flaming fountain. He led them to one of the glass and iron tables next to the cascading streams of flaming water spilling from the stone and copper waterfall.

A waiter came over promptly to take their drink order, and Daisy mischievously said, "I will have one of your famous Hurricanes."

Paris and Shirree both chimed in, "We'll have three Hurricanes."

Paris looked around at the brightly lit torches circling around the patio and said, with a smile on her face, "This has been a great day."

"Enough of this idle chit chat," Shirree demanded, giggling. "Tell us about Mr. O'Connor!"

Daisy looked at Paris smirking. "No more small talk, tell us about your new burning hunk of love."

At that moment, their large pink Hurricanes arrived at the table and the girls began to sip the strong, delicious elixir. Paris stalled, taking a large sip of her drink, savoring the sweet heavily laden rum concoction.

"This is the best," she sighed.

"Enough," said Shirree. "Tell us about Doyle! Why have you been hiding him from me?"

Paris looked at her cousin and Daisy. "There is nothing more to tell. He rescued my hat after I tripped on the steps after mass. He picked up my hat from the dirt and as he handed it back to me. It started to rain. We ran to La Madeleine to get out of the rain. He invited me to lunch. I told him I was having lunch with friends, and invited him to join us. Look at my wilted hat!" she said, as she lifted her bedraggled white hat from the chair next to her.

"I think you have left something out of this puzzle, and I don't mean the éclairs," Shirree retorted. "What else happened?"

Paris smiled, "He asked me out for Friday night, and I agreed to have dinner with him."

There was a pregnant pause. Shirree said, "Paris we have known each other forever. I know you are not telling me everything, you naughty girl."

"All right," Paris said blushing, "when we were standing close together, or should I say molded together by the crowd, I felt very aroused, so aroused that I could feel my nipples harden under my bra. He smelled so good. I could feel myself kissing him; I could feel his hands on my breasts. I felt my body become hot and wet inside. I know this sounds crazy, but I have never been as aroused and he was only touching my hand. I had only met him ten minutes before and I was ready to jump his bones!" she said blushing and stammering.

"Oh. You go girl!" squealed Shirree. "He is the one."

"What do you mean, 'the one'?" Paris asked breathlessly.

"I've been really worried about you," Shirree said laughing. "Paris, you are twenty years old and still a virgin. You have a great body, even if you don't have my great boobs," she said as she proudly displayed her cleavage by pulling down the front of her T-shirt. "You and I both have the Viverette creamy white skin and blue-black hair. You are a luscious babe, just like me, and you ain't done the nasty yet! What is wrong with this picture? You needed an exciting man to get your juices flowing. He just walked into your life. He is over six feet tall, eyes of blue, and he has a beautiful body. Even more amazing, you met him in church."

"I need another drink," Paris said as she signaled the waiter. "Make it three more Hurricanes please."

"Shirree, I cannot believe how vain you are. You are too much. You are really in love with yourself!" squealed Daisy.

Shirree replied, "If I do not love myself no one else will love me. Daisy, you are fabulous looking. You have thick blonde hair, a small waist and a well-endowed bootie. Your hazel eyes are much prettier than mine, and you have full sexy lips. We three are very beautiful chicks!"

"I will drink to that," said Daisy, mollified by Shirree's compliments.

"I agree with Shirree," Daisy said to Paris. "Doyle is 'the one.' He is very, very sexy. He couldn't take his eyes off you! I watched the way he looked at you...."

"How did he look at me?" asked Paris.

Daisy replied, "He looked at you the way a dog looks at a bone he wants to lick and eat. It makes me shiver just looking at him looking at you."

Paris retorted, "I think our magic elixirs are affecting us and we are slightly drunk."

The orange red sun was setting and the blue sky was streaked with pink. The fountain was a brilliant red flame of water and the torches seemed to reflect the colors of the sky. The girls sat quietly enjoying the beauty of the night as they savored their drinks.

"This was a lot of fun," Daisy said dreamily. "What a great way to spend Easter, but I think I am toasted and have to go home."

"I concur. I hope I will be able to walk home," Shirree said as she quickly rushed to the ladies room.

The other two girls laughed at Shirree, even as they also made their way to the toilet right behind her.

The girls walked through the quarter, which was filled with mulling crowds of people. Shirree and Paris waited until Daisy was safely in her cab before walking to the apartment they shared in the Pontalba Building.

They entered their apartment and Shirree said, "I had an extraordinary time, but I am really tired and gloriously inebriated."

"That makes two of us. I am intoxicated!" Paris said tittering. "Goodnight night, sweet dreams Shirree," she said as she walked to her bedroom at the opposite end of the hall.

Paris entered her bedroom shut her door, took all of her clothes off and tossed them on a large blue chair, and dived into bed. The softness of her lavender-scented sheets felt very sensuous against her body. She closed her eyes and pictured Doyle's face in front of her. She felt his presence so strongly that her whole body became hot and wet. She touched herself and began rubbing herself very gently. She felt her nipples harden and her vagina swell between her fingers. Her body began shivering and contracting. Her touch became deeper and faster, her fingers moved of their own volition. Her body filled with sweet warm passion as she gasped in pleasure. She quickly fell asleep without brushing her teeth or saying her prayers.

17

Chapter 3

Paris walked across the street to the cathedral to attend morning mass. She entered the church and walked to the table holding votive candles. As was her custom when she came to the cathedral, she said a prayer for her sister as she lit a candle.

"I know you are in heaven Suzette, looking down upon me and the whole family. We all miss you very much. I pray for you every day. God bless you."

After mass she walked across the street to La Madeleine for breakfast and stood in line debating between an almond croissant and a chocolate croissant to accompany her coffee. She chose the almond croissant. The smell of chicory coffee was pleasantly invigorating. She sat on a long wood bench placed next to an old wooden table scarred with age.

She placed her tray on the table and quickly devoured her flaky croissant and hot chicory coffee, reflecting on the day before and her encounter with Doyle. Just the memory of her feelings caused her to blush.

She walked out to Jackson Square, which surrounded the perimeter of the park in front of the cathedral, and surveyed the artists, mimes and tarot card readers who were busily sitting in front of their tables and plying their various trades. Paris never tired of watching the animation of the square. Every day brought new mimes, exciting bands and fresh people to participate in novel situations. Hemingway had his "movable feast," and she had her kaleidoscope of moveable people. People from all over the world came to Jackson Square. Young, old, men, women and combinations of both, mingled with white people, black people, Asians—Jessie Jackson's "Rainbow Coalition" were all part of the everyday scene.

There was a clown, dressed in red and white stripes topped by a black hat, juggling balls which he threw up in the air for a group of enthralled tourists. A mime, his skin painted silver, wearing what appeared to be silver armor, was standing motionless on a silver table holding a silver sword. A crowd of people surrounded him, cajoling him in a most aggressive manner to see if he would move or blink. She took some bills out of her purse and placed them in the mime's silver tip bucket.

Paris walked around the square admiring the work of artists who were creating caricatures of tourists. She watched other artists painting portraits of people with pastel chalk and acrylic paints. Other artists were painting scenes of the people in the square as they were doing their sightseeing. She watched the psychics at work. They sat on their folding chairs in front of their card tables hungrily watching as people passed by. Signs on their tables announced to everyone passing that they were the greatest palm reader, crystal ball reader, tarot card reader, mind reader or psychic in the whole world. All the readers wore brightly colored garish clothing. Some of the women, as well as the men, wore strange turbans wrapped around their heads. Their arms and necks dripped with outlandish jewelry and many sported colorful tattoos. Paris was surprised to see most of the readers had lines of people waiting around their tables for readings so early in the day.

She walked to the front of the square and saw the mule-driven carriages lined up to take people for a tour of the quarter, their drivers standing in front of their carriage calling out to the people passing. Their mules clean and shiny, wearing small flowered straw hats with holes poked out to accommodate their ears. Paris gently petted the mane of a brown mule that tried to show his appreciation by licking her hand with his enormous pink tongue.

The Square of today was quite different from the Jackson Square of the past when prisoners were dragged from jail to this very same spot and their punishments publicly meted out. Thousands of prisoners were beaten or hung in public executions. People fascinated by the spectacle of seeing men and women tortured, beaten and executed would sit around eating and laughing, enjoying the exhibition as entertainment.

Paris walked to her apartment, which was on the side of the square above a doll shop in the Pontalba Building. She daydreamed of Doyle, feeling foolish that she was expending so much energy thinking about a man she barely knew. She walked up the stairs to her apartment and checked her phone messages. The only message she received was her friend Sadie canceling their tennis match for this afternoon. She walked to the music room off the kitchen and played some of her favorite music on her black, baby grand piano. She found herself very sleepy and decided to take a nap on the comfortable couch beside the piano.

Paris awoke to the voices of Shirree and Daisy giggling and

laughing as they fixed lunch. She was about to join them when she overheard Shirree talking about her.

"Daisy, I am so happy that Paris is coming out of her funk. The whole family's worried about her. Yesterday she seemed her old self. She was talking, laughing and interacting with the group."

"I know. I remember what a fun-loving person she was when I first met her. She was full of life and everything was a new adventure to her. After her sister died she withdrew into a shell. She hardly did anything but go to school and play the piano."

"Daisy you have no idea how horrible it was right after Suzette died. Paris stayed in her room, in bed, and cried constantly. We couldn't get her to eat or even leave her room. She wouldn't bathe or even comb her hair. Maman Sophie made her milkshakes and smoothies; she would take them to her room and stay with her until she drank them. This went on for weeks. Everyone in the family was in mourning after Suzette died."

"No one was thinking clearly, Ante Lilly Anne and Oncle Louis were devastated and very irrational. Grand-mère Madeline draped herself and the whole house in black. Finally, Maman Sophie had to call Dr. Charles Le Blanc to check on Paris."

"I am so glad that she is taking an interest in dating and having a relationship."

Daisy nodded. "Yes Shirree, but we want her to have a happy relationship with a man who's going to be good to her. She doesn't know this man; we don't want to see her hurt."

"You are right. We were drinking last night and today I realized that by telling Paris she was too old to be a virgin I might be pushing her into a situation she's not ready to handle. It was wrong of me to chide her about her sexuality."

Paris entered the room announcing, "I could not help overhearing your conversation. Shirree, please do not blame yourself for anything. I am attracted to Doyle, but I do not expect to jump into bed with him. I want to go out with him and get to know him before I become sexually involved with him. I am happy because I am finally feeling sensual and very alive. I haven't felt this way since Suzette died."

Paris looked at her friends with a big smile on her face as she announced, "I'd like to go shopping for some new clothes. Would y'all like to come with me?"

Daisy replied instantly, "Did you say shopping? You know that is my favorite form of exercise. I would love to go shopping today."

"Shopping, absolutely," Shirree agreed. "Canal Place? We haven't gone hunting for clothes together in a long time. The white silk dress you wore yesterday looked great on you, but you have been wearing it for all occasions for the past three years. It is time for a change."

Paris thought to herself, "I am starting a new chapter in my life. New clothes, new life. I have come out of my cocoon and now I am a butterfly."

Chapter 4

Doyle called Paris on Tuesday evening and they made dinner plans for Friday evening. He said he would make reservations at the Redfish Grill. The conversation was short and direct. She invited him to her apartment before dinner for cocktails. Paris loved the sound of his voice and she loved his take-charge attitude. Friday night could not come fast enough for her. Paris went to Shirree's room modeling one of the dresses she had purchased at Saks.

"Look, this dress is fabulous," Paris smiled, as she walked in and did a pirouette in a sky-blue halter dress cut very low in the back.

Shirree exclaimed, "It fits you perfectly and it shows off your toned arms. Put the jacket on. So how does it look with the plaid sandals we bought?"

Paris placed the matching fitted jacket over the halter dress and buttoned it at the waist.

"That is a great look for you, very demure with the jacket on, and very hot with the jacket off. The blue plaid mini purse we bought matches the plaid sandals perfectly. I'm glad I convinced you to buy it."

Shirree and Paris went into the kitchen to complete their set up for cocktail hour. Shirree carefully removed the *piece de résistance* from the oven. It was baked brie covered with phyllo dough and filled with praline sauce.

Paris looked longingly at the brie, "Shirree you did a great job with the brie. This definitely is a work of art."

Paris removed the warm French bread from the oven and placed it next to the brie on the marble top of the bar. Shirree took out several boxes of cheese and crackers and artistically placed them on flowered, small-boned China plates next to a large bouquet of red tulips and violet colored jonquils.

"Everything looks yummy. I could demolish all the brie by myself!"

Shirree replied, "No you couldn't, because I would fight you for my fair share."

Promptly at seven the security system phone rang. Paris answered and quickly went down to open the door for him.

"Paris," Doyle greeted her with a smile. "You look amazing and you smell fabulous."

"Thank you Doyle," she replied, blushing. "You look pretty amazing yourself."

Doyle followed Paris into her apartment. The unique furniture, the tremendously high ceilings and the spaciousness of the rooms impressed him.

Shirree greeted him with a big smile saying, "I am opening a bottle of champagne, would you like some or would you prefer something else to drink?"

"Champagne sounds great."

The security phone rang again and Shirree said, "That's David calling; I'm going downstairs to let him in."

"Is David her boyfriend?"

"Yes. Well I should say *kind of*. We grew up with David. Our parents and David's parents have been friends for years."

Shirree walked into the room, and introduced David to Doyle. The two men shook hands.

"Why don't we sit on the terrace?"

"That's a good idea. David, you bring the champagne in the ice bucket while Paris and I move the hors d' oeuvres outside."

They sat down on the thick black cushions atop the white iron chairs. Paris poured a glass of champagne for Doyle as they nibbled on the delicacies atop the table.

Doyle pointed to the Brie: "This looks good. What is it?"

"Brie," Paris explained simply.

She took a small plate and put a piece of French bread on it. She then used a large spoon to scoop up the warm brie and, with another large spoon, ladled a mixture of praline sauce over phyllo dough on his bread.

Tasting the warm sweet mixture Doyle exclaimed with pleasure, "This tastes amazing! I have never tasted brie before, but I know now that I really like it."

Paris replied, "This is a real Creole dish. I'm glad you're enjoying it."

Doyle looked in admiration at the various colored morning glories entwined on the black iron railings and the pots of red roses next to them. "You have a remarkable patio and a great view of the square; I can sit here and see all of Jackson Square beneath your balcony."

"We do. I believe this is the best view of the statue of Andrew Jackson sitting on his horse from any place in the quarter." Paris pointed across the way to the statue of a man on a horse.

They sat there quietly sipping their champagne and enjoying the sight of people parading beneath them in the square.

"What school do you go to?" Doyle asked David.

"I'm a resident at LSU. I am studying to be a general surgeon. What about you?"

"I am going to Tulane. I'm in my third year of law school."

"David, finish your drink. We have to leave we have reservations at Antoine's for nine. Paris and I are going to bring the food inside so it doesn't spoil."

David looked thoughtfully at his watch, "I believe we have just enough time to finish this great bottle of champagne. It would be a sin to waste it."

After the food was put away, Shirree handed David his suit jacket saying, "Dr. La Blanc, our table awaits."

"I am at your service madam."

The couple said their goodbyes as they left the apartment. Paris locked the doors and they held hands as they walked down the street in the direction of the Red Fish Grill.

The waiter showed them to their table immediately. Paris gracefully sat down and slowly removed her jacket to reveal her halter top and her bare back. She watched with satisfaction as Doyle stared admiringly at her. They both ordered the blackened red fish as an entrée and Doyle ordered a bottle of white wine to complement the fish. They were sitting side-by-side in a small booth. Paris felt Doyle position his leg against her thigh and she felt intoxicated by his proximity, but also a little annoyed at his brazenness. The food was delicious, but she only picked at it because her appetite wasn't for the food. They savored the wine and each other as they talked about school and their favorite movies.

After dinner Doyle asked Paris if she would like to go to the bar in the Bombay Club for a drink. She quickly acquiesced. They walked arm-in-arm the few blocks to the hotel and made their way to the bar where they sat at a small table in the back of the dark room. The music was roaring and the atmosphere was sultry.

Paris and Doyle ordered Cosmopolitans to drink. Paris took one sip and realized that after champagne and half a bottle of wine at dinner it was not a good decision to drink more. She felt very tipsy and light headed.

The band started to play sultry music, perfect for slow dancing.

Doyle looked at her as he held out his hand. "May I have the honor of this dance?"

"My dance card's filled, but I think I can fit you in," Paris quipped.

He led her to the small crowded dance floor and wrapped her in his arms.

Paris moved away, putting distance between them, but he pulled her closer to him and whispered in her ear her as they danced, "I love your scent. What is the name of the perfume you wear?"

"Sweet Olive Flower. It's made from the flowers of the sweet olive trees that grow here."

"I think you are the most beautiful woman in this room."

She giggled, "It is so dark and smoky in this room you can't see any woman besides me."

"You're right, but I can feel you. And what I feel is beautiful," he said, as he pulled her body closer to him.

She found herself putting her arms around his neck and melting into his body.

"This is so nice," he murmured softly to her as he put his hands on her bottom, caressing her as they danced.

She gasped in pleasure as she felt his hard manliness pressing into her. She pressed back, enjoying the madness that he was creating in her body. She wanted to stay joined like this forever. His hands cupped her buttocks, pulling her into his erection. She gasped and pulled away.

"It's late and I'm tired. Will you please take me home?"

"Of course," he replied, "just let me pay the check."

He put his arm around her as they walked to her apartment, saying very little to each other. Paris thought to herself, "If he thinks I'm going to invite him up to my apartment, he is going to be very surprised."

They arrived at the door to her apartment and Paris kissed him on the cheek. "Doyle, thank you for a great evening, I really enjoyed myself."

Before she could pull away he put his arms around her and kissed her deeply, sliding one hand under her halter-top and slowly caressing her breast. She felt her nipples harden and the heat of his body inflame her. She melted and savored the raw passion that permeated her body.

It took all of her self-discipline to separate her body from his, saying softly, "Goodnight. I will be thinking of you."

She put her key in the lock and as she walked in the door, she turned and blew him a kiss.

*****

Doyle called early the next morning inviting her to dinner at his apartment. Paris told him blithely that she had other plans for the evening, but she invited him to a jazz brunch the following Sunday.

She could tell by his voice that he was very surprised that she wouldn't jump at chance to have dinner with him at his house. But he accepted her invitation.

Paris hung up the phone feeling very self-satisfied. Shirree walked into the room.

"Are you ready to go to breakfast?"

"Yes Shirree I am ready, where do you want to go?"

"The Bluebird Café. Those pecan pancakes are calling my name. Bring your tennis racket and wear shorts so we can play tennis after we gorge ourselves on pancakes."

An hour later the girls were seated at a small table covered by a red and white checkered oil cloth; a large ceiling fan buzzed noisily above them. A waitress came to their table to take their order. She had a hairnet covering her gray hair, and wore an old-fashioned white uniform with a black apron. Shirree ordered pecan pancakes for the two of them with lots of syrup.

"I can hardly wait to hear about your evening. Tell me everything that happened last night!"

"We had a fabulous dinner at the Red Fish Grill. We sat at a booth and he kept rubbing his leg against my thigh, which excited me and annoyed me at the same time. We went dancing at the Bombay Club and he was all over me. I enjoyed it. I went along with the program, but it was not the way to act on a first date." Paris sighed.

"He walked me home and I felt as if I could read his mind. He thought I was going to invite him in and we were going to sleep together. I kissed him good night and he put his hand underneath my dress. I removed his hand and I turned away, opened the door and blew him a kiss goodnight."

"He sure is something," Shirree exclaimed as she swallowed a piece of her pecan pancake. "I thought he was well mannered. I am sorry I made those silly remarks about Doyle being your 'Prince Charming.' It sounds as if he is only looking for some action."

Paris responded thoughtfully, "He called this morning and invited me to his house; for dinner, no less!"

Shirree replied, annoyed, "He has some nerve! He must think that he's God's gift to womankind. Did the jerk think you would quiver and say, 'I will be there promptly at eight wearing no panties under my skirt, and a bottle of your favorite wine'?"

"I guess he did," Paris said laughing. "What I did say was that I had plans but I would like to invite him to brunch next Sunday as my guest. I could tell the he was flabbergasted. There was a pregnant pause before he accepted my invitation."

"That was very clever. You put him in his place and took control of the situation. He is so sexy and charming I imagine few women turn him down for dinner and 'entertainment' at his house. You inviting him as your guest for brunch, now that is class—dinner would have been sexually aggressive, but a jazz brunch is pure genius.

"Paris what are you going to gain by seeing Doyle again?"

"I'm very attracted to him. I don't intend to let him bed me any time in the near future. Perhaps we can have a romance together. Maybe he will be able to view me as a person, rather than an object to temporarily use and then discard when he's bored."

Shirree looked at her cousin sympathetically, "Paris, please be careful. He seems very slick. I will never forgive myself if I encouraged you to do anything that turns out to be harmful to you. You know he can never be just a friend."

"I know you love me Shirree, and you're right he can never be just a friend. But he is the only man who has ever really excited me. I enjoy being with him. I'm going to be very careful. Please don't worry about me."

Shirree thoughtfully sipped her lemonade. Doyle O'Connor, who seemed so perfect yesterday, seemed very menacing today.

Chapter 5

Doyle sat on his comfortable seat in the first-class cabin of his plane waiting for takeoff. He was looking forward to a well-earned vacation.

His thoughts drifted to Paris and he felt somewhat guilty for the way he treated her the night before. He was very angry at her and he acknowledged the root of his antagonism: he felt like a gigolo. He had very little money of his own and it would take him years as an attorney to be able to afford the lifestyle that the Viverettes provided for him.

When they were first married her family bought them their house, their furniture, his office—everything of value. At first he was ecstatic. The Viverettes provided him with the lifestyle he always dreamed of. There was only one problem, and that was everything they purchased was in the name of the Viverette trust. Nothing belonged to him, nor would anything they purchased for him and Paris ever belong to him. Every time he thought of his situation he became more resentful toward Paris.

He also dwelled on the miscarriages she suffered. He so desperately wanted a son and she seemed incapable of bearing children. He blamed that on her.

He was in deep thought when an attractive, well-built blonde said, "Excuse me, that's my seat. Can I get through?" She gestured to the window seat beside him.

Doyle replied, "No problem."

He got up and moved to the aisle so she could comfortably seat herself at the window. He got a good look at her when she was moving to her seat.

"She has a great body," he thought to himself. "Especially her ass."

Doyle turned to her, smiled, and said smoothly, "My name is Doyle O'Connor."

"Kathleen Reynolds. I saw you on television earlier today. You were walking out of the courtroom with your client. You're the attorney who defended Antonio Leon."

"Guilty as charged," he replied laughing.

"You certainly worked hard to defend your client. Everyone thought he would be found guilty. Congratulations!"

"Thank you, for the compliment. I appreciate it very much."

The plane geared up for takeoff, they both tightened their seat belts and sat back in their seats. The captain made the usual announcements: they would be in Martinique on schedule, they would be flying into the city of Le Lamentin and the temperature was seventy-five degrees.

The flight attendant came to take their drink orders—they both ordered the rum punch—and the flight attendant skillfully poured their drinks into tall glasses.

Kathleen took a sip of her drink and said flirtatiously. "This is a very potent drink! A couple more of these and I will forget I am supposed to meet my husband at the hotel."

Doyle replied, "Kathleen, drink up. I promise I won't take advantage of you. After all, these seats are too small."

She giggled and said, "You're charming. I can see how you were able to charm the jury. I have read many contradictory stories in the newspaper about Alberto Leon in the newspaper." She leaned closer and whispered, "Was he really innocent?"

"Let me tell you the true story Kathleen," Doyle said in his most earnest voice. "But first let me catch the flight attendant's eye so she can bring us another drink.

"The DEA has been trying to arrest Antonio for a long time; they think he's involved with a Columbian drug cartel because his brother is José Leon."

"Oh, I didn't realize they were brothers," exclaimed Kathleen. "I see José Leon's pictures in the paper and on TV all the time. He's a fugitive. He left the country before they—the FBI—could prosecute him for smuggling millions and millions of dollars' worth of cocaine into the country. He just disappeared. I saw him on that *Most Wanted* show! They are offering a million dollars to anyone who has information about his whereabouts."

"They are desperate to find José," Doyle agreed. "That is why they're trying so hard to find Antonio guilty of a crime—they feel he will lead them to José, or perhaps turn his brother in to save himself."

"The government will try to use him in any way possible to find his brother. They have never found any evidence to charge Alberto with a crime. He is a respectable businessperson and a great philanthropist. He is certainly not responsible for the acts of his brother José."

Kathleen looked thoughtful. "Why then did they charge him with conspiracy to murder Charlie Roe?"

"Do you really want to hear all the details?"

"Yes, please. I'm really interested."

Doyle's eyes lit up at the opportunity to talk about his work. "Pepe Rios murdered Charlie Roe and he confessed to the murder."

Kathleen leaned forward, intrigued. "Why did Pepe confess to the police that he murdered Charlie Roe?"

"It is a very funny story," Doyle said laughing, relishing his own cleverness. "Pepe is not the brightest guy in the world. He shot Charlie dead center in the chest as Charlie was unlocking the door to his house. It was after midnight. Pepe used a silencer so none of the neighbors heard the shot. He wiped his fingerprints off the gun and he filed the registration numbers off the gun. He put the gun in a pail and covered it with cement. He dumped the pail into the inter-coastal waterway."

Doyle paused for effect. "He committed a perfect murder. The police had no clues. They finally put Charlie in their cold-case files. Pepe was very pleased with himself. He knew he committed a perfect murder. Months after Charlie died and all the publicity stopped, Pepe felt he was in the clear. One night he went to his favorite bar and proceeded to get drunk."

Kathleen began to smile—she could guess where this was heading.

"He wanted to brag about how clever he was to his bartender friend. The bar was very noisy and Pepe had to speak loudly so the bartender would hear him. Unfortunately for him, the man sitting on the barstool next to him was a detective who had investigated the murder of Charlie and he heard Pepe's confession. Less than fifteen minutes after he shared his perfect murder with the bartender, a drunken and befuddled Pepe was in the police station being booked for his perfect murder.

"It was apparent that Pepe would say anything rather than go to jail for first-degree murder. He knew that he could plea bargain and his sentence would be drastically reduced if he pinned the murder on Antonio." Doyle was almost laughing at this point. "Pepe knew he had no defense. He also knew that the police would do anything if they could charge Alberto with a crime, so he claimed that Alberto had hired him to commit the murder. The prosecutor promised that he would reduce Pepe's sentence if he could prove Alberto hired him."

Doyle explained, "The DEA were desperate to get their hands on Alberto, so they chose to believe Pepe's story and charged Alberto. He was accused of hiring Pepe to murder Charlie Roe. When I questioned Pepe about why he claimed Antonio had hired him to kill Charlie, he stated a man, who he knew very well, offered him $20,000 to do the murder. The man who hired him claimed he represented Antonio Leon. The police couldn't find this guy who supposedly gave Pepe Leon's order to dispose of Charlie. Apparently he disappeared from the face of the earth.

"I stressed to the jury that Antonio Leon was a successful kind generous man, who was unjustly hounded by the government because of his brother. The jury took only one hour to find Antonio innocent; this was American justice at its best." As Doyle was vigorously proclaiming his client's innocence, he was thinking to himself, "And above all, Alberto pays me very generously for my work."

"Now Kathleen," he said as he took her slender fingers and gently caressed them, "I have been monopolizing this conversation. I want to hear all about you. You strike me as a beautiful and exciting lady."

"On one condition," she replied, her voice serious. "My husband is meeting me at the airport and he is very jealous, so we cannot walk out of the plane together."

"No problem." His hand gently caressed her arm as he rubbed his leg on hers.

The flight attendant served dinner and they ate while talking and laughing as if they were old friends. After dinner, Doyle asked for pillows and blankets. Doyle surveyed their cabin—the other passengers appeared to be fast asleep. All the seats around them were in total darkness. No lights appeared anywhere and the sound of snoring pervaded the cabin.

Doyle whispered in her ear, "Kathleen, we are going to have our own little pajama party."

She giggled as she turned off their lights. "What are we going to do at our pajama party?" Doyle laughed, "What would you like to do?"

He unzipped his pants and their arms crossed as she slipped her slender fingers inside his opened fly and wrapped her fingers around his penis as he put his hand underneath her skirt and moved her panties firmly to one side so he could put his fingers in her warm hot center. He slowly caressed her. She made soft mewing sounds as his fingers probed deeply inside of her.

She grasped his penis and murmured, "You're big. I want to feel that big boy inside of my pussy."

Whispering in her ear he said, "You have the softest little pussy. Come on baby purr for me." He felt her wetness as his fingers touched her little man in the boat, causing her to sigh deeply.

She squeezed her fingers around his cock and said coquettishly, "You're a big boy. I never had a man as big as you. I don't know if my little pussy is big enough to handle you."

"Would you like to try to handle me?"

"I'm willing to give it a whirl."

"Kathleen,I need to go to the *restroom*," Doyle said quietly with a wink.

He got up from his seat. She waited a moment before following.

*****

The plane disembarked at the small Le Lamentin airport in Martinique. As Doyle stepped out of the plane he was greeted by a short Hispanic man with a heavily lined face. He wore a captain's hat jauntily perched to the side of his head revealing his thick gray hair.

"Señor Doyle O'Connor!" hailed the little man.

Doyle nodded to him, "Yes I'm Doyle. Who are you?"

"I am Carlo. Señor Alberto sent me to pick you up. Please give me your passport and luggage so I can speed up the formalities."

Doyle handed it over to him. "Carlo, how did you recognized me?"

"Oh I saw you on television with Señor Alberto. You are a celebrity now."

Doyle puffed up with pride. They entered the minuscule airport crowded with people from Doyle's flight.

Carlo said, "I will only be a few minutes, Please wait for me here."

Doyle waited and watched as Carlo slipped the passport to a man in a dark blue uniform who greeted him with a hearty slap on the back. The man walked into the customs office and returned a few minutes later, handing the passport back to Carlo who shook hands with the official and beckoned Doyle to follow. Doyle glanced back at the large disgruntled crowd waiting in the customs line as he and Carlo sailed through the front door.

Carlo led him to a black limousine, opened the trunk, and placed the luggage inside. He opened the back door of the car for Doyle saying, with an expansive smile on his round face, "Welcome to Martinique! We are going to the city of Marin where Señor Albert's yacht is docked at the Port De Plaisanca harbor."

"It is too bad you came in at night," Carlo continued as they pulled away from the airport. "It is a beautiful ride through the city. In the daytime you can see the mountains and the volcano. This the most interesting Island in the West Indies. If you like I will take you on a tour tomorrow."

"That would be great! I'd enjoy that!"

They arrived at the yacht harbor where Leon's craft was docked. Doyle was amazed at how large the yacht was.

"Welcome to the Christopher Columbus! I will take you to your stateroom. I know you have had a busy day and you are probably very tired. Señor Alberto will be here tomorrow afternoon. Would you like to have dinner in your room?"

"Yes that's a good idea. I'm very tired."

Carlo led the way up a winding staircase. "As you can see, this yacht is almost as big as a cruise ship. It is very easy to get lost in it. This is your stateroom: the green suite. Dinner will be served shortly. Is there anything else I can bring you now?"

"No," Doyle replied, looking around his mammoth suite. "Everything is perfect."

All the furniture in the suite was designed to resemble aged driftwood buffed to a silver patina. He sat on the large soft bed in the center of the room and took off his shoes, placing his feet on the lush green carpet. His tired feet felt as if they were enclosed in velvet. He looked around his surroundings and noticed a large remote on the large desk adjacent to the bed. He stood up and picked up the remote turning it over to examine the extensive menu on the back. He pushed one button and the silky green curtains parted exposing panoramic windows. Outside, white foam swirled on the dark ocean. He pushed another button and an overhead panel opened exposing a large plasma TV. He pressed another button and a large table opened to display a sizeable, well-stocked wet bar.

Doyle ventured out to the deck and inhaled the smell of fresh ocean saltwater. The waves bounced on the side of the boat and sprayed him with cool droplets of brine. The sun had set and when he looked up to the heavens he saw a blood-red moon fluttering through the sky and illuminating the blackness. The luxury of the yacht intoxicated him.

Doyle mused to himself, "I knew Alberto was rich but I had no idea that he was this rich."

Carlo was back in a few minutes carrying lobster salad and wine in a silver ice bucket. Doyle lingered over his dinner and wine enjoying the peace and quiet of his luxurious surroundings. He walked back into his room and found his bed turned down, his suitcase unpacked, and his clothes put away. The bed was soft and inviting, with silky sea-green sheets. He lay his head on the soft pillow and tried to fall asleep.

Now that his mind was still and his busy day had passed, thoughts of his wife Paris pervaded him. He could not totally erase the burden of guilt mixed with anger that languished in his head. The dissolution of her pregnancies changed her from a gay, thrilling, affectionate girl, to a sad, tired woman. He knew he was also to blame for her withdrawing from life and becoming the lifeless entity she had become. He pictured her at their home saddened and frightened by his behavior toward her. Tears came to his eyes, not for himself, but for Paris who had always shown him nothing but love and compassion and received scorn and hate in return. Their marriage was a paradox; he was primarily attracted to her for her money and lifestyle, but over the years he began to hate her for the same things that made their marriage attractive.

Doyle finally fell asleep thinking of Paris and New Orleans. He recognized he had a love-hate relationship with her and he felt very guilty for the ugly things he had done to her in the past months. She never argued with him she quietly accepted his malice. He could smell her scent, the scent of sweet olive blossoms on his pillow. He promised himself that in the future he would be kinder to her. He knew he had verbally and physically abused her, he swore to himself that he would never do any of those things again. She was his wife, and he would treat her with the love and dignity she deserved.

His unconscious mind wandered back to the time he met her on the steps of the cathedral. The look of surprise on her face when her hat had blown away was that of an innocent child. He remembered the excitement that he experienced when he returned her hat and she looked up at him with her big, beautiful, blue eyes and her heart-shaped face, which glowed as she spoke to him. He knew at that moment that he wanted to possess her.

Chapter 6

After he left Paris and her friends at Pat O'Brien's, he walked to Canal Street, hopped on the streetcar, and got off at the closest stop to his house. He enjoyed the walk from St. Charles Avenue to his apartment on Oak Street because he liked to see the large stately mansions in the Garden District.

Wealthy Americans moved to that area after the Louisiana Purchase. They wanted to build homes that rivaled the homes of Creoles who lived in the French quarter and Esplanade Avenue. Canal Street was the street that divided the property holdings of French and English.

A potpourri of sweet-smelling lush flowers and verdant gardens surrounded the magnificent homes. Magnolia trees, roses, honeysuckle and jasmine provided just a few of the blossoms to perfume the streets with their syrupy scents. The great gardens of flowers earned the area name The Garden District. Originally, the homes were painted a pristine white color. Now, they were cloaked in a palette of colors that ranged from delicate pastels to deep violets. With age, the green tentacles of assorted vines had curled around the intricate wrought iron fences of the mansions and became part of the decor of each house.

The twisted roots of the large oak trees dominated the sidewalks and the streets, creating an obstacle course of uprooted brick sidewalks. The roots tore up the tar streets causing an explosion of holes and gaps in the roads. This made it difficult to drive a car and keep your tires from being torn apart in a pothole.

Doyle had tripped, lost his balance, and fell over the tentacles of tangled roots on numerous occasions. He felt it was small price to pay for seeing the glory of a golden era of American architecture. He daydreamed about one day owning a beautiful sprawling mansion equal to the ones he gazed at longingly.

Doyle arrived at his apartment and rapidly changed his clothes. He and his roommate Alex shared the first floor of a faded-lavender Victorian house. He sat on a black leather couch and began to study.

He heard whistling at the door and opened it, yelling," Alex, bro, did you lose your keys?"

Alex came in and flopped down on a large orange chair in the

35

corner and replied, "No amigo I did not lose my keys. They are on the top of my dresser where I left them. I just forgot to bring my keys with me. Have you been studying all day?"

"Actually," Doyle replied, "I went to mass, met a beautiful girl named Paris, and had a great lunch at the dock with three great looking babes. I've just been home studying for about an hour. Alex, I think I am in love."

Alex replied flippantly, "Amigo, you are always in love. I am not surprised."

"No bro, I am really in love this time."

"How many times have I heard the same story?"

"She has long shiny black hair, great legs, and a lot of class. She is unique. I just looked at her Alex and I knew we were destined to be together."

"You are loco man!" Alex said with a laugh.

"You're probably right, but let me enjoy my fantasy."

The phone rang and Alex answered, "He's right here, hold on," and handed the phone to Doyle.

Doyle took the phone. "Hi Beverly, I was just thinking about you." Alex snickered in the background as Doyle said, "Beverly can I see you tomorrow night? That is, if you have no other plans."

There was an extended pause before Alex heard, "Great, I'll meet you at your house at seven. Take care sweetheart, I'll see you soon."

Alex looked at Doyle and said, "I guess Beverly is still your main squeeze. You are too much Doyle. You love all the women, and all the women love you. I envy you. You have a horde of women, and no one wants to go out with me."

Doyle looked at Alex, his curly hair falling over his thin face and his kind large brown eyes. Alex's clothes were tailored in beautiful fabrics but always seemed too big for his thin body.

"Bro, you are the greatest guy in the world. You have a super sense of humor, you're goodhearted, generous, and you're one of a hell of a lot of fun. One of these days you are going to meet a lady who is worthy of you. She will love you and you are going to have a great life together and be very happy. I'm a tomcat. I will never be faithful to anyone, so Alex you are really the lucky one because I will always be on the prowl."

"That sounds good, amigo, but in the meantime you're up to your eyeballs in booty, and I can't get anything. Right now you are luckier than I am," he growled as he picked up a pillow from the couch and threw it at Doyle, who flung it right back to him.

"I'm hungry. Want to go to Camilla Grill and have some of those great burgers topped with onions? How about fried pecan pie and great chocolate milkshakes? I think that would fill me up."

Doyle divided his life into two parts: his life before he met Alex, and after he met Alex. They both attended the same Catholic school and played on the school football team. Doyle's father was an enlisted man in the Navy. Doyle and his family had moved so many times that he had lost track of all the places where they had lived.

Doyle's father retired from the Navy with a small pension and became a mechanic in a used car dealership. The family moved to a small house in Miami in a very dismal area. His mother worked as a waitress in a small diner near their home and she also did alterations in their house. His brother Brandon attended the University of Florida on a football scholarship. He worked in the school cafeteria for his spending money and books.

When Doyle was sixteen, he became a busboy at the Venetia restaurant. The restaurant had excellent Italian food and was always busy, having established a reputation for its food. The food was expensive and the tips were very good. The only drawback was that he was exhausted at the end of the night. Sometimes he wouldn't get home from work until midnight. He was constantly groggy when he arrived at school at eight the following morning.

He had been working at the Venetia for several months when he looked up and saw Alex sitting at a table with his family in the dining room.

"Alex, you've selected a great restaurant; best food in town."

"We think so," Alex said as he smiled at him. "I'd like to introduce you to my family. This is my mother Maria Garcia, this is my sister Serena Garcia, and this is my father Roberto Garcia."

Meeting Alex's family was the turning point in Doyle's life. Alex's father was a business owner who owned the Venetia and a car dealership, among other things. Knowing something about Doyle's financial situation from his son, Roberto offered Doyle a position as his Alex's English tutor. He later offered Doyle's father a job at his Cadillac dealership.

Doyle and Alex became fast friends. They spent a lot of time studying together and Alex's grades improved tremendously. Daniel

O'Connor was delighted to be in a position of management. He enjoyed working with cars and was very happy to have the opportunity to make more money. The timing was perfect. Daniel O'Connor had just sworn off drinking because of liver damage. He was finally able to channel his energy into working rather than wandering around to every bar in town. Doyle's mother no longer had to work as a waitress. The O'Connors were able to buy a home in a better section of Miami.

Doyle observed how the Garcia family lived. He studied their manners and mannerisms. He watched how they ate and what type of fork they used for each course of food. He assimilated their attitudes and carriage. He learned how to treat women and incorporated their panache. He emerged a gentleman and left the impoverished Doyle behind him.

Chapter 7

Doyle did not sleep well that night. He was sound asleep when he heard Carlo's wake up call. He dressed hurriedly. He was looking forward to tour the island which was considered the most beautiful and most cosmopolitan island in the West Indies.

He went into the bathroom, quickly shaved, and threw on a pair of jeans and a T-shirt. When he came out of the bathroom Carlo was in his bedroom placing a breakfast tray of croissants, orange juice, coffee and a cheese omelet on a table.

"*Bueno,* Señor I will wait for you, we will have a good trip today. You will like my Island. First I am going to take you on a quick tour of Marin and then we will go to the country side and the beach. So Señor, bring your bathing suit."

Doyle finished his breakfast, grabbed his swim trunks and they walked around the complicated maze of the yacht, disembarked and went to the limousine. Carlo wore a flowered island shirt over his jeans, which emphasized his thick body and short stature. His captain's hat sat on a thick head of gray-black hair. They entered the black limousine and began their journey with Carlo in the front seat and Doyle making himself comfortable on the supple gray leather seats in the rear of the car. No sooner did Doyle get into the car than it started to rain heavily.

"I hope it is not going to rain all day and spoil our sight-seeing trip."

"Oh no, it rains everyday here for about an hour and then it stops raining and the sun shines and we have a beautiful day."

Doyle looked around at the brightly painted pastel houses and the people in vividly colored clothes running into their homes to avoid getting wet. He noted how neat and clean the city was and how well maintained the roads were. No pot holes or cracks on these streets.

"Señor Doyle, look over at the area of small houses across the street from us. Josephine was born in 1763 on this land." Carlo handed Doyle a brochure about Empress Joséphine saying, "I think you will find this very interesting, it was recently printed by the department of tourism. Everyone has a curiosity about Josephine, so there is a lot of material printed about her."

Doyle nodded in agreement. "I have seen portraits of Joséphine in New Orleans and heard tales that she screwed half of Paris before she married Napoleon, and the other half after." He began reading the brochure, "This is really interesting. I never knew she was of African descent."

"At birth, she was named, Marie Josephe Rose Tasher de la Pagerie and everyone called her Rose. When she married Napoleon Bonaparte in 1795, he changed her name to Josephine because he disliked the name Rose. From the time she married Napoleon she was known only as the Empress Joséphine.

"The place I am taking you to swim is supposedly the place she liked to swim when she was a young girl. You are going to get to swim, drink, eat and watch tits all at the same time. We are going to Le Francois where we will take a boat to the white sand basins, known as Fonds Blancs."

They arrived at Le Francois and went aboard a sightseeing boat with 30 other people. In the men's room and put on their bathing suits. The boat went out a distance before it anchored in a section of shallow water. Everyone went into the water.

This was the first time he had ever co-mingled with women bathing bare-breasted. His eyes were magnetically drawn to the variety of jutting nipples surrounding him. Women of a variety of ages went topless and their breasts were happily bobbing in the water; he studiously looked at Carlo to keep from staring at the sea of floating tits.

Waiters in bathing suits were serving food and drink on large trays—rum punch and some type of fritter—to the bathers who were standing in water up to their waist. Doyle watched the bathers around him laughing and eating. He noticed females, as well as males, were casually smoking cigars as they stood in the water socializing.

"Carlo, this is really something!" Doyle exclaimed laughing. "I'm really enjoying this."

They stayed in the water for about an hour enjoying the unique sensation of eating and drinking in the clear water in the shallow white sand basin. After a couple hours, they reluctantly left the boat and were on the road again.

Carlo announced, "Our next stop is the ruins of the island's oldest city, St. Pierre."

"What makes St. Pierre so special?"

"St. Pierre was known as the Paris of the West Indies. In 1902, the volcano Mount Pelée erupted and over 30,000 people died in two minutes." Carlo shook his head in wonderment.

"I can see the volcano from here. Wow, what a sight!"

Next, they visited the rain forest and Doyle viewed plants and insects that he had never seen before. They stopped to see a waterfall, which rapidly cascaded down the side of the mountain. Hundreds of vivid brilliant butterflies swarmed around the swirling water.

They returned to the *Christopher Columbus* by nightfall. Doyle immediately jumped into a shower and changed into fresh clothes. He was standing on the deck when Carlo called and told him that Señor Alberto wanted to meet him in the game room. Doyle was anxious to see Alberto and hungry for the praise he knew Alberto would lavish on him for the splendid way he handled his murder case.

The walk seemed to last forever as they turned down corridors and walked up winding stairways to reach the game room. They walked and walked for about ten minutes before they reached their destination. Doyle walked in the room with a big smile on his face as he went over to shake hands with Alberto.

Alberto greeted him with affection, saying, "It is so good to see you Doyle." Then Alberto lowered the timbre of his voice, "Doyle I would like you to meet my brother José."

Doyle's hands went cold and clammy; he could feel his heart beating rapidly in his chest. He could be disbarred if anyone found out he was socializing with a wanted man and His career would shrivel up like a dried raisin. He knew it was very important for him not to show fear in front of these men.

Doyle, a big warm smile on his face, took José's outstretched hand and shook it vigorously saying, "You are really much better looking in person than on your wanted posters."

There was a pregnant pause before José smiled and burst out in loud, hardy laughter. He looked Doyle in the eye saying, "There are not too many man in the world who would have the *chutzpah* to say that to my face. I like you."

Doyle smiled, breathing a sigh of relief. "I do not believe I know what 'chutzpah' is, sir."

Once again José burst out laughing, "*Chutzpah* is big balls. Doyle you created a brilliant defense for my brother."

Alberto interjected, "You are a great attorney. You had the jury in the palm of your hand. You convinced all of them of my innocence."

"Carlo," he commanded, "please open the Champagne. We are going to celebrate."

"Doyle," José said, "I would like you to meet two of my associates. This is Fidel."

Doyle extended his hand to Fidel who almost crushed Doyle's fingers as they shook hands. "Nice meeting you Fidel."

Fidel mumbled, "Likewise," and returned to his chair.

Doyle was amazed to realize that he was so focused and fearful of José that he never noticed Fidel. How could anyone not notice a man, who looked like a Hispanic Mr. Clean? Fidel had a gourd-like nose, arms the size of ham hocks, and the smile of an alligator.

"This is my other fellow traveler, Peligro," José said as he patted a large brown and black Rottweiler. Its enormous pink tongue dangled from his open mouth. Peligro opened his mouth wider, exposing humongous white teeth that looked like fangs, and then lazily lay his head at his master's feet.

Carlo nimbly poured the champagne and handed each man a glass.

José stood up, "I would like to make a toast to family, friendship, health and prosperity!"

Alberto, who had been silent up until now, smiled as he held up his glass, "That covers all the important things in our lives. Once again I would like to thank you Doyle, my good friend."

Doyle retorted, "You were innocent of those charges."

José looked at Doyle, a sardonic smile on his face, "As you know, innocence does not guarantee an acquittal. Doyle, you were brilliant in court. You made mincemeat of the prosecution's witnesses and you also cast doubt on the credibility of the prosecution's reasons for trying to convict Alberto."

"How do you know so much about the court proceedings?"

"I was in the courtroom every day in disguise, observing the way you handled the case."

Doyle looked at José with surprise. "You're the one with *chutzpah*!"

"I believe in taking a hands-on approach when it comes to the welfare of my family." José paused looked at Doyle. "This brings me to a new page in our association. The Leon family takes care of its own. I am the head of the family and as the head of my family it is my responsibility to make sure that my family is protected."

Doyle sensed the tension in the room was directed at him.

"Doyle, I believe you are well acquainted with Adriana Franco, who is the youngest daughter of my sister Carmen."

Doyle's throat constricted, his heart was pounding very fast, his hands were ice cold; with great difficulty he said, "Yes, I am."

A mental picture of Adriana flashed through his mind. She was a petite redhead with buxom breasts, short legs and a plump body who drove a red corvette. He had met her in a lounge right before closing time one evening when he was very, very, drunk. She took him home with her and he fucked the life out of her. She reminded him of the Pillsbury Doughboy—soft and squishy.

She kept screaming, "Oh poppy! Oh poppy!" as she violently came, scratching his back with her long purple fingernails. He made the mistake of giving her his business card and she kept calling him at his office. Occasionally when he was bored and she called he would see her.

José continued, "I want to congratulate you; she is pregnant with your child. I know you are married. I have heard your wife has not been able to carry a baby full term and I am aware that you desperately want a child.

"I know this is a surprise to you Doyle, but everything you want is in your grasp. Adriana told us that you are in love with her. She was very happy when you told her you loved her because she fell in love with you on your first date. All of your dreams are coming true. Adriana is a beautiful girl she will be a good wife to you and she will give you a beautiful baby. I know it will take you a few months to settle your affairs. You understand you will have to marry her before the baby is born, or my sister Carmen will make my life a living hell."

José's tone gave no room for argument.

Alberto held his glass up, turned towards Doyle and with a big smile on his face said, "Doyle welcome to our family."

Doyle forced himself to smile happily as he drank his champagne. He did remember telling Adriana he loved her—it was while he was fucking her and stoned out of his mind. Doyle was in a state of shock. As an attorney he knew not to react in an emotional situation. He had the ability to disassociate himself from the problem and try to view it in a logical way. But this was a disaster, not a just a problem, and he needed time to figure out what his options were.

Carlo announced that dinner is ready and he is serving it on the deck so everyone could enjoy the fresh ocean breeze while they eat.

As Doyle attempted to eat his seafood salad, he observed José dominating the conversation. The man was charismatic, a natural-born leader, and very dangerous. José gestured with his hands as he spoke, and nodded his head, which emphasized his snow-white hair and deeply tanned face. He and Alberto shared large Roman noses, which dominated their handsome faces; they were tall, muscular and agile in their movements. The greatest difference between the brothers, aside from the fact that Alberto had curly brown hair, was their eyes. Alberto's eyes were big brown and peaceful while José's were black and menacing.

José looked at Doyle with his dark, hawk eyes, "You are not eating, what is wrong?"

He looked at José trying to sound sincere as he replied, "I am overwhelmed with thoughts of my new life."

"Another toast," José raised his glass. "To your future and Adriana's!"

Doyle was too stunned to say anything. His tongue and brain were frozen. He sat perfectly still, his face a perfect blank. At Doyle's unenthusiastic response, José's voice became rough and menacing. "I am giving you five months to rid yourself of your wife and marry Adriana."

José's face subtly changed, his black eyes seemed to narrow and Doyle could see a spasm of irritation cross his reddened face. He said with rancor in his tone, "Doyle O'Conner you will be married to Adriana by October of this year. I will not allow anyone to hurt my family. Do you understand?"

Doyle felt his eye ticking and his fingers shake. He looked at José, and then Alberto, forcing himself to speak the words that came out of his mouth in a lifeless monotone, "I do love Adriana; I am thrilled about her having my baby. It will be an honor to be part of your family. October." He knew he sounded like a parrot, but apparently they believed him.

Alberto looked at him and nodded as he smiled, "This is what we wanted you to say. Congratulations."

Doyle glanced at Fidel who was staring at him with a fixed stony expression on his ugly face. Peligro, who was sitting at José's feet, seemed to be at attention and staring at him as if he was waiting for his master's order to tear him apart with his large white teeth.

Doyle pasted a wide grin on his face and looked first at José and then Alberto, "I am honored by your generosity. It will be an honor to be part of the Leon family."

Doyle was still shaking and his body felt icy cold when he entered his room. He had the worst headache of his life and he felt like a trapped animal on the way to the slaughterhouse. He lay on his bed and pondered about what he was going to do. He acknowledged the fact that his life was entangled in a dangerous, perhaps deadly, dilemma.

He heard Carlo calling his name as he knocked on his door. Doyle opened the door and Carlo looked at him with a big smile on his face.

"Mr. Alberto has sent you a present!"

Before Doyle could say anything, a beautiful girl walked into the room carrying a silver tray in her hands.

She gave Doyle a sultry smile and said, "My name is Bella. I am here to serve you."

Doyle, his voice muted with fatigue replied, "Bella, you are beautiful, but I am exhausted."

Bella handed him a small glass flute filled with a green cloudy liquid, saying, "Drink this. You will feel better. You will relax and sleep like a baby."

He took the drink she handed him and swallowed all of it. It was so strong that his throat felt like it was on fire."

What am I drinking?" Doyle asked, "I have never tasted anything this strong!"

She did not answer him. Instead, she lit a small silver pipe and blew the smoke in his face. He repeated his question, "Bella, what was in that drink?"

Bella replied with a sultry voice, "It was absinthe; on the island we call it the Green Goddess. You are going to be very relaxed now, I promise you."

She began undressing him and the next thing he knew he was floating in the warm soothing water of the Jacuzzi. She was naked, her firm caramel breasts were gently pressing against his lips. He put his arms around her small waist and hugged her slender body against his. Her long curly hair was the color of cinnamon. The water seemed alive with movement and he felt like a babe being rocked in a cradle. He fell asleep and woke up to Bella's arms around him and her magical probing fingers touching his body. He felt so good that he didn't want to move—he only wanted to melt in the water.

Bella stood up and helped him out of the Jacuzzi. She draped a towel around his shivering body and dried him with a plush towel and a soft touch. She pulled him towards the bed, removed the bedspread and maneuvered his inert body onto the sheets. She slowly massaged his toes with warm scented oil. Slowly her delightful fingers worked their way to his thighs. His penis suddenly came alive as she teased him with her light but firm touch. She took a glassine envelope out of her purse and rubbed a white powder in his mouth, on his penis, and around the periphery of his anus. She cupped his balls and started to suck his cock as she gently placed her adroit finger around the inside of his anus. He moaned in pleasure, and she rolled him to the side and placed her tongue in his anus as she squeezed his cock.

Doyle felt as if he was he was in another dimension. His body was warm and he was experiencing sensations he had never felt before. His body re-charged and he moved over Bella so he could suck her breasts and put his fingers in her thick bush at the same time. He then rolled on top of her and put his face between her thighs. He teased her with his tongue, gently nibbling and biting the inside of her thigh. She let out a shriek of pleasure as she forcibly pushed his head against her clit, moving him to the spot that aroused her the most. Her supple body squirmed in delight, as she began to moan.

Doyle mounted her, pushing his cock deep inside of her. She snaked her fingers between his legs and placed them deep into his ass. He succumbed and screamed at the pain and pleasure she was giving him. When he could no longer hold back, he pulled her long hair and slapped her hard buttocks.

She screamed with all her might, "Harder, harder, give me all of that big cock!"

Within a few minutes he came, but his cock was still as hard as steel. He could not believe it. He embraced her saying, "Bella I cannot move a muscle."

She laughed as she sat on his lap, put his penis back inside her, and rode him like a stallion. She squirmed in pleasure and screamed his name. He came, he came, and he came until he thought he would never stop.

She was gone when he woke up the next morning and he momentarily thought Bella was a dream until he touched the soiled, wet sheets and felt the ache in his legs. The phone rang and Carlo greeted him cheerfully asking him if he enjoyed his evening.

Doyle laughed and said, "All I can say is, 'wow'!"

As Doyle dressed for breakfast, all of his fears and anxiety returned to him. He could feel his left eye twitching and his stomach began to ache at the thought of spending hours with the Leon family. He tried to compose and detach himself from the political/social quicksand that defined the Leon family. He pasted a smile on his face and forced his quivering mind and body to relax.

Doyle endured a stressful day of fishing, drinking and making small talk with his new family. His face felt stiff from smiling. He was thrilled that he was returning to Miami the next day. He felt as if he had been emancipated, but he knew his problems were not over—they were just really beginning.

Carlo escorted Doyle back to his stateroom and bade him goodnight. A few minutes after he entered his room, he had a knock on the door. He opened to find Bella dressed in a red sarong carrying her silver tray. All thoughts of fear melted away. She took the clicker off the dresser and pressed the button to start the stereo. She then began a little dance as she slowly stripped off her red sarong. It was an enjoyable night for both of them.

Chapter 8

Maman Sophia rose at dawn. She quickly bathed, dressed, and packed. She called Paris' phone number in Miami—no one answered the phone. After five rings the answering machine came on and she left a message asking Paris to call her immediately. She woke up Papa Joe and started to tell him that she was leaving for Miami.

He interrupted her and said calmly, "I know Sophia, I heard you crying out Paris' name in your sleep all night."

The tantalizing aroma of fresh coffee wafted through their bedroom.

"Joe, who is that making coffee in my kitchen? It smells mighty good."

"Cher, Tante Seri spent the night and she is probably cooking up a storm for our breakfast."

"Bless her heart. She must have gotten up very early this morning to cook."

"Breakfast is ready! Come and eat before the cinnamon buns cool!" Tante Seri called out as she knocked on their bedroom door.

Joe and Sophia walked down the hall to the kitchen to savor Tante Seri's cooking. Seri had set the table with Sophia's favorite brightly flowered plates and a white damask tablecloth. There were freshly baked cinnamon buns, pecan bread and brioche on the table.

Sophia's fluffy white bichon frisé dogs Lulu and Beau were sitting patiently under the table hoping that some goodies would be dropped on the floor for their own enjoyment.

"This looks wonderful, Tante," Sophie said as she hugged the smiling, diminutive, fragile woman.

Tante was wearing gold tear-drop earrings, a long purple silk dress and gold sandals.

"She may be old, she might be wrinkled," Sophia thought, "but she's always elegantly dressed."

Sitting at the head of the table was a smiling Charles, Tante Seri's faithful companion of many decades. He had been a prizefighter in his youth and his crooked nose and thick ropey arms were quite visible under his blue T-shirt. He had a big grin on his smooth, round face, and chalk-white teeth that stood out like headlights against his dark skin.

He got up from the table and walked over to Sophia, giving her a giant hug as he said, "Lordy, girl, you look prettier every time I see you."

"Mr. Charles, go on with your bad self. You are such a flatterer! You always make me feel like a young girl."

Tante Seri bade everyone to be seated, as she poured the coffee and sat down to say grace. Everyone bowed their head as she said, "Heavenly father, Loas, and sacred ancestors, we thank you all for our bountiful blessings. We ask you to sanctify Sophia's trip to Miami and ask you to protect Paris."

"How did you know I was going to Miami, and how did you know I am worried about Paris?"

"Maman Sophia, have you forgotten that I am not only your Tante, but I am also the current Queen of Voodoo in New Orleans? When I die you will be my successor, so I better know what is happening to you. I know all of your sorrows. I promise you that there will be justice for Paris, and at the end of her journey she will be blessed with much happiness."

The phone rang and Sophia quickly left the table to answer it.

"Sophia, I have been trying to call Paris for the past two days. I have been leaving messages on her answering machine, but she is not returning my calls. It is not like her to disregard our calls. We speak to her a few days a week. Have you spoken to her?"

Louis, Paris' father, was calling from Spain where he and his wife Lilly were vacationing. Louis's voice was agitated as he spoke. "I've not been able to reach her either. If she had gone on a trip, she would've called one of us. I was planning to visit her in Miami this month. I decided to go today. I was just getting ready to book a flight to Miami when you called."

"The key to Paris' house is in my office where I keep my other keys. The phone number for the security gate at Palm Island is also in my office."

"I'll take care of everything. Stop worrying Louis, there is probably nothing wrong. Her answering machine may not be working."

"I know, Sophia. I'm being an alarmist. Please call me after you speak to her."

"You know I will," Sophia murmured into the phone. "Please give my love to Lilly."

When Sophia hung up she turned to her family and said, "Tante, breakfast was something good. I really enjoyed it. I would love to sit visit with you, but excuse me. I have to get ready for my trip."

Papa Joe asked, "Cher, what can I do to help you get ready for your flight?"

"Joe, why don't you get dressed and meet me at Bayou House? I need to find some things I will be taking with me to Miami."

"Don't be anxious Sophia, Mr. Charles and I will make sure your man and your dogs will be well fed and happy while you are gone."

"Tante, my only fear is that you're going to fatten up my man while I am gone and he will be too fat and lazy to give me any loving," Sophia said laughing.

Sophia called the airline and made reservations for the first available flight to Miami. She went to the Viverette household and quickly found the keys and phone numbers they needed.

Sophia called the security gate at Palm Island. A few minutes later, a man came to the phone and introduced himself as Dave Waters. She explained that she hadn't been able to reach Paris by phone for a few days and wanted to know if Paris left the neighborhood.

"Mrs. Moses, Mrs. O'Conner has not left Island for the past four days. The only guests she received were from her maid service last Friday."

Her next call was to Dr. Charles Le Blanc, the Viverette family's doctor. She left him a message that she was leaving for Miami this afternoon to see Paris, and that she'd like his son Christopher's phone number. Christopher was a neurosurgeon at Mount Sinai hospital in Miami Beach. Sophia had known Christopher since he was an infant. She didn't know what she'd face in Miami, but she felt better knowing that she could contact Christopher if there was a problem.

She checked her suitcase to make she sure she had packed all of her necessities, assured that whatever she forgot she would buy when she arrived in Miami. She hugged and thanked Tante Seri and kissed Mr. Charles on the cheek as she flew out the door where Joe was waiting in their car to rush her to the airport.

Papa Joe opened the car door for her saying, "You sure do clean up good. All the young bucks in Miami are going to think you look real fine Miss Sophia."

She laughed at him. "They should! Lilly brought me this linen suit at Chanel when she went to Paris last year."

She had chosen a designer brown purse and shoes to match her beige suit. Her motto was "the more affluent you looked the more respect you received," especially if you were a black woman.

They arrived at the airport and Papa Joe walked Sophia to her gate. He held her tightly, asking: "Sophia, did you bring your oils and herbs with you?"

"Of course I did, Joe. And a special *gris-gris* bag for protection."

"Honey, Tante Seri and I are going to have a special prayer meeting for Paris tonight. Now girl you remember, you better stay away from them young bucks."

Sophia laughed, "You are so pitiful. I will try to be good Joe. Love you." She kissed him and walked away to board her plane.

*****

Every time she came to Miami she saw new construction going on. The city was always working on more major highways and contractors were always building more condominiums. The charm of the magical tropical city, the amazing look of wild jungle plants, and the beauty of the beaches, were obscured by a sea of large concrete buildings.

The O'Connor House was in a gated community called Palm Island. Not really an Island, it was a man-made oasis of palm trees, tropical gardens and waterfalls. Everyone had a swimming pool and a cabana in his or her backyard and the expensive landscaping created the feeling of being on an island. The developers had created a pristine, expensive version of the Garden of Eden.

She arrived at the sparkling white gatehouse and greeted the security guards who stood tall in their white starched hats and uniforms. She opened her expensive handbag, showing them her identification and keys to the O'Connor house.

Dave and two of his men insisted upon escorting Sophia to the O'Connor's home. They followed her car in their sparkling white Jeep.

She went to the house and rang the tinkling chime of the doorbell. There was no answer. She unlocked the door with her key and she asked the guards to accompany her into the house. She called Paris' name and Tou-Tou ran down the stairs barking loudly to greet Sophia. He darted up the stairs and when he reached the second floor the little white dog started to howl as if he were in pain. Sophia ran after Tou-Tou and the guards ran after Sophia. Tou-Tou led Sophia to the nursery.

Sophia gasped in horror when she saw Paris, motionless on the floor covered with blood. She was wearing a sullied blue nightgown and holding a white stuffed lamb in her arms. Tou-Tou stood over Paris' prone body as if he were guarding her.

Security called an ambulance as Sophia sat down on the floor and cradled Paris in her arms, rocking her back and forth. She checked Paris' pulse, and gently rolled back her eyelids. Sofia was thankful she was still alive.

The ambulance arrived in a matter of minutes. They checked Paris' vital signs and immediately administered oxygen as they placed her in the ambulance.

They asked Sophia what hospital she wanted Paris to go to and she quickly replied, "Mount Sinai Hospital." Sophia called Christopher and told him.

In about ten minutes, they arrived at the emergency room at Mount Sinai. Christopher appeared a few minutes later. Christopher deftly examined her and requested a nurse to start an IV. Christopher and the nurses wheeled Paris away on a gurney for further tests. Sofia waited impatiently in the waiting area until the doctor returned.

"Sophia, do you know how long she was on the floor or what happened to her?"

"I have no idea what happened to her. I tried calling her several times in the last few days, but she never returned my calls. It was so unlike her. I just knew something was wrong. When I went to her house, I found her on the floor of the nursery unconscious covered with blood."

"Sophia, it appears she has a concussion which has caused her to fall into a coma. She is also very weak and has lost a lot of blood. The tests will hopefully help us determine how much damage has been done to her brain."

Sophia started crying. "My poor baby! Brain damage! She has to get well."

"Where is Louis? I will call him and explain Paris' condition. I know he'll want to be contacted as soon as possible."

"He's in Spain," Sophia murmured as she searched her purse for his phone number.

"Give me Doyle's number as well. He should be here with his wife."

"I don't know where Doyle is. I called his office and his service told me he was out of town until Monday. They told me they didn't have a contact number for him."

A nurse came in and told them they had a room ready for Paris. Sophia followed the orderly as he wheeled Paris through the hospital. They took Paris to a private room on the third floor. A nurse came to give her a sponge bath and remove the dried blood from her face and hair. Within a short time Paris was clean and dressed in a hospital gown.

After an eternity of waiting, Christopher came back. "Sophia the tests showed a severe concussion. The only thing we can do is to let her be. The IV will supply all the nutrients her body needs and I have ordered a transfusion to replace the blood she has lost."

Paris was attached to several serious-looking machines, her arms covered with IVs, and her bed surrounded by monitors. She appeared small and frail.

"How badly is she injured?" Sophia asked, her voice sounding panicky.

"Her brain is swollen from the impact to her head. We have to wait and see if the swelling goes down. I don't know at this time if she has any brain damage. I did not see any, but we have to be prepared for all contingencies. She could possibly wake up tomorrow and be fine; on the other hand, she may be in a coma for some time."

Sophia looked at Christopher, tears streaming down her face. She choked out, "This is going to be a waiting game; we just have to wait and pray for the best."

"I want to drive you back to Paris' house," Christopher said, "and I would like to look around the house to see if I can see where she was injured. It will be helpful in diagnosing her condition."

"That is fine with me; I appreciate your driving me home. I will leave my rental car in the parking lot and you can bring me back to the hospital. I sure could use the company."

They arrived at Paris' house and Tou-Tou welcomed them with his loud barking. They walked up the long staircase and entered the bedroom that Paris and Doyle occupied. Tou-Tou trailed closely behind them. Christopher looked all over the room for some clue that might tell him what happened to her.

"This is strange. Doyle's clothes are in his closet but there's nothing of Paris' in her closet," Christopher said. "I cannot imagine why she would have moved her clothes."

Christopher intently followed the path of blood. "I see a trail of droplets of blood on the carpet. It seems she walked all over the house after her injury. Perhaps she fell after her original trauma and caused the wound to bleed more."

They checked all the bedrooms on the second floor and could not find Paris' things. They went to the downstairs bedroom suite where they found Paris' clothes hanging in the closet. There was blood spattered all over the carpet and a blood-covered hand towel was lying on the floor.

Sophia said, "How was she able to walk around the house with an injury like that?"

"It takes a while for the swelling to start. She probably had a terrible headache, but was able to walk around before the swelling became a major problem."

Christopher followed Sophia down the hall to the nursery.

"My God!" he exclaimed, seeing the white baby furniture smeared with blood and baby clothes strewn in all directions. "She must have been beside herself to have done this."

Sophia remembered when Paris became pregnant for the second time and they went shopping for this beautiful white baby furniture. They bought all types of baby toys and a big gorgeous multi-colored fluffy wool rug covered with bears and clowns. They had laughed as they hung colored fish mobiles over the crib. Paris suggested they paint colorful rainbow murals on the walls of the nursery. They had gone to a paint store and came home with a lot of paint and paint brushes.

While they were busily painting the happy rainbows, Sophia had had a sinking premonition that Paris' happiness would be short lived. Paris had lost a baby only four months before and she had been delighted to be pregnant again. But Sophia had felt that she needed more time between pregnancies. She'd never mentioned her feelings to Paris. How could she say anything when Paris was so blissfully happy? Three months later Paris miscarried again.

Christopher looked at the blood on the white lamb, the floor, and the furniture. He shuddered as he imagined her suffering and pain.

Sophia watched the blood drain from Christopher's face and tears start to form in his eyes. She took his hand and said, "Come to the kitchen and let me brew some Louisiana coffee with chicory for you."

Tou-Tou was in the kitchen, lying motionless on the floor when they walked in.

Sophia petted the dog. "I know that you miss Paris, but she will soon be home to play with you."

Sophia brewed coffee while Christopher composed himself. He found a green tennis ball on the floor, which he tossed back and forth to Tou-Tou. She looked at the kindness on Christopher's face, and remembered him as a small, quiet boy with long arms and a small slim body. He had a mop of sun bleached brown hair, which covered half of his freckled face, and his eyes were the color of copper pennies.

Christopher had grown into his long arms. Although he was not excitingly handsome like Doyle, he was pleasant looking. More importantly, he exuded empathy and stability, two traits that Doyle sadly lacked. Sophia realized that he was in love with Paris. She could see his love when he examined her in the hospital with such great tenderness and concern on his face.

Christopher said, "I forgot to tell you I called Louis. The Viverettes will be here tomorrow morning. They chartered a private plane and will be flying in from Madrid. It's the quickest way they could get here." He finished his coffee and turned to Sophia, "Are you ready to go?"

"Five minutes. I just want to pack an overnight bag with my toiletries. I'm spending the night with Paris. I don't want her to wake up alone in a hospital room."

Sophia was back in a flash. "Christopher, I don't know how I could have managed without you," she said as she gave him a big hug.

Christopher looked at her with tears in his eyes, "I love Paris, too, I will do whatever I can to help her." He kissed Sophia on the cheek and assured her that Paris was getting the best medical care.

They were both quiet as they drove to the hospital.

Chapter 9

Paris' body was in Miami, but her mind was floating in the past. She was happy, carefree and in New Orleans.

Doyle arrived at Paris' apartment promptly at noon on Sunday. Paris greeted him wearing a very short jean skirt and a clingy white T-shirt. She had pulled her shiny mane of black hair back and tied it into a ponytail.

Doyle took one look at her and said, "You look like you're in middle school. Are you sure I am not too old for you?"

She blushed, and in a coquettish voice whispered, "Well maybe you are?"

"Where are you taking me to brunch? I have looked forward to this all week."

"It is a restaurant in a small old hotel, a few blocks away."

Doyle took her hand in his, and asked, "Does the hotel have a name?"

"It's Pinot House. Tourists seldom come to this section of the quarter. Mostly local people go there to eat."

Paris felt good walking next to him. She felt his energy as she held his hand. He was wearing a T-shirt and jeans. She could see his toned body, and she felt the heat of his body next to hers.

"This is it. It looks run down from the outside, but the inside is lovely." Doyle looked at the modest, small, white hotel with little interest.

They walked into the lobby and Doyle was amazed to see that the floor and columns were made of black marble. The art deco furniture was striking in red and black plush velvet. Large framed drawings from the art deco period covered the walls and the black lacquered tables had crystal bowls with flowers in them. The contrast of the shabby exterior to the sophisticated interior was surprising. He knew little about furniture, but he appreciated the uniqueness of everything he saw in the room.

A maître d' dressed in all-white linen greeted them. "Miss Paris, I have your reservation. Please follow me to your table."

As they followed the maître d' Paris noticed the men staring at her as she walked by, and the women staring at Doyle. "We make a nice looking couple," she thought to herself.

They were seated at a round table covered with a snow white tablecloth. They were in middle of the courtyard next to a large pond where big, fat, golden-orange koi swam around in circles in the crystal blue water. Doyle looked around the courtyard and saw hanging baskets overflowing with big pink flowers and ferns hanging from the top of the wrought iron fence.

In the center of the room a jazz band was playing "St. Louis Blues." There was a pianist, a trumpeter, a guitarist and a drummer. They played their music with soul and gusto. The waiter brought their menus and they both ordered Bellini's to drink.

Paris said, "I would like to recommend the eggs sardin, the pain perdu and Andouille sausage. These are the house specials."

"I do not know what any of that is, but I love it when you speak French to me," he replied, laughing. "I am taking your recommendations."

"You are a sly devil, my *beau homme*."

"What are you saying to me, you vixen?"

"You will never know," she said, rapidly fluttering her eyelashes. They sat back sipped their Bellini's and enjoyed listening to the band play "One for My Baby."

The food arrived and Doyle carefully studied it. "Paris, I cannot figure out what the sausage is. It tastes very good. Paris burst out laughing.

"Andouille is a soft smoked spicy Cajun pork sausage. You can only find the good Andouille in Louisiana. I am very glad you are enjoying your food."

They both ordered another drink and quietly sat savoring the music. Doyle took her hand and slowly kissed her fingertips. He looked into her eyes and said. "I want to thank you for a beautiful day. I love being with you. When I'm with you everything becomes magical."

Paris turned beet red. She could feel her whole body melting. Mentally, she could feel him kissing her body, as he had kissed her fingertips. She looked at him, hoping he could not read her mind, and softly said, "What a beautiful thing to say."

Later they walked out of the hotel and Doyle put his arms around her waist, gently kissing her on the mouth. Paris' face turned red. He whispered in her ear, "Thank you for a lovely brunch. I love to watch you blush."

They reached Paris' apartment and Doyle walked her up the stairs. Paris looked at him archly and asked, "Would you like to come upstairs with me?"

"I would be happy to."

Paris opened the door and Doyle took her hand and kissed her palm. He took her face between his hands and gently kissed her eyelids, her cheeks, her mouth, and her neck.

Before he was able to kiss her breasts, Shirree opened the door with a cheery, "Hi guys! Did you have a pleasant brunch?"

Doyle and Paris guiltily pulled apart and greeted Shirree. "I was just going to play some music for Doyle, would you like to join us Shirree?"

"That sounds great. I will be there in a few minutes."

Paris led Doyle, to a small sitting room, with a black baby grand piano in the center and a few chairs surrounding it.

"What would you like me to play for you?" Paris asked.

"I really like 'Don't Cry for Me, Argentina.' Can you play that?"

"No problem," Paris said as she began to play and sing a rendition of the song.

Shirree came in and joined the singing. The girls coaxed Doyle to sing with them and Paris played everything from Beethoven to "When the Saints Come Marching In." Shirree went to the bar and fixed everyone Cosmopolitans. After a couple of those they were giggling and singing with enthusiasm.

Doyle looked at his watch and said, "I can't believe it's seven! I have to go home and study."

"Did you say it was seven?" Shirree echoed. "I was supposed to meet Daisy at seven. I am out of here! I will you see you later. Have a good evening."

It did not take more than five minutes after Shirree left before Paris and Doyle were on the floor. After the Bellini's and Cosmopolitans they were both giddy. Doyle lifted Paris' shirt and undid her bra. He put his mouth on her breasts and slowly started to caress her nipples. She pulled him closer to savor the feeling of his hard body against her. Paris felt herself become hot and dripping wet. Doyle put his hand up her skirt and ripped her silk panties off her. He unzipped himself and dropped his pants to the ground. Paris gasped at the size of engorged penis. He took her hand and placed it over his hardness. She gingerly stroked him.

"I'm sorry Doyle," she said panting as she spoke, "I'm a virgin. I didn't mean to you lead you on, but I do not want to lose my virginity on the floor."

"You're the first girl I've been with who was a virgin," Doyle said in amazement. He brought his arms around her and held her in his arms. "I do not want your first time to be on the floor either. It should be in a romantic place."

Paris looked at him her eyes big as saucers, "Doyle I want you to make love to me, but I hardly know you. Are you willing to wait a little while for me to make up my mind?"

"Of course, baby; as long as it takes I understand. I want you to lie back and relax. I want to make you feel really good."

He put his fingers very gently between her legs. She was sopping wet and moaning. He slowly ran his tongue up and down her legs. He could feel her trembling when his tongue reached her thick, curly mound. He spread her legs apart and started to suck her warm center. She tasted like sweet flowers. She moaned and pushed his head deeply into her. He worked himself into a position where his fingers and tongue were working in sweet harmony with one another. She was screaming his name and her body was moving with his tongue. She came and he kept sucking the sweet honey that emanated from her body until her contractions and moaning stopped.

He gently kissed her on the lips and said, "You taste like sweet honey. You have the sweetest pussy in the world."

She threw her arms around him whispering, "I have never felt like this before. Oh my God, I never knew anything could feel this good."

Doyle laughed. "I have to go now. Will you walk me to the door?"

They dressed and walked down the stairs together.

Paris stopped him. "Doyle, my family is having a crayfish boil next Saturday afternoon. We'll be spending the night at my family's house and come back Sunday. Shirree's boyfriend will be driving. Would you like to come?"

"Count me in! I would really like that." He kissed her deeply and passionately as he walked out the door.

When he arrived at his house, he called Beverly and apologized for running late. He walked quickly towards Beverly's apartment as he hummed Evita to himself.

Chapter 10

The next day Doyle called. "Paris, I'll be finished with my exams early Thursday afternoon. I'd like to see the King Tut exhibit at the museum. Would you like to see it with me?"

"My last class ends at eleven-thirty, so that would be perfect. We can walk to Esplanade Ave and take the bus.

"I will see you at twelve. I hear the exhibit is great."

Shirree looked at her shaking her head, "It must be love. How many times have we gone to the King Tut exhibit, not counting the grand opening party?"

"Maybe three. I love the exhibit! It probably won't come back to New Orleans for many years."

"Oh, you are a great liar! Would you like a sandwich? After all, passion works up a great appetite?"

When Paris came back to the kitchen, Shirree had ham and Swiss cheese sandwiches on rye bread with potato salad on the side.

"I see your romance is going well. Do you still find him distastefully aggressive?"

"I told him that I'm attracted to him, but I do not believe in one night stands. I confided that I was a virgin, and I want my first time to be spectacular. Shirree, he makes me so hot and sexy, but I want him never to forget me. I want him to feel horny every time he thinks of me and be haunted by the scent of my perfume."

"Alright Paris, you've convinced me. You go girl!" Shirree cheered, panting with laughter. "You are the drama queen of the family. Do you want him to scatter rose pedals on the sheets for you?"

The girls giggled as they cleaned up their mess. Shirree looked at Paris, smiling at her like a Cheshire cat.

"By the way Paris, did you tell Doyle about your father?"

"No it never came up in our conversations," she replied archly.

"He will be in for a surprise. You are too much Paris."

*****

Thursday arrived quickly. The couple walked rapidly to the bus stop on Esplanade Avenue, and within five minutes, their bus arrived.

As soon as they sat down, Doyle turned to Paris and said, "This is the last day of the exhibit. I hope we won't have to wait in line for hours to get in."

"I have some friends who work for the museum. I promise you that we will not have to wait in line for hours. Doyle, this is where we get off the bus. We are in front of St. Louis Cemetery number three. You can see sweet olive trees planted all around the cemetery."

"I saw this cemetery on one of my tours. The tour director told us these trees were planted around the cemetery to overcome the smell of death."

"I love their smell. My perfume is made from the flowers of the sweet olive tree," Paris said as she plucked some of the flowers off the tree and gave them to Doyle to smell.

Doyle put the flowers to his nose enjoying their smell. "Every time I smell the sweet olive trees I will think of you," he said, putting his arm around her and pulling her close to his body.

Paris felt her heart begin to beat faster and she knew her face was beginning to flush with excitement. "You are such a flatterer, you scoundrel. That is why you will make a marvelous attorney."

"Now Paris," Doyle said laughing, "Was that a compliment or an insult? I was only telling you the truth."

Paris laughed as she looked up at him and said, "You are a born rogue. I have a feeling that you've had more girlfriends than hair on your head."

"You are probably right and I have a thick head of hair. But remember there are many churches but only one cathedral, and I sense that you will be my cathedral."

Paris stammered and blushed with pleasure. "You are full of blarney!" She began to stutter as she quickly changed the subject, "Do you remember what the tour director told you about St. Louis number three?"

"There you go, I give you a compliment and you change the subject." Doyle looked around the cemetery with admiration "I can see why they call the cemeteries here 'cities of the dead.' The tombs look like miniature houses."

"These tombs or crypts are houses for the soul. Family members of every generation are buried in their own family's vault. My sister Suzette is buried in St. Louis number two. We have our family tomb there. I frequently go there to pray and leave flowers for her."

"I remember the tour director saying that in New Orleans the water table is too high to put coffins in the ground. If it rained hard the ground would become too soggy and the caskets would pop open and the corpses would float away."

"Yes that's true, so the Spanish custom of burying people above ground in vaults was adopted."

"Is it true that Voodoo is practiced in the cemetery at night and all sorts of Voodoo relics can be found around the tombs."

"Some of the cemeteries contain the remains of Voodoo Queens. You can see flowers, votive candles, bones and food around the graves."

"There are all sorts of tales about hauntings and strange things that happen at the cemeteries at night. The gates of all the cemeteries are locked at dusk, and everyone is warned never to go to any cemetery at night unless they go with a tour group." Paris stopped and pointed across the cemetery. "Look Doyle. You can see the museum from the cemetery."

As they were talking, they walked over the bayou on St. John Bridge and entered City Park. They walked up a path lined with large oak trees laden with streamers of moss. The ponds surrounding the museum abounded with ducks, swans and geese floating peacefully in the water waiting for someone to throw them food. They became creatures of the wild when people tossed food to them; once bread and seeds were tossed by kind humans, the wildlife descended upon them. Within seconds hordes of birds would aggressively follow, making quacking noises and pecking them.

"Look around the park Doyle. One hundred or so years ago men dueled under the large oak trees we are walking under."

Doyle admired the museum from a distance. "Paris, This museum looks like a temple. The closer we get to it, the bigger it looks. I enjoy coming here and just looking at the outside of the museum."

"We are very proud of our museum. It is among the top twenty-five museums in the country. It was built on a manmade hill so that it could be seen from blocks away and to protect it from flooding."

As they approached the museum, a crowd of people came into view. "The line is very long, Paris. I hope your friend will be able to get us in. I really want to see the exhibit before it leaves."

"Come with me," she said, taking his hand.

They circumvented the crowd and walked to the front door of the museum. Doyle skeptically followed her, noting the glares from those waiting in the long line. There were two guards standing in the entranceway. The guard on the left tipped his hat to them.

"It is good to see you again, Ms. Paris, have a good day."

"Thank you, Edward," she replied smiling.

Doyle followed Paris to the reception desk where a middle-aged woman greeted her warmly.

"Claudia, this is my friend Doyle O'Connor. We are going find a tour guide to introduce him to King Tutankhamen."

"Your timing is perfect. There is a tour starting in five minutes. It is so nice to see you again."

"It is good seeing you too, Claudia. As soon as the semester is over Shirree and I will be back to volunteer."

"It was nice meeting you, Doyle. I hope you enjoy the exhibit."

"I am sure I will. I've always been interested in King Tut."

They walked over to the tour group and Paris introduced Doyle to Jordan, who was their guide.

"We are lucky to get you as a guide, Jordan, you are the best!"

"Flattery will get you anywhere," the tall blonde replied smoothing back her long hair. "I think I have done three tours already and I know I will be doing three more. I hope I don't lose my voice," she said wearily.

The tour began and they enjoyed seeing the golden mummy and all of his gold ornaments. They both agreed that the King's royal gold diadem and the gold inlaid canopic coffinette, which contained his mummified internal organs, were the most interesting objects of the exhibit. The tour moved slowly among the swarm of people. It lasted two hours.

Doyle looked at Paris and asked, "How many times have you seen this exhibit?"

Paris looked at him with a smile on her face, "Three times, but I have enjoyed the exhibit more and more each time I have seen it. It may not return to America for decades. The golden mummy is an exciting exhibit. King Tut and his gold ornaments are magical to me."

Paris tugged on his arm. "I'd like to show you my favorite exhibit: the Faberge collection of golden eggs. It's here permanently on the second floor."

They walked up the stairs and down a long corridor. They entered a small dimly lit room. It was dark and cold. Doyle exclaimed to Paris, "I can hardly see anything and I think I am getting frost bite."

"Your eyes will get used to the muted light. If the Faberge eggs are exposed to light or heat they will deteriorate."

Paris showed Doyle one ornately decorated gold egg when Doyle became distracted. "Paris, I'm really not into jewelry, but I'd eat."

They walked to the main floor where Paris was greeted by a full-figured redhead who came up and hugged her.

"Miranda," she said as she hugged her back, "it is so good to see you!"

Miranda breathlessly sighed, "I have been looking all over the building for you, Paris. Your father heard you were here with a friend and would like to invite both of you for cocktails."

"I thought he was still in Greece, or I would have gone to say hello to him in his office. Oh Doyle, I am sorry I didn't introduce you sooner. This is my father's secretary and my friend Miranda. Miranda, this is my friend Doyle."

Doyle had no idea what was going on, he was confused but he had enough aplomb to take Michelle's hand and say, "It is very nice to meet you."

"I hope you enjoyed the King Tut exhibit."

"Paris," Doyle asked emphatically, "Who is your father?" "Louis Henri Viverette."

"No, I mean what is your father's connection to the museum?"

"He's the curator."

"You never mentioned it to me before."

"I had no reason to, Doyle. What difference does it make to you what my father does?" she said defensively.

"You're right Paris, but it was a big surprise to me! I felt embarrassed because everyone knew accept me."

"I did not mean to embarrass you. I apologize for my thoughtlessness."

"I accept your apology. How do you know where to meet your father for cocktails?"

"My father always goes to the same place. Tavern on the Park is a few blocks from here. You'll love it. It's an old bar and restaurant which has the original furniture from the early nineteen hundreds."

"I am sure I will love the bar, but the question is: am I going to love your father?"

"He is a very interesting man with a great sense of humor. Everyone likes him," Paris assured.

A maître d' met them at the door and Paris saw her father and uncle's booth at the end of the room.

"Papa," she said, turning to a slightly plump olive skinned man with thinning hair. Mr. Viverette sported a well-trimmed mustache and goatee. Paris kissed him lightly on his cheek and smiled as she made introductions. "This is my friend Doyle. Doyle this is my father."

Louis Viverette shook Doyle's hand and said, "It is very nice meeting you. I am so glad you could join us. Please sit down."

Doyle sat down and Paris went up to her uncle and kissed him on his cheek.

"Oncle Pierre this is my friend Doyle, and Doyle this is my Oncle Pierre."

Doyle thought that there was very little similarity between the brothers. Louis was thick set, with a round distinguished face and an aquiline nose. He was about five-foot-eleven and his brother was slightly taller. Pierre, as well as Louis, had a round face even though he was leaner than his brother. He possessed a full head of dark hair graying at the temples and his face was clean-shaven. Both men shared the art of congeniality and an aristocratic air of graciousness. Paris sat next to her father and Doyle sat across from her next to her uncle.

"What would you like to drink? Pierre and I are having scotch. I don't see many young people drinking scotch."

"Louis, scotch is too strong for the youngins. It is an acquired taste, like caviar. Scotch is for real men like me and old men like you." They all burst out laughing, breaking the ice." You have to understand Doyle, I am only two years older than my brother, and now that we are older, he will not let me forget it!"

Louis looked at Doyle and said, "Are you attending college here?"

"I'm attending Tulane. I am in my second year of law school."

"Good for you. Lawyers make a lot of money. My brother Pierre is an attorney and he has done very well for himself."

Pierre spoke up jovially, "I enjoy being an attorney. I especially enjoy the drama of being a trial attorney. I have twenty-two attorneys working for me, and they all practice different aspects of law."

"I would like to be a trial attorney. That is what I want to specialize in when I finish law school."

Pierre handed his business card to Doyle saying, "Call me when you have free time, and if I am trying a case in court you are welcome to come and observe me."

"Thank you, I appreciate your offer. I'm going take you up on it as soon as I can."

"I wanted my son Andre to follow in my footsteps, become an attorney and join my law firm. Andre had other ideas. He graduated from Tulane and then he decided he wanted to become a chef rather than an attorney. Now he owns a restaurant in Paris and my dreams of Viverette and Viverette law firm have passed."

"Pierre, Andre attended Le Cordon Bleu culinary school in Paris. He worked at a four-star restaurant in Paris as head chef for two years and then opened his own restaurant in Paris, which he named Vivi in honor of our family spice business. He is a famous chef and he is very happy with it."

"Louis, you are right and I am pleased my son is happy. His restaurant is successful and he is married to a very beautiful lady. And Marisol is pregnant with my first grandchild. However, I did want him to be in business with me." Pierre had to take his leave early. "Paris, Doyle, I am afraid I have to leave now. Your lovely Ante Juliet is waiting for me at home. She invited some people for dinner, and if I am late she will be upset."

Louis looked at him innocently, "I assume you are leaving me with the check?"

Pierre, a big smile on his face, said, "Yes, I am, and with great pleasure." He shook hands with Doyle saying, "I hope I will be seeing you soon." He gave Paris a big kiss on her cheek. He then glanced at his brother, smiling roguishly at him, "It is always enjoyable seeing my much older brother." Everyone at the table laughed heartily.

When Doyle shook hands with Pierre, he felt his firm grip and soft hands. He scrutinized Louis, holding his scotch glass with his long fingers and well-manicured nails, and thought to himself that Louis and Pierre exuded money. Their clothes were custom made for them. He could tell by the stitching, the fit, and the unusual texture of the fabric. More importantly, they had the panache of men who were in control of others.

Louis smiled at Doyle, "I would like to invite you and Paris for dinner, unless you have made other plans."

"That is fine with me. I was planning to take Paris for dinner anyway."

Doyle watched Louis motion for the check, as he slowly sipped his scotch.

"We will go to Café Degas. It is cool enough to eat outside on the patio and they have excellent food."

The parking lot attendant brought Louis's shiny black Jaguar to the door and Paris sat in the front with her father.

"This is a very nice car Mr. Viverette, it smells of new leather."

"Please call me Louis—Mr. Viverette sounds too formal. This car is only a week old. It is the third Jaguar I have had in the past three years. I really like the way the Jaguars handle the road."

They arrived at Café Degas, a charming café decorated with many paintings and packed with people. Luckily, some people had finished dinner and were leaving the patio just as they came in.

Louis commented, "This is not a very posh restaurant, but the food is excellent and the atmosphere is very colorful."

The manager, an elderly-looking blond woman with a heavy French accent, came to the table and handed out menus.

"It eez a pleasure to see you here again," she said.

Louis said to Doyle, "The owner is an artist from France; he opened the café in 1980 and tried to replicate the feel of a small, intimate, Parisian bistro. Edgar Degas lived a few blocks away from here with his relatives. That's the reason the café is called Café Degas."

After they ordered and their food was brought out to their table, the conversation turned to the museum. Doyle asked, "Louis, what made you choose your unique vocation?"

Louis paused for a second and replied, "I have always been interested in art and antiquities. A curator has the opportunity to explore both. I became interested in art because my great, great-grandfather met Edgar Degas when Degas lived with his mother's relatives in New Orleans for a year."

"I had no idea Degas visited New Orleans until Paris told me today."

"Yes he lived in New Orleans for about a year and created some amazing works while he was here."

"Degas was a great man. My great, great-grandfather Jon Charles Viverette was a struggling artist who went to visit Degas when he was here. Jon was so impressed with Degas' work, he begged Degas to allow him to go to Paris to study with him.

"Unfortunately, only small groups of people were interested in buying his work, but Jon still kept painting because he enjoyed it. An odd thing happened about eighty years ago: one of the descendants of the original owners of his artwork donated the paintings he inherited to several museums and Grandfather Jon's work suddenly became famous. His talent was recognized and soon many art collectors started to search out his work to buy. His art work does not bring in the money of a Degas or Monet, but it brings in a tidy sum."

"Papa I am sure Doyle is not interested in our ancestor's art work."

"I am very interested in art history. Please tell me more."

Louis continued, "When I was a young boy I found some of Grandfather Jon's paintings stored in the attic. I was very impressed by his talent; this sparked my interest in art. I had no interest in painting, but I discovered I was interested in collecting. Our family always collected antiques and our house contains a multitude of collectibles handed down from generation to generation and I always enjoyed researching their origins.

"I am very lucky to be able to be a curator because I am doing what I love. I travel all over the world and visit many museums. I see exhibits of fine art and antiquities and I buy for the museum and my personal collection and get paid for it."

"Did you ever find any more of your grandfather Jon's work?"

"I have never found any more of his art work. According to the records he kept there are many more paintings hidden away on our property. Every five years or so we have a scavenger hunt, but so far we have not found all of the missing paintings."

After they finished dinner and their snifters of Grand Marnier, Louis said, "I should be getting home. Lilly and Lady Madeline should be finished with their bridge party by now."

Paris said, "Papa thank you for a lovely evening."

Louis replied, "It was my pleasure. I am glad you could join me. Doyle, I want you and Paris to take a cab home. It is too dangerous to walk the streets of mid-city at night."

He handed Doyle some bills and called for a cab with his cellphone.

Doyle replied, "Louis, that's not necessary. I will pay for our cab."

"Doyle, you and Paris are my guests. I insist on paying."

"You can't argue with my father, you will never win. Papa thanks again for a lovely dinner."

"Louis, I appreciate your generosity. I have enjoyed this evening very much."

Louis kissed his daughter and shook hands with Doyle as he departed.

The cab stopped at Paris' apartment first. Doyle walked her to the door and kissed her passionately goodnight. After Paris was dropped off, the taxi delivered Doyle to his home. Alex was already asleep. Doyle went to bed shortly after.

He thought of Paris and her family. The Viverettes had everything he ever wanted. They did not have to live in near-poverty wondering where their next meal was coming from. At ten years old, he had to start work-cutting lawns, as did his brother Brandon. It wasn't for their spending money, but to contribute money for the survival of their family.

He shuddered when he remembered the times his father spent all of the money he received from the Navy on booze and his mother learned how to prepare Spam in ten different ways. He had to wear Brandon's old clothes, which were sometimes threadbare by the time he got them. He never had more than one pair of shoes at a time; sometimes he had to wear them with holes in them because they could not afford another pair.

The Viverette family lived in the same house for generations; they had roots, whereas his family wandered from place to place living in small ugly apartments and matchbox houses. He decided at that moment, he was going to marry Paris. Did he love her? He didn't really know, but he did know that he coveted her lifestyle with a strong passion.

Chapter 11

Sophia stood over Paris as she lay unconscious in her hospital bed. She chanted softly as she anointed Paris' hands and feet with a sweet cream she had specifically made for this the previous evening. The cream contained an assortment of herbs, sweetened almond oil and oil of sweet olive trees.

Sophia had brought her healing book with her from New Orleans. Joseph laughingly called her book *The Handy Voodoo Book of Spells*.

When her ancestors came from Africa, they brought their skills in healing herbs with them. They could not find the same herbs and plants in Louisiana, but by trial and error, they created new mixtures to minister to the sick. As time went on, they added spells for love, luck, fertility, money and anything that would improve their position in life. The first Voodoo queens were unable to read or write so the information was passed on orally to the next queen.

The massive book was old and worn. The entries were all hand-written and each new queen entered her new chants, spells and recipes for *gris-gris* bags that she personally developed. *Gris-gris* bags were small bags of herbs and other magical items that were made to be carried by the supplicant to bring love, luck, health, money and a myriad of other things they might desire.

Sophia quietly sat on the chair next to Paris' bed. She held her hand and prayed for her recovery. Paris looked so frail and defenseless with the IV in her arm and the other monitors that connected her limbs and body to the apparatus next to the bed. Sophia stood up and felt compelled to examine Paris' arms and shoulders carefully. For the first time she noticed that Paris had numerous small, faded bruises on her skin. She could not believe she hadn't noticed them before but initially she had been focusing on Paris' bruised face and injured head.

Christopher came in the room with another doctor whom he introduced as Harrison Michael a specialist in head injuries. Dr. Michael had already studied Paris' X-rays and the results of her tests before he came to examine her. He thoroughly checked her bodily reflexes and raised her eyelids to check her eyes.

"The last X-ray shows the swelling of her brain is receding. Her reflexes appear normal. Her blood work shows no abnormalities. The coma is helping her heal by removing stress from her mind and body. I don't know when she will come out of her coma and I don't know if she will have any memory loss. All we can do is hope for the best. I am sorry that I cannot give you a specific timeline."

Sophia looked up at the white-haired, bearded Dr. Michael, who had a very serious look on his angular face. "I appreciate your coming here. I am glad you explained everything to me."

Dr. Michael removed his horn-rimmed glasses and smiled at Sophia. "It is amazing how many inexplicable cures have come from hope and prayer. I hope Paris will regain her health soon."

Several hours later, Louis and Lilly entered Paris' room with trepidation. Lilly took one look at her daughter's inert body hooked up to monitors and IVs and began to sob. Sophia stood up and went to hug Lilly and both women began to cry.

"She is going to be fine. Please sit next to her. Christopher was just here with a specialist from Mayo Clinic. He will be back shortly. He can explain what has happened to Paris more accurately then I can."

As if on cue Christopher walked into the room and greeted the grief-stricken Viverettes. He hugged Lilly and shook Louis's hand. He then repeated what he and Dr. Michael had told Sophia.

Louis' face was ashen when Christopher finished speaking. He went over to his wife and put his arms around her as she cried hysterically. Lilly went over to Paris and kissed her bruised face and hugged her prostrate body. She gained her composure and began talking to Paris as if she were cognizant of what happens around her. Louis and Sophia sat as still as statues as they watched Lilly's attempts to communicate with her daughter.

Sophia invited Christopher for a cup of coffee asking Lilly and Louis if they would like something from the hospital café, but they declined. When they reached the café Christopher brought two hot steaming cups of coffee to the table and asked Sophia what she would like to discuss with him.

She replied, "Christopher and I found faded bruises on Paris' arms and shoulders and wrists. I did not see them before because I was concentrating on her face and all the monitors she is hooked up to."

"I noticed them immediately Sophia. My guess is that Doyle forcefully grasped her in a fit of anger. I am convinced he has been abusing her and that he is responsible for her concussion. I will speak to him about it. I do not want to upset Louis and Lilly at this time; I feel it would be too much for them to deal with."

"I agree with you Christopher," Sophia retorted in a soft, angry voice.

Doyle arrived in Miami in late afternoon. The first thing he did when he returned to Miami was to contact his office and speak to his private secretary, Miranda, whom he paid well and who was the personification of discretion.

"You have quite a few calls," Miranda said. "Sophia Moses and Mr. Viverette called to tell you your wife Paris is in Mount Sinai hospital, in room 1040, and he asked you call him on his cellphone. He said you have the number. And an Adriana Franco called you twice. She said that you have her phone number. Would you like the names and telephone numbers of the clients who called?"

"Miranda, what did my father-in-law say?" Doyle asked in a breathless voice.

"He asked where you were and when you would return to Miami."

"What did you tell him?"

"I told him you were away on business and you would be back this afternoon; and you did not tell me where you were going."

"Miranda, please call Ms. Franco and tell her I have a family emergency and I will call her as soon as I can. Call all of my other clients and tell them the same thing. Tell my brother that Paris is in the hospital and I am on my way to see her. If any of my clients need urgent help, please have Brandon speak to them for me. And Miranda, thanks for handling everything so efficiently for me."

"That's what you pay me for, Doyle. Good luck."

He immediately called Louis. "Louis, what is wrong with Paris? Why is she in the hospital?"

"She has a concussion and is in a coma."

"Oh my god. I'll be right there." Doyle hung up quickly.

"Louis, is he coming to the hospital? Where was he this weekend?"

"Lilly, I didn't ask him where he was. All I know is that he was not with our daughter, so you ask him where he spent his weekend if you like."

"Louis, don't be rude to me!" she snapped as tears poured out of her bright blue eyes and rolled down her pale cheeks.

Louis walked over to his wife and embraced her slender body tightly. He smoothed back a blonde tendril of hair that had fallen out of her chignon.

"I'm sorry I was rude. I don't give a damn about what he did this weekend. All I care about is our daughter."

Christopher entered the room and said, "I have ordered more tests for Paris. An orderly is going to take her for X-rays. It would be better if you all waited here. We should be finished in an hour."

"Please, Christopher, I can't bear to lose another child. You must promise me you will do everything possible to save Paris," Lilly pleaded. She was on the verge of hysteria.

"Lilly, believe me. I am doing everything feasible to get Paris well as soon as possible. I have had consultations with all the doctors in the hospital and, as I told you, a colleague of mine from Mayo Clinic has examined her. We just have to give her injury time to heal."

Sophie walked over to Lilly and said to her, "I promise you Paris will be well very soon."

Their eyes met and Lilly stopped crying. She tried to put a smile on her face as she said, "Christopher, I apologize for my ridiculous words. I know you are doing everything in your power to help Paris and you do not want to make any false promises to me. Is it possible for me to spend the night in the hospital with Paris?"

"Yes of course. I will ask the nurse for an extra bed for you. It will be no problem. Why don't you go to the hospital restaurant and have something to eat. It will make you feel better."

The three of them sat in the room talking about nothing for what seemed an eternity, but what was only a couple of hours. All eyes were focused on Paris who lay limp and motionless, her body attached to wires as if she were a puppet.

Doyle entered the room, greeted everyone hurriedly and dashed to Paris' bedside.

"What happened to my wife?" he asked passionately, as he looked at her swollen, bruised face.

Three pairs of eyes watched him as he went to sit next to his comatose wife.

He gushed, "Paris I am so sorry you are hurt and I was away. Oh baby I am so sorry!" He kissed her cheek and took her limp hand and kissed her fingertips. A sprinkle of teardrops fell down his well-tanned face.

Christopher came into the room and greeted Doyle coldly. He directed his conversation to Paris' parents. "We just examined Paris' latest X-rays and her condition is unchanged."

"What is her condition?" asked Doyle.

Christopher explained Paris' state to Doyle and emphasized the trauma to her head that initiated her coma. After the explanation, he looked at Doyle directly and said, "Do you have any idea what might have happened to Paris to cause her concussion?"

"I cannot imagine what happened to her. I have been out of town this weekend. I tried calling her, but I was in Martinique fishing and the phone service is not very dependable there."

Christopher looked at the Viverettes and Sophia and said, "You must be very hungry. The dining room on third floor has a panoramic view of the intercoastal water way. Also, the food is much better than the other restaurants in the hospital."

Doyle said, "I am here now. I will sit with my wife."

Louis looked quizzically at Christopher. "We just returned from the dining room I don't think we're hungry at this time."

Sophia replied quickly, "That is a good idea. We need to leave the room for a while and walk around. Lilly, you are going to need clothes and some toiletries if you intend to spend the night at the hospital. We can buy everything at the gift store here in the hospital."

The three of them walked silently out of the room and located the elevator, which would take them to the first floor where the gift shop was located.

Sophia looked at Louis and Lilly and said, "I believe Christopher wishes to speak to Doyle alone."

"Ah," Louis nodded.

As soon as the family left, Christopher confronted Doyle. "I know that you had something to do with Paris' injuries. I have no way of proving it: but I promise you if she dies you will pay for it."

Doyle responded, ferociously, "You've been reading too many novels. I love my wife! I would never do anything to hurt her!"

Christopher turned his back on Doyle and walked out of the room abruptly. He could not prove any of his accusations, but in his heart, he knew Doyle had done something to hurt Paris.

Doyle sat next to his prostrate wife who appeared small and helpless in her hospital bed. He stared at the IV attached to her hand and all the devises she was hooked up to and felt waves of guilt wash over him as he was fascinated by her bruised and swollen face. He knew he had caused the trauma to her head. After he had tried to pick her up and carry her out of the bedroom, she fell to the floor hitting her head on the sharp corner of their marble end table. He remembered the resonance of the thud when she struck her head and the sound of her piteous sobbing reverberated in his mind. He was sure that the collision of her head against the table caused her concussion. He was so angry about her waking him up that he never bothered to check to see if she was hurt.

He leaned over Paris and whispered in her ear, "I am so sorry, baby; I never meant to hurt you. I must have been out of my mind. Please forgive me."

He sat watching her still body for quite some time and then he realized that no matter what happened to her he had to pick up the pieces of his life and continue to function. He took his cellphone out of his pocket and called the main number of the hospital requesting the gift shop. He ordered their biggest bouquet of flowers sent to his wife's room. He regretted his actions toward her, but he could not allow anyone to find out what he had done to her.

In the dining room, the family ordered dinner and once again picked at the bland, unseasoned, unappetizing food that was placed in front of them.

"I just have a feeling there is something wrong with their marriage. My intuition tells me that there is something not right with their relationship," said Louis.

Lilly turned to her husband. "Do not become paranoid, Louis. We cannot fault Doyle for having to go away on a business trip. You are away on business all the time. I never doubt your love for me just because you do a lot of traveling."

"You're right Lilly," Louis relented sheepishly. "I'm being stupid. Paris has never complained about Doyle; she adores him. I am sure he loves her as much as we do. However I am certain about one thing: the food in this hospital is horrible." Louis pushed away his barely touched plate.

"My love, hospital food is always dreadful. Look on the bright side: you need to lose weight and the hospital cooking will help."

Lilly and Sophia laughed at the look of embarrassment on Louis's face.

"Lilly," he laughing jovially, "I think I married you for your sense of your humor."

The three of them laughed heartily together. After hours of worry, laughter was the catharsis they needed to ease their anxiety.

"There is a chapel in the hospital and I'd like to go there to pray. Will you accompany us Sophia?"

"Of course, Lilly, I'll go with you. I think that's a good idea. All prayer is good."

After looking in on Paris once again, Lilly stayed behind in the hospital with her daughter and Doyle, while Sophia and Louis decided to go back to the house for some rest.

Tou-Tou greeted them as soon as they walked in the door. He jumped all over them and then started yelping pitifully. Sophia refilled his automatic feeder and put water in his aerated doggy waterfall.

"He misses Paris," Sophia explained.

She had been so upset about Paris' trauma she had not noticed that Paris' beautiful antiques had been replaced with ultra-modern décor pieces. In the middle of the room stood a couch, which looked like an overgrown, fuchsia kidney. The table next to it looked like a bottle-green mushroom held up by a long chrome stem. She stared at a large, framed picture of a large red can of Campbell's tomato soup above the couch.

Sophia shook her head saying, "Lordy, Lordy. I know Doyle chose this furniture."

Tou-Tou followed Sophia to her bedroom and watched her every move. He could not find Paris so he paid close attention to Sophia; he wanted to make sure she would not abandon him. Tou-Tou barked, vigorously licked her face and fell asleep beside her.

Sophia decided to sleep in the downstairs suite where Paris' clothes were hanging. She knew she would feel closer to Paris by sleeping there. She brought her suitcase to Paris' bedroom.

Sophia lay in bed with Tou-Tou and thought of how she helped Paris move into this house four years ago. Paris had hired a closet designer to remake her and Doyle's walk-in closets. She made sure there were special cabinets for her shoes and handbags. She had special sections made to separate her sports clothes from the casual clothes, and her cocktail dresses were color-coded. She was thrilled by the way the closets looked. There was no way she would have voluntarily moved her clothes to another closet and have them placed there in a hap-hazard way. Something out of the ordinary had to have happened. She would contact the maids first thing in the morning and try to find out when Paris moved her belongings to another room.

Doyle returned to his house about two hours after Sophia and

Louis. He made as little noise as possible. He didn't want to wake them up and be forced to make conversation with them.

Tou-Tou heard him enter his room and followed right behind him. The small white dog started to howl as loud as he could, and Doyle tried to kick him away, but Tou-Tou was quicker than he and sunk his sharp little teeth in Doyle's ankle. Sophia heard the noise and knocked on Doyle's door asking him what was wrong. When Tou-Tou heard her voice he started howl again, waking Louis who came into the room as quickly as possible.

Doyle angrily showed Louis and Sophia his bloody ankle, hissing, "This animal is dangerous."

Sophia replied, "Doyle, this dog weighs less than twelve pounds, maybe you stepped on his tail by accident and that is why he bit you."

Louis looked at Doyle and said, "Sophia will keep her door shut. That should solve this problem."

Sophia kissed Tou-Tou and whispered to him as she put him in bed beside her. "I know what you wanted to tell me. Everything is going to be alright. We need to go to sleep now."

Doyle was furious at Tou-Tou. The dog had hated him from the minute Paris had brought him home. He washed his bloody ankle and put a bandage on it. He was tired, but unable to fall asleep and kept thinking about his predicament.

The Viverette family owned his house, his car, the furniture in his house and his office. He only had about a hundred thousand dollars in his own name; not enough money to support his lifestyle or business for any length of time. Everyone thought that he was a successful shrewd businessman to be able to afford his extravagant lifestyle. He knew he would end up penniless if he divorced Paris.

He certainly could not afford the humiliation of the Leon family becoming aware of his real financial situation. They would lose all respect for him. He would no longer be their peer. The more he thought of his situation, the more fearful he became. He felt his hands grow cold and his body stiffen with apprehension.

He thought of leaving Miami and running away to another part of the country where no one would know him, change his name, and start a new life. He decided that would be his best option if he wanted to stay alive. In Miami everyone was impressed by one's façade and trappings of success. You had to look rich to become rich. Wealthy clients would not be drawn to an attorney who looked poor; they gravitated to an attorney who exuded prosperity. They equated money with power, and only a powerful attorney would be able to protect their interests.

The Viverettes were never overly fond of him. They tolerated him because Paris loved him. Everything they did for him was to make their daughter happy. If Paris were to die he would receive nothing from them. His lifestyle would evaporate and so would his status.

On the day that they announced their engagement, Louis welcomed Doyle to the family and said, "Treat my daughter with love and respect, keep her out of harm's way, and be loyal to her. If you do hurt her, you will live to regret it."

Louis's words reverberated in Doyle's mind as he took a long, hot shower. He put on a dressing gown and quietly walked down the stairway to his wet bar where he poured himself a large stiff drink of scotch. Of course, the bane of his existence, Tou-Tou, started to bark as he moved around his house.

Carlo had packed his bag for him and everything was neatly in place. At the bottom of his suitcase he found a souvenir of the yacht, a plush large green hand towel that was tidily folded over something thick and heavy. He unfolded the towel and found a huge stack of bills, very tightly packed together. There was a small note on top of the stack with one word on it "enjoy." He counted the hundred dollar bills—there were 500 of them.

"What a welcome surprise," he said to himself.

He opened the door of the walk-in, custom-made closet that contained his private safe. Paris had an interior designer create special cabinets and drawers for both their closets. Hidden behind a maze of cabinets, he could hardly find the safe himself. He finally opened it and placed his cash inside. As he placed the money in the very back of the safe, a large brown envelope dropped to the floor. He opened the envelope, curious since he couldn't remember what it held. There were two life insurance policies: one for Paris' life worth two millions dollars and one for his life for the same amount. Each was the beneficiary of the other. Doyle had completely forgotten about the policies.

He breathed a sigh of relief and muttered to himself, "Jesus, Mary and Joseph, thank you God."

He kissed the policies. He was briefly jubilant before he had a reality check. Paris is alive, so what good are the policies? Two million dollars would make life much easier for him. He could build up his practice and not worry about money.

He checked his cellphone for messages. He had one from Alberto telling him he was saddened to hear Paris is in the hospital, but Adriana was waiting for his call. He called Adriana and listened to her gush about their wedding. When she asked him where he wanted their wedding reception to be, he felt nauseated. He told her he was feeling ill and had to go to sleep and promised her he would call her back in the morning when he's feeling better. His last thought before he fell asleep was that he knew he was destined to sell his soul to the devil one way or another.

*****

Early the next morning he was awakened by a knock on his bedroom door.

He heard Louis's deep voice saying, "Doyle I must speak with you."

Doyle's heart began to pound rapidly in his chest. Louis was going to give him the news that Paris had died during the night. A feeling of exhilaration and happiness swept through his body. All his problems are solved! Doyle opened the door and Louis embraced him, gushing happily.

"Paris opened her eyes and she recognized Lilly! But she fell back to sleep. The doctor assured us Paris was on the road to recovery. She might be in and out of consciousness until she is fully recovered. The important thing the doctor said was that she recognized her mother and she could speak, so her brain is functioning."

Doyle looked at Louis's beaming face and replied, "I am so happy I don't know what to say. I am going to dress quickly so I can be with her. I have been up all night praying for her recovery."

Louis looked at Doyle's bloodshot eyes and haggard face and cursed himself for doubting his son-in-law's devotion to his daughter. Lilly was right: he had been acting like a paranoid fool.

Chapter 12

Paris lay in her hospital bed oblivious to her surroundings, her limbs confined by tubes and monitoring devices. Her dreams and thoughts visited the past when her life was filled with fun and anticipation of a happy, promising future.

She and Doyle were sitting in the back seat of David's vintage Mercedes quietly holding hands. Shirree and David were laughing and bantering in the front seat as David drove to the Viverettes' crayfish boil.

Shirree turned to look at Doyle and said, "We live in the woods with nothing around us but the bayou, ancient oak trees and the brown, muddy Mississippi River."

"Shirree, I didn't know that you and Paris lived in the same house."

"We don't Doyle. There are two family homes on our plantation. My home is a mile down the road from Paris'."

David turned down a winding road flanked by thick masses of brightly colored wild flowers. He took an exaggerated breath through his nose.

"We are almost there. I can smell the crawfish boiling from here! Mmm! Mmm! I'm starved! I can hardly wait to attack a mound of boiled crawfish."

"Shirree, my mouth is starting to water. I think I can smell them already. What about you, Doyle? Can you smell them?"

Doyle nodded enthusiastically, "And I am starved. I hope there is a lot of crawfish for us to eat."

Paris laughed, "My parents always have a lot of crawfish to cook for a boil. About forty pounds of crawfish makes only ten pounds of meat, which serves eight to ten people, so they always have two pots cooking when they have a lot of people coming over."

One minute they were on a deserted road and the next minute a huge, white manor house loomed in front of them. The large house was built on land that was much higher than the road and looked quite majestic as they approached it. The mansion literally took Doyle's breath away. There were four ionic columns in the front of the manse. The second floor had a white wrought-iron fence surrounding it. On each side of the house was a slanting staircase to the second floor. The staircases intercepted each other and joined at the center.

The pristine white manor was cradled by masses of deep pink crepe myrtle and large red azaleas, whose wild, fiery blossoms grew jungle-like tentacles all over the front and sides of the enormous house. There were clusters of magnolia trees on the outer perimeter of the house, their large white flowers contributing to the look of an untamed tropical garden.

David drove to the back of the house and parked alongside many other cars. They walked into a large, covered pavilion where many long wooden tables and benches had been set up. The tops of the tables were covered with newspapers. On a few tables there were piles of small, cooked, blood-red crawfish and individual piles of boiled corn, onions, and potatoes that had been boiled with the crawfish.

Paris looked at her father standing over a huge pot of boiling water happily dropping vegetables and spices into the swirling water. He was wearing a white chef's hat and apron and he appeared sublimely enthralled by his cooking. Several feet from him stood Papa Joe, also wearing a white apron, but sans chef hat. He was holding a large colander of grayish-looking crawfish that he dipped in and out of a large tub of cool water to clean the mud off.

Paris took Doyle's hand and said, "I want you to meet Papa Joe. He's cleaning the crayfish. He's my godfather and his wife Maman Sophia is my godmother."

Doyle looked up at Papa Joe and shook his calloused hand, which felt like a vise around his fingers. Papa Joe smiled.

"Nice to meet you," he said to Papa Joe, slightly intimidated by the six-foot tall man built like Paul Bunyan.

Joe greeted Paris with a big hug saying, "Lordy girl, you get prettier and prettier every time I see you. Doyle, you treat my godchild good or you will be dealing with me. Hear?"

Paris blushed as she looked at Doyle. "Papa Joe is just being funny. Papa is waving to us. He wants to say hello." She smiled at Papa Joe and said, "We'll see you later."

They walked over to Louis' cooking station and he welcomed his daughter with a big hug and kiss and then shook Doyle's hand.

"Doyle welcome to Bayou House! I hope you two are hungry. We have plenty of food for you. Doyle, do you like crawdaddys?"

"I love these little creatures, but it takes me forever to get any meat out of them."

"Let me show how to eat crawfish Loozy-anna style."

He took a cooked crawfish from the pile on the table and twisted the head apart from the tail and set it aside. He peeled a couple of segments of shells from the table to expose more meat and pinched the bottom end of the tail and pulled the meat out of the shell. Then he grabbed the head and sucked the seasoned juices out of it."

Now you try it Doyle," he said as he handed him a large crawfish.

It took Doyle twice as long to extract the meat. "I think I have the hang of doing it the Louisiana way. This is the best crawfish I've ever tasted."

"That is because I boil it in my secret seasonings handed down from generation to generation. In fact, we sell our private recipe seasonings all over the world. Papa Joe and Maman Sophia run my import-export business for me."

"Papa you sound like a Louisiana Colonial Saunders, talking about your secret seasonings."

"Honey, I'm not exaggerating. The Viverette family spice recipes are our money secret."

Paris handed Doyle a washcloth dipped in lemon water and said, "My mother, aunt, and grandmother are on the other side of the pavilion. I want to introduce you to them."

Paris and Doyle took their leave. "Thanks for the lesson on crawfish eating Louis. I appreciate it," Doyle said in parting.

Louis smiled at the young lovers, "Have a good time guys. Good friends, good food, and good music—that's what it is like down here on the Bayou."

Doyle looked around and realized there were almost a hundred people milling around eating and drinking from the kegs of beer on the tables.

Paris glanced over at Doyle. "I know my father is a trip, but we humor him."

"Paris, he's a great guy. I really like him."

Paris smiled at him warmly. "I am glad. But what's not to like, really? He has fundraisers for charities all the time and he tries to help people less fortunate than us."

Paris steered him to the other side of the pavilion where a bunch of women were sitting at a round table sipping white wine in long stemmed glasses. They reached the table and Paris began the introductions.

"Maman, this is my friend Doyle. Doyle, this is my mother; everyone calls her Miss Lilly."

Lilly shook Doyle's hand. "Welcome to our home. I hope you enjoy your visit with us. Please bring two more chairs so you and Paris can sit down. I'll introduce you to the rest of the family."

Doyle stood up and fetched two chairs.

"Doyle, this is my mother Madeline Dior, Paris' grandmother; she prefers to be called Lady Madeline."

Lady Madeline extended her hand to Doyle and said in her heavily accented English, "So nice to meet you Doyle."

Lady Madeline was most likely in her late eighties. She had long white hair which she wore neatly pulled back from her face in a bun. Her sparkling green eyes didn't appear to miss anything around her. She was much taller than her daughters and her granddaughters and she carried her slender body with grace.

"Doyle, this is my sister Miss Juliet."

Juliet was a slightly buxom, vivacious redhead who dressed in bright colors.

Doyle shook hands and said, "Miss Juliet, I have met your lovely daughter Shirree. It's a pleasure to meet you."

Within a few minutes Miss Lilly had skillfully introduced him to at least twenty relatives and friends. Papa Joe sat next to Maman Sophia and Doyle thought that they seemed to be a happy couple. Sophia had golden skin and large sienna-colored eyes. Papa Joe was the color of polished ebony and when Doyle looked at him he thought of a well-muscled panther.

There was the constant sound of laughter. Pierre kept everyone laughing with his zings directed at his brother Louis, and Louis always had a witty jibe for him in return. He compared Paris' family with his and inwardly winced. Louis was well groomed, dressed well, was unfailingly gracious and had a coterie of friends; his brother Pierre seemed to share all of his brother's traits and in addition had a quick wit.

Doyle thought of his father Daniel O'Connor, who was a tall man with a potbelly. His face was red and lined, his nose was bulbous and when he smiled neither his eyes nor his demeanor smiled along with his lips. He had few friends and rarely spoke more than a few words to anyone. Foulness seemed to cling to him. When the priests and nuns spoke about evil and the devil at the Church of the Little Flower where

Doyle had attended grade school, Daniel O'Connor's face would pop into Doyle's mind as the evil they referred to.

Doyle pictured his mother Cristina at the Viverette table laughing with the family. He remembered her from when he was very young; she was not a beautiful woman but she was pleasant looking with her black shiny hair and dark brown eyes that glittered like stars when she laughed. Over the years the bleakness of her life took away her laughter and sweetness and left in their place a thin, faded, joyless woman.

He and Paris sat and spoke with her family for a short time and then Paris said, "Doyle, you must be starved."

They politely said goodbye to everyone and excused themselves from the table. They quickly walked back to the pavilion where more people had joined the festivities and they all were happily talking, eating, and drinking. David and Shirree were at the first table they came to.

Shirree said merrily, "We've been looking for you! I'm glad you found us. Grab the plates at the end of the table and dig in."

There was no cutlery on the table, just paper plates, paper towels, piles of food and kegs of beer. They grabbed their plates and began eating the red-hot crawfish and the seasoned potatoes, corn and onions that were cooked with the crawfish.

There was no talking for at least twenty minutes while everyone sat chewing. Then the music began; someone went to the front of the pavilion and started to play the horn. Then another man brought his drums to the front and a woman joined them with her guitar. Papa Joe went to the front with his trombone and Oncle Pierre walked up with his clarinet and they all started to jam. The sound of "Tin Roof Blues" resonated through the room. Everyone started to clap hands and sing along with the band.

Stealthily, a troop of cleaning people came and started to clean the tables and gather the remnants of the food to take home to their families. Hot towels, bowls of lemon water and cut lemons were placed in front of all the diners to wash off their grubby hands. A large square table was set up to accommodate heaps of cupcakes, pralines and French pastries for the guests to enjoy for desert.

Louis finished his cooking and cleaning and grabbed his clarinet and joined the band. The music was hot, the moon was out, and almost everyone in the crowd was participating by clapping, singing or stomping their feet. The tables and chairs were pushed to one side to make room for dancing. Paris and Doyle went to dance on the makeshift dance floor, joined by David and Shirree. The floor became jam-packed by couples, singles and groups of people line dancing.

"When the Saints Come Marching In" signaled the end of the evening. People grabbed their napkins and marched in a line, happily waving their white napkins and singing to the music. Doyle looked at his watch and was amazed that it was two in the morning. He suddenly felt very tired. He couldn't believe all the food he had eaten and all the beer he had consumed.

He had expected to have a little sex play with Paris this evening, but he was too exhausted to think about it, let alone do it. Everyone left except the immediate family. Doyle was wondering where his room was and stood politely waiting for guidance. Paris was standing next to him but she hadn't mentioned the sleeping arrangements.

Lilly called out to them, "We are serving brunch at twelve-thirty tomorrow because we are going to the eleven o'clock mass at Saint Rose of Lima Church. David and Doyle, you're welcome to join us."

David replied, "I would really like to join you but I am really wiped out, Miss Lilly. I can hardly keep my eyes open. I have been studying like crazy for the past few days."

Doyle also declined the offer. "I am going to sleep in. I have had a real tough week, but thank you for inviting me."

"I understand pre-med students and law students study very hard. Sleep well boys. I will see you at brunch tomorrow. Papa Joe will take you to the *garçonnière*."

Doyle looked up and there was Papa Joe, a big smile on his face as he looked at Doyle and David. "I will walk with you men. I am sure the young ladies are ready to turn in."

"We young ladies are very tired," said Paris as she gave Doyle a chaste kiss on the cheek.

Shirree kissed David on the cheek goodnight and both girls giggled as they walked up the stairs to their rooms.

David said, "Let's get our things from the car and go with Papa Joe."

Doyle was puzzled as to why Papa Joe was taking them to their rooms. He was looking forward to Paris showing him to his room. Papa Joe was right behind them as they took their belongings out of the car.

They walked down the path to a small white house with pillars on the front porch. Papa Joe took a set of keys from his pocket and opened the door saying, "I hope you two gentlemen sleep well. There is food in the kitchen if you get hungry. I will see you tomorrow."

Doyle looked around and saw that there were six double beds lined up side by side in what appeared to be the main room of the house.

"Welcome to the *garçonnière*," David deadpanned.

"What the hell is a *garçonnière*?" Doyle exclaimed.

"It is a French word for bachelor quarters. They were built a distance from the main house to keep the young bucks away from the unmarried ladies in the house. Every plantation had a *garçonnière*. After all southern belles have to be protected from the wiles of horny young men."

Doyle didn't share David's humor. "I assume there are bathrooms in this house."

David replied with an amused look on his face, "Absolutely. You can have your choice of beds. There is a small kitchen down the hall. We have a pantry filled with snacks and a refrigerator filled with orange juice, milk, and cold cuts. We even have a coffee maker and full wet bar stocked with liquor. The only downside is that there are no young ladies here."

Doyle started to laugh saying, "This could only happen in Louisiana. The south takes very good care of their bachelors. They may segregate us, but they make sure that we have bed and board."

David joined his laughter as he said in his best southern accent, "Welcome to the deep South, you Yankee carpetbagger! Now let me get some sleep."

*****

Doyle was awakened next morning by the phone on the wall next to David's bed.

David answered and said groggily, "Thanks for waking us, Paris. We'll meet on the verandah in about twenty minutes."

David and he walked on the path to the main house and climbed up the stairs to the veranda. The family greeted them warmly. Paris beckoned to him, and he made his way next to her.

"Good morning," she said smiling. "Did you sleep well?"

"I did, you little vixen. The bachelor quarters are equipped with great mattresses and feathery pillows. I think I fell asleep before my head hit the pillow. I really enjoyed the party last night. It was one of the best parties I have ever been to. Everything was perfect," he pouted, "but there was one little thing missing: you were not in my bed."

Paris giggled and chose to ignore his statement. "I am glad you enjoyed the party. My family enjoys entertaining and we are always having parties with different themes. And the themes change with the seasons of the year!"

They were seated at a large rectangular table covered with a snow-white tablecloth. The verandah was spacious and was enclosed with a white wrought-iron fence. Small vases of fragrant apricot-colored roses were scattered on the table with matching dishes and napkins.

A tall, plump woman stood at the doorway and announced, "Your brunch buffet is all laid out for you on the table. Please help yourself."

Lady Madeline was the first in line. Louis and Lilly followed. The table was on the back of the porch. Paris and Doyle were among the last in line.

"What a spread!" thought Doyle, eager to try the different entrées. There was caviar with capers, finally chopped onions, chopped eggs and toast points. He had never tasted caviar before, so he eagerly put a spoonful on his plate. He also helped himself to the accompaniments and the toast points. Paris put some on her plate, too. They helped themselves to the smoked salmon and smoked trout. Doyle noticed that everyone took small helpings of each dish. It was not like a restaurant buffet where everyone tried to heap as much food on their plates as possible. When everyone was seated Louis said grace and all began to eat.

Doyle was disappointed in the caviar. He placed the caviar on a toast point with chopped egg and onions on top of it. He took a bite of the combination and found the caviar to have a bite to it, but it was too salty for his palette. He decided the small, shiny, black eggs were an acquired taste.

After the plates were cleared, Paris invited Doyle to see the inside of her house. He followed her inside and was surprised at the size of the house and how many different types of furniture and antiques were represented in the rooms. He admired the various styles of glittering shaped crystal chandeliers that seemed to be in every room. He noticed a wooden butter churner in the dining room, which Paris confirmed was authentic and dated back to colonial days. Doyle stopped to look at a dappled rocking horse carved in wood with realistic looking amber glass eyes. He stroked the back of the horse and realized it was covered with horsehair.

"Come to the living room and I will show you one of my favorite pieces."

They went to the living room where Paris pointed to large mellow light amber pear standing in one corner of the room. Doyle went to look at the carving and marveled at the fact that the closer you looked at the polished patina of the pear, the more it appeared to be a giant pear. Paris opened the hinged pear and showed Doyle that it was a tea caddy; with a silver teapot, sugar bowl and creamer in it.

"This pear was carved by hand in the early eighteen hundreds in England. This is a work of art that must have taken a craftsman years to make."

Paris led him to the room where some of her ancestor Jon Viverette's paintings hung. A few of them were muted pastel-colored landscapes and some were the vividly colored voluptuous nudes who seemed to ascend from a sea of lilies, roses or poppies.

Doyle said, "Paris, the nudes are amazing. Do you have any more of them?"

"According to the records grandfather Jon Charles kept, he hid the paintings all over our property so the Yankees wouldn't find them. He was senile when he painted the nudes, and we have only been able to find a few of them."

"How does your father keep track of all of his collectables in the house?"

"He and his secretary catalogue all of his collections. Every time he buys something new it is cataloged."

"Paris, you grew up in a museum. How lucky you are to live with all of these beautiful treasures around you."

"I am very lucky to have a great family around me who I love very much and who have always been very supportive of me. The antiques are just objects. But, you're right. I have been very blessed."

Shirree entered the room and said, "I am glad I finally found you. I have been looking all over for you. David and I are ready to leave. He has a lot studying to do. Are you and Doyle ready to go?"

Doyle nodded. "My clothes are in the car. Are you ready to go Paris?"

"I will be. I have some clothes to get from my room. It will only take a few minutes I will meet you on the veranda."

Shirree and Doyle went to the veranda to say goodbye to everyone. David was talking to his brother Christopher when Shirree and Doyle walked in. David introduced Doyle to Christopher, saying with great pride, "This is my big brother, a neurosurgeon who is in the top ten percentile in his graduating class!"

Christopher shook hands with Doyle and said, "I am glad to meet you. Officially I won't be a neurosurgeon for another month. I'm waiting for Duke University to present me with my degree.

Doyle replied jovially, "It is very nice to meet you. Congratulations on graduating from Duke! The top ten percentile is quite an accomplishment. You should be very proud of yourself."

Doyle then excused himself to get something he had forgotten in his sleeping quarters.

The brothers continued to chat outside. "David, How are you doing at LSU?"

"Great, bro! I love being a resident there. Charity Hospital is my second home. I must have patched up hundreds of bullet holes already. It seems as if the same people come back week after week, or maybe they are all beginning to look alike…."

Christopher laughed at David's comments. "Unfortunately, that is the way it is late at night at most emergency rooms—stabbings and shootings, mixed with a sprinkling of accidents, a small number of ruptured appendixes and some premature babies. It gives you the opportunity to experience a myriad of medical problems in a short period of time."

Paris walked into the terrace and saw David and Christopher talking together. She raced up to Christopher and gave him a big hug and kiss. "It is so good to see you Dr. Le Blanc."

Christopher hugged her back and said, "Paris you look great. I'm glad to see you. After graduation I am going to work at Mount Sinai hospital in Miami, so I'm glad to see you before I leave."

"I'm sure your father and mother must be proud of you. Three doctors in the family!"

Doyle watched the three of them from the other side of the room. Paris looked very happy to see Christopher and was in an animated conversation with him. Christopher was tall, slender and covered with freckles and his hair was an unruly light brown. David apparently had the looks in the family with his muscular build, blonde hair, and wide smile. David and Paris came over to where Doyle was standing.

"Are you ready to go?"

"Absolutely," said Doyle. "I have said goodbye to everyone and thanked your family for their hospitality."

Shirree joined them and they were on their way back to New Orleans. On the way back Doyle and Paris held hands and teased one another. David dropped the girls off and took Doyle home.

Paris said, "I had a great time Shirree, what about you?"

"I had a fine time, Paris. And your man Doyle looks as if he's very charmed by you."

"He should be, damned Yankee. He'd never seen a plantation home before!" And they both giggled happily.

Chapter 13

Louis, Lilly and Doyle sat in Paris' room watching for more signs of recovery. The mood was much more upbeat than before.

Sophia stayed home to try to locate the maids. She called the guardhouse for the phone number of Happy Maids. Sophia called and learned that the maids are scheduled to work at Palm Island today and to arrive in a few hours.

Two hours later the three girls arrived at the house in their pretty pink uniforms with a look of fear on their young faces. Lola explained the frightening and bloody scene that they encountered that day. She tearfully explained how Paris refused any help to clean up the blood and had screamed at her and yelled at her to leave. They didn't know what else to do, so they left. Lola insisted that in the past Paris was always kind to them and was never rude.

When the maids left Sophia took a cab to the hospital to join the family at Paris' bedside. Lilly was doing needlepoint and Louis was pouring over the *Wall Street Journal.*

Doyle excused himself, explaining he had a business meeting to attend. Doyle rushed to his office to take care of any emergencies that had arisen. On the way to his office he received a call from Adriana reminding him of their date for lunch. He had forgotten all about it. He dare not break the date, so he asked her if he could change the time and make it a late lunch. She acquiesced and they agreed to meet at a little Cuban restaurant on Southwest Eighth Street.

Adriana was already at the restaurant when he arrived. He realized that he had eaten no breakfast and was starved. The specialty of the house was paella with yellow rice. He and Adriana both ordered it.

He looked at Adriana sitting across the table from him chattering away: her little plump face beaming with happiness. She rattled on about her family and how happy everyone is about their wedding. He kept a smile pasted on his face as he quickly consumed his salad and bread.

Doyle had eaten about two thirds of his paella when his cellphone rang. He looked at his caller ID: it was his father. Doyle decided to ignore the call and keep eating. The phone rang again and again and Doyle finally decided to take his call.

He answered with a curt, "Hello."

He heard his father's icy voice, "Your mother just dropped dead so you and your brother better get over to Sullivan's funeral home now! You two make arrangements for her funeral." And being the moron he was, he hung up before Doyle could ask him any questions.

Doyle sat motionless at the table in shock. Tears ran down his ashen face.

"Doyle what's wrong?"

"My mother just died. I have to leave now. I have to go to the funeral parlor."

He threw some money on the table as he walked out of the restaurant with Adriana trailing after him. Adriana hugged him and kissed him on the cheek. He was oblivious to her ministrations as he rapidly walked to his car.

Once in his car he called his brother Brandon. He speedily relayed his father's message and they agreed to meet at Sullivan's Funeral parlor. Doyle sat in his car and mechanically made the requisite phone calls. He called Paris' family at the hospital, then called his office and spoke to Miranda—he won't be in the office for a few days.

Doyle rushed to the Sullivan Funeral home where Brandon and his father were waiting. He was filled with rage at his father and guilt at himself for being so involved with his own life that he neglected his mother. He occasionally called her, promising to take her out to dinner in the next week or so, but he never did have the time for their dinner. He would then apologize for not spending more time with her. She would gently tell him that she was very proud of him and she understood how busy he was. She never chastised him for ignoring her for months at a time nor would she ever call him.

When he asked her why she never called, her answer was always the same: "I know how busy you are and I don't want to intrude in your life."

Doyle knew she was intimidated by the wealth and sophistication of the Viverette family. On the rare family occasions they were together, his mother stiffly sat on a chair and never joined in their conversation. It was obvious she was not enjoying being with her daughter-in-law or her family. He had to admit to himself that he was ashamed of his own mother. She always looked so shabby and downtrodden that he did not want to be seen in public with her. She reminded him of the life of poverty he experienced growing up, which was something he wanted to forget. He reinvented himself.

The people he surrounded himself with were of a different class than his mother and father. He felt his face become hot and redden with color as he acknowledged the snob he had become. Doyle gave her large amounts of money for birthdays and holidays to salve his conscience, but he was unable to give her his love or time. He was glad that Brandon his wife Annie and their two boys spent time with his mother; somehow it seemed that their consideration towards his mother mitigated his responsibilities toward her.

He arrived at the funeral home, acknowledged his father, and embraced his brother. He quickly made and paid for the arrangements of his mother's funeral. He spared no expense—at least she would be buried in luxury.

"Pop, what happened?"

"She died of a stroke. If you had come to visit your Ma you would have known that she had many strokes. In fact, she was paralyzed on her left side from one of them."

Doyle looked at his brother Brandon in astonishment.

Brandon nodded mournfully, "She's been partially parallelized for the past four months."

"Why didn't either of you let me know how sick she was?"

"She made me and your brother promise not to tell you, Mr. Bigshot," his father said scornfully. "You were too busy to be disturbed. You were too good for the likes of your Ma and me. Do you think I don't know you're ashamed of your own family?" he spat out with contempt.

"You shouldn't talk, Pop. You beat and verbally abused her ever since I can remember! Now that she's dead you're going to pretend that you were a caring husband?"

"Don't throw your big words at me Doyle. I admit I hit your Ma sometimes and I wasn't the best husband, but it doesn't change the fact that you were ashamed of us and didn't want to be around us. You were a lousy son!"

Brandon, who had been silent, suddenly intervened: "Pa, Doyle, Ma is dead! So stop fighting. For her sake let's try to get along. We should be mourning her death, not fighting among ourselves."

"You two boys come with me and we'll down some Irish whisky. A lot of time has passed since I went drinking with my sons. We can talk about the nice things your Ma did for all of us," he said, as tears suddenly sprang from bloodshot eyes and rolled down his weathered face.

"That sounds great Pa," Doyle spontaneously agreed. "We'll go wherever you want to go."

After a great deal of scotch, tall stories and tears, they left the bar leaning on each other and temporarily forgetting they were a dysfunctional family. Brandon was the first one to leave. Doyle drove his inebriated father home and to assuage his guilt he even helped him stumble into his house and undress for bed. His father fell into bed and managed to sing several verses of "Oh Danny Boy" before he passed out.

Doyle drove to the first restaurant he saw and quickly ordered a cheeseburger, fries, a side of chili and a pot of coffee to sober him up. After he devoured the food and drank several cups of coffee he called the hospital and his father-in-law answered the phone bubbling over with happy news about Paris. She had momentarily opened her eyes, recognized him, and called out his name. Louis was convinced that she would awaken soon.

After he heard Louis's jubilation, Doyle forced himself to sound thrilled by Paris' progress and expressed eagerness to see her as soon as possible.

Louis expressed his sympathy, as well as Lilly's and Sophia's, for the loss of his mother. Doyle thanked Louis for his condolences and told him he would be at the hospital shortly. He then went to the men's room and tried to wash the death, alcohol and fear from his hands and his life.

Doyle stopped to buy Paris another bouquet of flowers on his way to the hospital. He bought her fragrant apricot-colored roses, which were her favorite rose. He thought, wryly, that it didn't matter what he bought her since she was still unconscious. He walked into Paris' hospital room and everyone again expressed their sympathies about his mother passing. He thanked them for their concern as he walked to his wife's bedside carrying the bouquet as if it were a burnt offering.

Doyle could see that the dour feeling of the hospital room had changed to one of hope. He immediately tried to emanate happiness about Paris' condition improving, but it was a difficult task. Lilly, Louis, and Sophia seemed relaxed, even cheerful.

Lilly looked at Doyle and said, "We are going to the dining room to have some dinner. I know you would like some time alone with your wife."

"Thank you Lilly, I would," Doyle replied.

He immediately sat down and kissed his wife on her pale face. The swelling of the side of her face had gone down and the bruises had faded a little more since he saw her that morning. Or perhaps earlier he had avoided looking at the wounds he had inflicted.

"Doyle," Louis asked compassionately, "what would you like to eat? Let us bring you some dinner."

Doyle replied, "I really don't care. Whatever you bring, I'll eat."

"I will surprise you then. I'll bring you the most appetizing thing on the menu. No Louisiana food, but it will be edible."

"Louis, give it up. Food is sustenance; it is fuel for our bodies. It really does not matter if it isn't gourmet. We have more important things to worry about," Lilly interjected.

In the dining room the conversation immediately turned to Doyle.

"Doyle looks ghastly," Louis observed. "He looks like he aged ten years since this morning!"

"He looks like he has been ridden hard and put away wet," Lilly agreed.

"There is something I have to tell you," Sophia said quietly. "I wanted to wait until Paris' condition improved before I brought this to your attention. I was sitting at Paris' bedside when I noticed small faded bruises on her wrists, shoulders and forearms. The bruises appeared to be made by someone grasping her forcefully with their hands, leaving their fingermarks on her skin. I mentioned the bruises to Christopher. He had already noticed them; he said that it looks like signs of abuse. We both felt it was wise to wait awhile before we made you aware of this."

Lilly and Louis exchanged grave looks.

"Also," she continued, "when I questioned the maids about that day, they said that Paris asked them to move her things out of her closet and into another bedroom. Paris was obsessed with her spacious closet! They must have had a fight if she was moving her things out of the master bedroom. And Tou-Tou was mighty unfriendly to Doyle when he dropped by the other day. I don't like what the evidence is pointing to."

When Sophia finished speaking there was dead silence for several moments before Louis angrily spoke. "I am going to seek Christopher's opinion about Paris' injuries. I will call my investigative agency tonight; I will call Pierre in a few minutes and tell him it's imperative that he and Juliet come here as soon as possible. I promise you we will find out what happened to Paris. Within a week we will find out everything about Doyle in all phases of his life. In the meantime we don't want Doyle to know we're suspicious of him, so we'll continue to treat him as our loving son-in-law...as difficult as that will be."

"By all means," Sophia proclaimed, "We'll give him enough rope to hang himself with."

"*Mon Dieu...*," Lilly breathed sadly. "What type of a monster has our daughter been living with? When she first married Doyle she always sounded so happy and excited when I saw her or spoke to her on the phone. I should have realized that something had changed."

Their unappetizing food arrived and Lilly gazed at Louis with a bemused "I do not want to hear one word about the quality of the food tonight; just glory in the fact that you are going to lose weight." Tears rolled down her face.

Louis leaned over and kissed his wife on the cheek replying, "I love you, even if you are a nag."

Chapter 14

Paris drifted back into a deep sleep, her mind wandering to her relationship with Doyle and their first jazz fest together. It was a day filled with good food, great music, and topped off with amazing sex.

It was the second weekend of the jazz fest and it was a bright, hot, sunny day. They were both dressed in khaki shorts, T-shirts and tennis shoes. Paris carried a backpack with sunblock, a lightweight cotton blanket, a huge wad of tissue for the portable potties, liquid hand sanitizer, hand cream and bottled water. They took the Esplanade bus to the nearest stop to the 145-acre Fair Grounds Race Track and walked the many blocks with hundreds of other people to the entrance. They walked past the shops into the food court where they were assailed by the delicious smells of the foods: peanut soup, shrimp etouffée, shrimp scampi, southern fried chicken, gumbo and many more delicious foods that made New Orleans famous.

They chose their food and drinks and sat down on the blanket Paris spread on the grass. Hundreds of other people were also sitting on the grass eating and listening to the music of the Neville Brothers. In the midst of all the luscious smells of food, the tangy scent of weed floated through the air, adding to the ambiance and enjoyment of the crowd.

"This is heaven" Doyle said, as he wolfed down his fried-shrimp po'boy and slurped down his icy cold beer.

The crowd roared as the Neville Brothers started to sing, "Ain't No Sunshine." The couple wandered through the stages, pausing to listen to Doctor John, Rockin' Dopsie Jr., and the Zydeco Twisters. Eventually, they made their way to the pavilion where Bruce Springsteen was going to perform and sat down on their blanket in the grass.

Doyle said, "I can't believe this, but I'm starving. I would love some spinach bread and a stuffed artichoke."

"I am hungry too; I could also use some more beer."

"I'll go to the refreshment area and load up on food and beer for us."

"Are you sure you'll be able to find me?" Paris asked. "Look at all these people sitting on the grass! There must be a thousand people sandwiched in this small area."

Doyle looked around and said, "You're right. I don't know if I can walk through the crowd without stepping on someone." He looked around and spotted a pole flying the American flag. "Paris, look that way," he said, pointing to the flag. "Move our things over there and I will be able to find you around the flag."

"Good thinking," she said, as she started to pick the blanket up and stuff it in her backpack. She thought for a moment and then took out the blanket and handed the backpack to Doyle. "You're going to need the backpack for the food."

Doyle gingerly walked through the masses of people who were sitting on the grass and on folding chairs. He left one section only to find the next section was equally crowded. It took him forever to navigate through the endless heap of bodies sitting, lying and walking on the grass. After he finally managed to walk away from the crowd, his next challenge was to steer through the people waiting in line at the concession booths. It seemed like an eternity before he was able to buy the food and beer. As he walked back to the Bruce Springsteen pavilion he saw the Lady Buckjumpers as they snaked through the crowd playing their soulful jazz music, spinning their parasols around their heads. Everywhere he walked or looked fabulous music was swirling around him.

It took forever for Doyle to find Paris. And when he finally located her, he almost had a heart attack. Beverly was sharing her blanket. He had to bluff his way through the situation. Paris saw him and waved. He looked at Beverly, her face mirrored her surprise as she stared at him, her mouth hung open in surprise. He casually made his way to the blanket stumbling over the quagmire of people who were packed together like sardines.

Paris said, "Well, you're finally back. I thought you might have deserted me. I want you to meet my new best friend Beverly. She lost her blanket and she may have lost her boyfriend, so I invited her to sit with me."

Doyle said, "Hi Beverly. How are you doing?"

Paris glanced at Doyle, as she unpacked the backpack and put the food on the blanket. "Do you two know each other?"

Beverly smiled like a Cheshire cat, "Doyle and I have some classes together."

"What a coincidence; thousands of people around and we bump into each other."

Paris noticed Doyle was unusually quiet. She thought, *"poor guy it must have been sheer agony to move through the crowd waiting in line for their food."*

"Doyle, thanks for going to get the food and beer in this mess. Beverly, please help yourself to some food—we have plenty."

The concert began. Bruce Springsteen started to sing his signature song, "Born in the USA." Beverly and half the crowd jumped up and started to sing with him as they swayed with the music.

Doyle watched Beverly as she moved with the tempo of the music. She was wearing tight short shorts and her round soft booty hung out of them. She was wearing a green halter-top that showed her abundant cleavage, her long curly red hair moved in all directions as she danced. His thoughts wandered to the thick curly red pelt between her legs and he felt himself swell underneath his shorts.

He glanced at Paris to see if she noticed his staring at Beverly, but she too was dancing on the grass. He watched as his two women danced together. He had a fantasy of Paris sitting on him with her silky long black hair cascading down her back like a waterfall. He was running his fingers up and down her soft white skin, as he gently kneaded her ass. Beverly was watching them fuck as she pleasured herself.

Paris was gently shaking him. "Wake up! I can't believe with all the noise and people around, you fell asleep."

He sat up, slightly dazed and looked around, the crowd was thinning out. People were packing up their belongings and leaving.

"You missed a great concert. Bruce sang my favorites '*Born to Run*,' '*Downbound Train*,' '*Thunder Road*' and '*Mansion on the Hill*.'"

"I'm sorry, Paris, it must have been the heat and the beer."

"Oh well, I had a good time dancing with Beverly. She left and asked me to say goodbye to you for her. We can sit here and eat the food you fetched. I'm really starving! But first I'm going to the portable potties; see you in a few minutes."

Doyle started eating the spinach bread and thinking about his sexy dream. After finishing their food, the couple wandered around again, catching performances from soul singer Irma Thomas and Harry Connick Jr., before it began to rain. Doyle and Paris decided to leave and search for shelter. The first place they found was the gospel tent and it was teeming with people, but dry. Doyle and Paris were wet, dirty and smelly. Paris' hair was wet and pasted over her face. With all the people around her she felt as if she was suffocating. They huddled together in the back of the tent listening to the rain pelt the tent.

Doyle's warm body pulsated next to hers and she began to throb with desire. She felt her body become hot, warm liquid seemed to trickle inside of her as the choir played, "Deep River."

"Doyle I can't breathe. I don't care if I drown in the rain, I have to get out of here."

"We'll probably float, but let's go for it."

They snaked through the people to get to the exit and out into the downpour. They walked for what seemed miles to get to the exit and then, a miracle; they were able to find a taxi to take them home. Paris had her key ready while Doyle paid the cab. She took off her soggy tennis shoes and ran up the stairs. Doyle was right behind her. She opened the door to the third floor and tore off her disgusting, wet, dirty clothes. She turned to Doyle and started to take off his clothes. He just stood there in shock, never expecting Paris to be so aggressive.

Shirree was in New York with Daisy for a long weekend, so Paris had the apartment to herself. She felt Doyle's fingers slowly caressing her butt and she felt she couldn't wait another moment. He followed her into the bathroom where she turned the shower on full blast. She dragged him in and they soaped each other and washed each other's hair. Paris handed Doyle a large towel and put her robe on. Paris ran down to the kitchen and grabbed a bottle of tequila and two glasses. She ran upstairs and filled them. She gave Doyle a glass and took one for herself. The tequila warmed her immediately.

"I want you now Doyle. I want you so much I think I'm going to burst," she said, taking another big slug of the tequila.

Doyle picked her up and cradled her in his arms, as he placed her on her bed." Paris, are you sure you want me to make love to you now?"

"Yes I want to feel you inside of me," she said as she got on top of him and started to kiss him.

They kissed slowly and gently. He rolled her over and said to her, "I just want you to lay there and let me satisfy you. I want to give you pleasure. I want to make you happy."

His tongue and fingers began to slowly caress her body. He opened the bottle of lotion on the table next to her bed and gently rubbed her with it. He smoothly sucked her nipples and licked her breasts. He kissed her stomach and her thighs, but he did not touch the furry mound between her legs. Instead he gently sucked her toes. She moaned in pleasure. He kissed her legs and thighs and she wriggled in delight. He separated her furry mound with his fingers and gently placed his fingers inside of her. He could hear her gasp in pleasure as he lightly flicked his tongue on her clit and inside of her.

She screamed, "Please stop, I want you inside of me!"

"Paris, if you want me inside of you, tell me, 'Doyle I want your cock inside of me'."

"Oh my God, Doyle, I want your cock inside of me!"

He slowly teased her by putting himself in her a little bit and then out. He did this until she was panting with desire and dripping wet. He then sat her on his stomach and said gruffly, "Put my cock inside of you."

She sat on his cock and felt a sharp pain as her hymen tore and blood trickled out of her. He took a towel from the side of the bed and tenderly wiped the blood off of her. He pulled out, laid her on the bed, put his tongue deep in her pussy, and ran his fingers playfully over her clit. He waited till she begged him for his cock before placing himself on top of her and thrusting himself inside her. She arched her back and wrapped her legs around his body, moving in concord with him. They fell asleep joined together.

Chapter 15

Doyle sat next to his wife's prone body and deliberated what he could do to preserve his sanity and his life. He had come to the realization that his best course of action, unfortunately, would be to kill Paris and to collect the two million dollars she had in life insurance. He could then marry Adriana and be a good father to their baby. He would make the Leon family very happy and they in turn would in all probability send him a lot of business.

The only problem was finding the best way to get rid of Paris while she was still in the hospital. He looked at her thin body, her white creamy skin and her shiny blue-black hair that fell around her face and shoulders, and he felt pangs of regret about what had to be done. It would be so easy to put a pillow over her mouth and smother her. He picked up a pillow and realized with Paris being unconscious there would be no struggle. She would just stop breathing. He looked around to see if there were any cameras in the room. He did not see any but he remembered Christopher's suspicion of him and he discarded the thought of asphyxiation for the time being.

Then sanity returned to his chaotic mind, and he began to think clearly; suffocating Paris in the hospital would be his death sentence. She was on all sorts of monitors and if she stopped breathing there would be a bevy of nurses in the room to save her. He was going to have to find another way to kill her.

He heard the family's voices in the hall and immediately took Paris' hand in his.

Louis handed Doyle a plastic container filled with food from the dining room saying, "Doyle you look exhausted. Please go home. We'll look after Paris. You've had a traumatic day and you need some rest."

To their amazement Doyle broke down and started to sob loudly. Sophia grabbed the tissue box from the table and started to gently blot Doyle's face.

"I'm going to take you home now Doyle. You're in no condition to drive."

She took him by the hand and led him to her car. Neither of them spoke until they arrived at the O'Connor house. Once inside, Doyle thanked Sophia profusely. Sophia asked him if he wanted her to make him a sandwich or some coffee.

Doyle replied "Thanks Sophia, I have the food Louis bought for me in the hospital. I'm going to microwave it and drink a cold beer after I go upstairs and shower."

Once more Tou-Tou chased after Doyle howling and trying to nip him on the ankles as Doyle walked rapidly to his room. Sophia fed and watered Tou-Tou and carried him to her room, shutting the door so he wouldn't wander. She then took a long relaxing bath. She massaged the fragrant body crème she had created all over body and put her pajamas and robe on. She held Tou-Tou in her arms as she walked to the kitchen to brew some herbal tea that she had made from an old, old recipe. She took the teapot and a cup back to her room where she sat on her bed and sipped the special tea that she used when she wanted to dream.

She called Papa Joe and he answered the phone saying, "How are you Cher? I have been missin' you so much. Now tell me what is happening in Miami?"

She told him that Doyle's mother had died of a stroke that day, what the maids had told her and all of the other happenings of her stressful day. She told him about Tou-Tou's response to Doyle.

"Joe, I feel Doyle is a mean man and he caused Paris' coma, but he broke down and sobbed at her bedside."

"Sugar, no one is all good or all bad. Good people do some bad things and bad people do some good things."

"I pray Paris is going to get better soon. Every time I look at her in her hospital bed I think of Suzette and how she died and I want to cry. It would be horrible if I lost Paris too."

"I know how you're hurtin' baby, but you have to think positive," her husband said consolingly. Sophia fell asleep with Tou-Tou snuggled next to her as soon as she said goodnight to her husband.

***

The viewing of Cristina O'Connor was a small affair. A few of her friends from church attended, and a few drinking buddies of her husband showed up. Annie's family came, as well as the Viverettes and Sophia, and a few associates of Brandon and Doyle came to pay their respects to the family.

Doyle stared at his mother lying in her coffin. Although the embalmers had enhanced her face with makeup, her once sweet fresh-looking face was drawn and lined. Doyle remembered her shiny chocolate brown hair framing her laughing face. He studied her short, unsightly, grayish brown hair which reminded him of dead leaves floating off the trees in late fall. She always had been a petite woman, but in her casket she appeared to be a shrunken doll, swathed in a large white gown, her gnarled thin fingers clutching her rosary beads.

This inert stranger did not look at all like his beautiful mother; his mother was a loving creature who sang to him as she bathed him, who kissed him, and caressed his hair as she read a book to him. His mother shared coloring books with him and laughed when they baked cookies together and he covered his hands and face with flour.

Cristina—the mother who was always hugging him and his brother, telling them how precious they were to her—had evaporated many years before she died. Whatever city they were living in, she managed to take them to the museums. Sometimes they had to take four buses to get to it, but they managed to get there. She stressed that without education they would never have a prosperous life, and they had to study now and do well in school in order to go to college because they would need scholarships to get into college. She also explained the importance of speaking English properly and constantly corrected their grammar and enunciation.

They both decided at a young age that they wanted to be attorneys; their mother encouraged them to follow their dreams. She achieved her goals for Brandon and Doyle, but she never thought she'd be discarded as her son Doyle's success blossomed.

Doyle contacted his old friend Alex the day before the funeral to reserve one of the private rooms at his family's Italian restaurant, the Venetia, for his mother's wake. Not having spoken to Alex in a while, Doyle only had distressing news for his old friend. Alex wanted to help Doyle any way he could.

"I'll be happy to take care of all the arrangements for the wake."

An ironic thought entered his Doyle's mind as he made his mother's funeral arrangements. He'd never had a party for his mother's birthday or Mother's Day, but here he was throwing a big catered wake for her death. He even ordered all of her favorite foods. During the wake, Miranda, wearing a black suit, stood, at the front door of the restaurant and showed the mourners where to go and answered any questions they had.

Pierre and Juliet had flown in from Miami in time for the mass, but not in time for the viewing. They arrived in a limousine with Lilly, Louis and Sophia. They greeted Doyle solemnly and expressed their condolences for the death of his mother. Doyle, weary from welcoming mourners, was shocked to see Alberto Leon walk in with his niece Adriana Franco.

Alberto hugged him and softly said, "My family offers you their deepest regrets."

Adriana stood on her tiptoes to kiss him on the cheek and said, "We are so sorry for your loss."

He looked at her short black dress with disdain as he thanked her for coming. Doyle held his breath fearing Adriana would say something else, but she and Alberto quickly walked into the bar for a drink, and then walked to the dining room.

In the dining room Alberto Leon went to a large table where the Viverette family was sitting. He introduced himself and his niece to the Viverettes, who were very cordial to him. The Viverettes and the Leons were sitting together at the same table having a lively conversation when Doyle walked in the room. The only thing that kept Doyle from having a heart attack was his exhaustion. He gave them all a weak smile and joined his father at the other end of the room.

Alex came over to console him—Alex, his best friend, who was so good and pure of heart, who always tried to be kind and help people. Alex was devoted to his parents, he always spent time with them, and he considered his father his best friend. He loved his children as well as every member of his family. Doyle knew Alex would never cheat on his wife and that he would never be in a similar predicament as Doyle.

"Alex, come with me while I go to the table to speak with my in-laws. They're very upset about Paris. I have so much on my mind. I am having difficulty dealing with everything. It'll be easier if you could take the pressure off of me."

"I understand, Doyle. I'll be more than happy to come with you. But what I do not understand is what is your client Alberto Leon doing at your mother's funeral with his niece?"

"Alex do you know the Leons?"

"Of course I know the Leons! Anyone who reads the newspaper or watches television knows of them!"

"They're here to pay their respects to me because of my mother's death. Alberto is my client and he was very grateful that I was able to have him exonerated from his murder charges."

"Doyle, don't fall into the clutches of the Leon family. If they become angry with you, they make your life a living hell."

"Believe me Alex, I know what they are capable of."

"Amigo, I know you love to live dangerously. I'll never forget the day you went to the jazz festival with Paris. There were over 100,000 people at jazz fest that day and guess who ends up sharing a blanket with their new girlfriend and your current sex buddy Beverly."

"That moment was messy, not funny, Alex," recalled Doyle, "laughing while walking around with my arms loaded with food and beer."

"Messy? The mess came the next day when Beverly showed up at our apartment and dropped off that bag for you. The look on your face was priceless when you came home and looked inside."

Doyle winced as he remembered that day. "I had no idea what to expect when I opened that bag. I knew it wouldn't be good, but I didn't anticipate my shirts and pants shredded into ragged little strips by a paper shredder. There was also a bunch of pictures taken of the two of us in the bag and she had cut my head off in all the pictures."

"She sent you a message, Doyle."

"Alex, you are the greatest, you always know how to make me laugh no matter how upset I am."

"Let's go and put your head in the Lion's den. Put a big smile on your face, Doyle."

"Good advice, Alex, but I believe I need a drink in my hand as well as a big smile on my face. Would you like one?"

"No thanks, I've had enough to drink."

Doyle returned with his drink. He and Alex walked to the table where the Leons and Viverettes were sitting, and joined them at their table.

Louis said, "Alex you're looking very well. I am sorry we have to see each other on such a sad occasion."

They shook hands and Alex politely greeted everyone at the table."

Adriana and I have to leave now, Doyle. I am very sorry about your mother." He turned to the Viverettes and said, "It has been a pleasure meeting you. I hope we will meet again and I hope your daughter recovers quickly."

The Viverettes smiled and Louis thanked Alberto for his good wishes for his daughter saying that he was delighted to meet him and his niece.

Doyle said, "Thank you so much for coming. I will walk you to your car."

Doyle accompanied Alberto and Adriana out of the restaurant to their waiting car and chauffer Andy. Doyle knew that Andy, a former Miami policeman, was his bodyguard as well as his driver. Andy opened the car door so Adriana and Alberto could seat themselves in the back seat of Alberto's shiny silver bullet-proof BMW.

"Adriana, Alberto, thank you so much for coming. I appreciate your attending my mother's wake."

Alberto had a big smile on his face as he entered his car, "Doyle this is what we do for members of our family, we share everything with them."

Doyle watched the car drive away and straightened his shoulders as he walked back into the restaurant and joined the Viverettes.

Chapter 16

Louis, realizing that Paris was going to be hospitalized for an indefinite amount of time, worked together with Christopher to secure a larger hospital room so that the family could stay at the hospital comfortably when they visited Paris. Christopher made all of the arrangements and the staff moved Paris and her belongings to the larger room.

When the Viverettes arrived back at the hospital, they were directed to the new room. They were pleased to find that the larger room had a sitting room adjacent to it, with couches that converted to beds. The décor was bright and cheerful, the chairs and couches were covered in beautiful posh fabrics, and the carpets were thick and plush. If monitors were not attached to Paris it could easily pass for a five-star hotel. There was enough room for eight or nine people to be in the suite together.

Lilly sat next to Paris' bed, talking to her as if Paris could hear and understand what she was saying. Sophia sat on the couch with Juliet and explained in great detail Paris' condition and her distrust of Doyle.

Doyle returned to the hospital when he left Alex. He went to Paris' room and found it empty, and all of Paris belongings gone. He sat down in one of the chairs in her room and said to himself, "Jesus, Mary and Joseph, Paris is dead. Hallelujah. My life has been saved." He breathed a sigh of relief. For the first time in a week, he felt very good.

A nurse walked into the room and said, "Oh, Mr. O'Connor. You must be wondering where your wife is. She has been moved to a suite on the fourteenth floor. Her room number is 1414."

Doyle felt the breath go out of his body.

The nurse looked at his chalk white face and said, "Oh I am so sorry. It must have been a shock when you came in the room and your wife wasn't here. Don't worry. She is doing just fine."

It took Doyle several minutes before he could speak and then the only words that he managed to say were a simple, "That's great."

He pasted a smile on his face when he entered Paris' new room. He now had five people to impress with his devotion for his wife. The family greeted him warmly when he walked into room 1414. They were all filled with smiles and happiness. He could not understand why, until he looked at Paris' bed. Paris was sitting up, a smile on her face as she called his name. He went to her and hugged her, tears of shock running down his face.

"Paris my love," he said, the words sticking in his throat, "I am so glad you're well."

She hugged him back and said, "Doyle I love you so much. It is so good to be awake."

Christopher walked over to Doyle and said, "She can't have too much excitement, and we don't want her to overdo anything. I am going to keep her in the hospital for another week for observation, and then I am sure she will be well enough to come home."

"Paris I have to go to my car for a moment. I left my cellphone there and I am waiting for a call from Brandon. My father's not well and Brandon said he might have to take him to the hospital. I will be right back."

Doyle walked out of Paris' room and down the hall. That was the last thing Doyle remembered before he fainted and fell to the floor. He must have been out for a good ten minutes before he came to. An orderly had come and moved him to Paris' former room and Christopher was on the phone ordering laboratory tests for him.

When he opened his eyes, Christopher asked gently, "Doyle when was the last time you had something to eat?"

"Christopher, I really don't remember."

Christopher ordered a tray of food for Doyle and an IV for him.

"Doyle I think you're dehydrated and probably haven't eaten all day. I'm sure you had a few drinks at the wake and before the wake. I'm going to keep you in the hospital overnight and order tests for you, just to make sure there is nothing else wrong."

Christopher went back in Paris' room and told her Doyle was not feeling well. He assured her that Doyle just needed some rest, and he would be fine.

Christopher met the Viverettes in the dining room: "I have good news for you. Paris is able to eat by herself. She is very alert. She remembers everything except what caused her injury. All of the monitors have been removed from her body. We are going to have a therapist work with her walking. Even though it is only a week since she's been able to walk, it is the prudent thing to do. He agrees with me that it is a good idea to keep her in the hospital for the next week for observation."

Paris' family was jubilant with joy over her recovery. Christopher explained to the family that she needed her rest. He did not want her to be stressed or over excited.

"What about Doyle? Do you really believe that Doyle is not sick?" Sophia asked.

"Absolutely. He had an anxiety attack. He did a lot of drinking and very little eating in the last couple of days. He should be fine after he rests for a while. I put him in Paris' former room."

"He was in a deep sleep when I went to check up on him," Sophia added. "I am sure Paris' illness and his mother's death had a lot to do with his stress. I also believe the visit of Alberto Leon and his niece did nothing to cheer him up."

Pierre said, "You are very intuitive Sophia. The visit of anyone from the Leon family is not a cheery event."

"I plan to stay with Paris tonight. That will give the four of you some time to catch up with everything that's happened."

"We will all go up to Paris' room to say goodnight."

"I will join you," Christopher chimed in. "I want to check Paris' vitals before I leave the hospital."

Louis said, "We are all appreciative of you, Christopher. I know that you are a brilliant doctor and we are lucky to have you as Paris' physician."

"Hey you guys are making me blush, but I appreciate the compliments."

They entered Paris' room where she was sitting up and watching television. The first thing on her mind was Doyle.

"Christopher, did you see Doyle again? How is he doing?"

"Paris, Doyle is going to be fine. He was very worried about you and very distraught about his mother. He is exhausted. I admitted him to the hospital so he could relax and get some rest."

"You aren't hiding anything from me are you? He's not sick is he?"

"No Paris, he's not sick, just worn out."

"I wish I could have been with him for her funeral. Do you think we should call Brandon and ask about his father's health?"

"I'll call Brandon. I'll get his number from Doyle. I don't want my favorite patient to be upset." Christopher gave her a teasing look before continuing, "You couldn't be at the funeral, but your family was at the funeral. Doyle is going to be fine."

"I feel very sleepy. I would like to go to sleep now. How long have I been here?"

"Six days," said Lilly.

"Oh Maman, who has been taking care of Tou-Tou while I've been in the hospital?"

"We are all taking care of Tou-Tou. He is fine. He is also very independent. He goes in and out through his doggy door. He has an automatic feeder and water system!"

"He is a truly pampered pup," Paris said laughing.

"Do I need to call anyone for you?"

Paris' eyes grew wide, "Oh no! I volunteer at Flagler school four days a week! My music pupils must be wondering where I am. I also promised to buy some musical instruments for the band. Maman, the principles name is Mark Stratton. Could you call him and tell him I have been ill? Tell him I'll be in next week and I will have the band instruments delivered to the school this week. The phone number is in my address book next to my bed."

Paris quickly fell asleep.

Chapter 17

Within a few minutes she was again dreaming of the past, the past in the city she loved, and where her life was filled with promise and gayety.

It was Halloween. Paris loved Halloween. She loved dressing up in costume and parading down Bourbon Street where there was a myriad of strange people dressed in wild costumes.

She and Doyle were an item now. He was addictive—she could not stop thinking of him. She was possessed by him. He would be graduating in June and she would not graduate for another year. He would probably move back to Miami and practice law with his brother Brandon and she would never see him again. She could not think about that without feeling great pain.

Paris dressed as a flapper. She wore a short silver beaded dress and a bobbed blonde wig over her hair with high silver heels. She learned the steps of the Charleston and practiced for hours to master the dance. Doyle was dressed as a vampire. He wore a black cape lined with a scarlet red lining. His face was painted chalk white and his lips were painted ruby red. Shirree was Cinderella. Her black hair was covered with a crown and she wore a long blue gown with a fake fur cape. She completed her outfit with clear plastic shoes. David hated dressing up in costumes so he decided to be a cowboy. He wore a red checked shirt, a pair of Levi jeans, Frye boots, and a battered cowboy hat.

The four of them met at Shirree and Paris' apartment for cocktails before they went parading down Bourbon Street. Shirree decided they would all drink blood-red cosmopolitans to complement Doyle's vampire costume.

Paris said, "All of our costumes are so dissimilar. A flapper, a vampire, Cinderella and a cowboy! We look strange together."

Doyle looked at her and the others, "You're right, we do look very strange and mismatched. But that's the fun of Halloween! Come on, do the Charleston for us."

Doyle tried to follow her quick steps and tripped over his feet, much to the amusement of Shirree and David.

They went to the restaurant on Bourbon Street where Paris took Doyle after they had just met on the steps of St. Louis Cathedral. They sat on the balcony where they could see masses of people in all ages and colors in wild clothes and without clothes. They ordered shrimp scampi, fried green tomatoes, a fried oyster loaf, grilled asparagus, plenty of French bread and plenty of wine. They drank, they ate and they laughed. They went to a couple of parties in the quarter and then ended up at The Dungeon. The Dungeon opened at midnight.

The four of them walked down a long narrow alleyway passage and crossed a moat where they walked into a darkened room called the Main Chamber Bar.

David asked, "Doyle have you ever been to the Dungeon before?"

"No, I haven't, but this looks like a bizarre place. The bar's menu is great! Witches' brew, dragon's blood. Look at the signs: 'Beware, for you have entered the Dungeon of the Prince.'"

They ordered drinks and went to the Venus room where skulls decorated the walls, and a hanging cage dangled from the ceiling. Paris looked around and pointed out about twenty vampires with fake fangs protruding from their red mouths.

Shirree tugged on Paris' arm. "Let's go upstairs to the Sound Bar and dance."

They walked upstairs to a crowded dance floor covered with costumed people wildly dancing and drinking. Shirree counted seven devils dressed in red with fake horns coming out of their hair. Doyle counted twelve transvestites, dressed beautifully until you looked down and saw their size-twelve shoes. The two couples started dancing with each other and ended up dancing and laughing with a group of masked people in the smoky room.

When they left it was morning and they were starved, so they decided to go to the Camellia Grill for breakfast.

Doyle said, "This is the best Halloween I have ever had. It was a great night."

Paris looked up at Doyle and touched his chin. "Oh Doyle, your lipstick is running all over your chin."

They all laughed loudly.

"Your blonde wig is hanging on your neck," Doyle pointed out in retaliation.

"So it is," she replied haughtily, replacing it upon her head.

*****

Paris didn't see Doyle for over a week. They spoke on the phone, but Doyle didn't ask her out and their conversations were always short because Doyle had to get back to his studies.

All week long she thought about him and wondered if he had become bored with her. At night in her bed she re-lived their lovemaking in her mind and she touched her body pretending his hands were on her. She would never forget the way he made her feel and how he pleasured her. He touched her in places she never thought anyone would explore on her body. But once his fingers and mouth were in her secret places, she never wanted him to stop. She wondered if he was turned on by her. She was inexperienced; he had to teach her everything. She remembered screaming with ecstasy when he was inside of her. She dug her fingernails in his back—she never knew she was capable of such passion. She wanted to sleep wrapped up around him. She felt no shame for her wildness. She just wanted more of his mouth, his fingers and his throbbing body connected to hers. She fell asleep praying she would be with him soon.

The next morning was Sunday and Paris went to the ten o'clock mass at St. Louis Cathedral. She walked in and as was her custom lit a candle and said a prayer for Suzette. She liked to sit in the front of the church because the beauty of the altar mesmerized her. She stared at the golden ceiling murals painted by an Alsatian artist in 1872.

Whenever she entered the cathedral, a feeling of peace and contentment came over her. The mass started and she was engulfed by the tranquility of the ritual. She participated in the prayers and went to the front of the altar to receive communion. She was among the last of the people to leave the church.

She started down the front stairs and realized that Doyle was at the bottom of the staircase.

He took her hand and said, "Paris Marie Viverette, will you be my wife?"

She looked into his deep purple blue eyes, smiled and replied, "Yes, I will be your wife."

He solemnly handed her a small jewelry box from his pocket. She opened the box and removed a small sparkling diamond engagement ring. She put it on her finger and exclaimed that it was beautiful as she embraced him and they passionately kissed. They slowly walked to La Madeleine where they momentarily sat and gazed at each other.

Doyle asked Paris what she would like to eat and she replied,

"Coffee with cream and an almond croissant." She stared lovingly at the engagement ring on her finger while Doyle went to get their food.

He came back with their food and said, "Paris this is our first day together as an engaged couple. What would you like to do?"

Paris thought a minute before she replied, "I would like a portrait painted of us by one of the artists in the square, so that we can always remember how happy we are today."

"What about your parents? I thought the first thing you would do, would be to call them and tell them you're engaged."

"I'll call them tonight. Today is just our day; our first official day as a couple."

Doyle took her hand and kissed her palm, her ring finger and then her fingertips. "Today we have made the commitment to officially belong to each other."

"Yes and then we will be married! You will be graduating in May. So…a June wedding!"

Doyle softly kissed her on her lips. "A June wedding will be fine for me. I love you Paris, and I don't care when and where we are married."

"I love you Doyle and I am very excited!"

They left the café and chose an artist on the square who did portraits. He first took a Polaroid picture of them and then started to paint in watercolors. He asked them to return in a couple of hours for their pictures.

"I have never taken a carriage ride, Paris. I would like to take one today."

"That is a great idea. Let's go choose our carriage."

They walked to the front of the square and found a carriage with a sturdy dappled mule wearing a straw hat decorated with big red roses. The hat had holes on each side to accommodate the mule's long ears. The tour guide introduced himself as Max and his animal as Maxine. They had to share the carriage with another young couple who were vacationing from Akron, Ohio.

Paris blushed as she confided, "We've just become engaged."

"We are on our honeymoon!" the couple said in unison, as the Max and Maxine began pulling them on the tour of the French Quarter.

Paris smiled at Doyle as she looked at the other couple and said, "This is my dream man. I am a very lucky lady to be engaged to him."

Paris and Doyle thanked Max for a great tour and bade goodbye to the couple from Ohio. Paris discreetly handed Max a folded ten dollar bill as a tip, receiving a smile in gratitude.

"Where would you like to eat Paris? I'm ready for lunch and I'm sure you are too."

"I'd like to go to Bacco's. We can have lunch in the patio and listen to some great jazz. You paid for the carriage ride, so I'm going to pay for lunch."

Doyle started to protest but Paris assured him, "We are students, and students take turns paying for things. I'm paying for the portrait also. After all, you spent a lot of money on my engagement ring."

She held out her hand and admired the ring on her finger. They finished their leisurely lunch and walked back holding hands to Jackson Square to pick up their portraits.

The artist smiled at them as he presented them with their picture.

"Doyle we look beautiful," Paris sighed happily as she stared at their images.

The artist, Peter Moore, looked at the happy couple and asked, "Do you two realize how much alike you look?"

Paris said, "I never noticed that we look alike."

"I never did either," Doyle replied.

Paris looked at the portrait of the two of them and said, "So we do. I guess we are narcissists. I have noticed a lot of married people look alike."

The painter looked at them and shook his head. "I do a lot of portraits for people, and I see a lot of similarities between them; but you two are so alike you could be brother and sister."

Doyle laughed as he looked at the painter, "We are both attractive people."

Paris paid for the portrait and handed it to Doyle to carry as they walked several blocks to a frame shop where they chose a simple frame for their picture. They walked to Paris' apartment where she called her parents.

Louis answered the phone and Paris said, "Papa put Maman on another phone. I have something wonderful I want to tell both of you at the same time."

Lilly picked up a phone and said, "Paris what's your good news?"

"Maman, Papa, Doyle and I are engaged!"

Lilly was the first one to speak, "I think that is wonderful! Why don't you and Doyle come here for dinner next Saturday night?"

"Let me check with Doyle." Paris glanced up at him.

"Paris, I will be happy to have dinner with your parents next Saturday night."

Paris, with much excitement and pride in her voice, told them about her beautiful engagement ring.

Shirree and Daisy came in while Paris was talking with her mother. Paris held up her finger with her engagement ring on it and both girls squealed with delight. After a quick goodbye to her parents, Paris embraced Shirree and Daisy, who wished them much happiness in their new life together. Shirree opened the bar and found a good bottle of wine to toast Paris and Doyle on their engagement.

Doyle looked at Paris' face beaming with happiness. She was wearing a purple jersey dress that clung to her body like a second skin. All day long he had been thinking of getting her in bed. The minute he gave her the engagement ring he felt himself get hard. All day he day dreamed about sucking her pert nipples which he could see through her skin-tight dress.

He watched her happily chatting with Daisy and about their engagement, and the beauty of the engagement ring he had given to her. He suddenly felt himself feeling trapped and suffocated. He didn't even know if he was marrying her because he loved heror because it was expedient to marry her for her money. He knew he needed time to get away from her and think. He went up to her and gave her a passionate kiss.

"Paris I have an important exam tomorrow I have to leave now."

"Oh Doyle, I thought we could have dinner tonight to celebrate our engagement."

"I will make it up to you honey. Will you walk me down the stairs?"

"Of course I will. I understand."

He said goodnight to Shirree and Daisy who happily congratulated him. He and Paris walked down the stairs and he embraced Paris as he gave her a loving kiss and wished her goodnight. Paris, Shirree and Daisy went to dinner at a small Italian restaurant down the street from where they lived. They drank lots of wine and ate great Italian food. Paris radiated happiness and could not stop talking about how lucky she was to be marrying Doyle and what a considerate man he was.

Shirree kept saying, "The minute I saw the two of you together I just knew he was the man for you."

Daisy sighed, "I am so happy the two of you are getting married. He is the most romantic man, proposing to you on the steps of the church where he first met you. That is true love."

"Daisy, what a beautiful thing to say. I want you to be one of bridesmaids and Shirree will be my maid of honor. You and Shirree have to come and help me choose my wedding gown. After all, you two were with me when I first met Doyle."

"Daisy and I would love to help you choose your gown and the bridesmaids' gowns. That way we'll be sure you don't choose gowns that make us look like clumsy lampshades."

"Shirree, you are too much! What you really mean is that you want to make sure your maid of honor gown will show off those humongous boobs."

"Paris, you're right. I could not bear to be your maid of honor in a dress that made me look like a librarian."

"Shirree, my love, I would never do that to you. I am so happy; I want to share my happiness with everyone."

Daisy looked at Paris with tears in her eyes and said, "We are thrilled that you're so much in love with a man who truly adores you."

They drank a toast to Paris' future, and talked about how beautiful her wedding would be.

Lilly was sitting in her living room with Maman Madeline and they were drinking a bottle of wine. Louis was pacing nervously in front of them with his wineglass in his hand. He had called his brother Pierre and asked him and Juliet to come over for dinner. He had also called Sophia and Papa Joe and invited them to join them, too.

Lilly smiled, trying to cheer up her husband's gloomy expression. "Louis, it is always a shock to a father when his daughter becomes engaged. Paris was depressed and deeply unhappy and withdrawn until she met Doyle. I am thrilled that she is in love…and more importantly…happy!"

"You're such a romantic, Lilly. We know nothing about Doyle or his family. I do not want my daughter to be hurt by anyone."

"He seems to adore Paris; that is what's important. He has a scholarship to Tulane, so we can assume that he is fairly intelligent," she said caustically. "Paris told me he is in the top ten percentile of his class. She is not marrying his family, she is marrying Doyle. I imagine his parents are not affluent. His father is a blue-collar worker, but that isn't significant. What matters is that they are in love."

Pierre and Juliet had walked in while Lilly was speaking and helped themselves to the open bottle of wine on the bar. Sophia and Papa Joe walked in right after.

Louis said, "Let's go outside and eat on the patio. It's a beautiful night. I'm going to grill some steaks and corn. Maryanne is going to make a salad and I'm going to grill some asparagus."

"That sounds good to me. Pierre and I love to come over here for dinner. You are a great chef Louis."

"But Juliet, you also tell me I am a great chef," said her husband.

"For the sake of peace and harmony, you are a chef extraordinaire," Juliet said laughing as she saw the look of feigned pain on Pierre's face.

Everyone laughed jovially as they made their way to the patio. Norris served wine to them on the patio and everyone relaxed as Louis barbecued. Norris spoke with a formal British accent and had worked for the Viverettes for years.

Louis finally said, "I think Paris is too young to be engaged."

"Lilly replied, "I agree with you, but if being engaged and married to Doyle makes her happy, I'm certainly not going to try to stop her. I'm going to do everything I can to make life easier for her."

"I agree," Sophia said firmly. "She has had so much unhappiness in her life. I am thrilled she has found someone who makes her happy."

Lady Madeline nodded her head in agreement. "She is twenty-one. Years ago girls married at seventeen."

Juliet looked at her mother and said, "I know you married Papa when you were twenty and your marriage was very happy."

Lilly said, "That settles it, we are going to make plans for Paris' engagement party and wedding. We will make her a beautiful wedding, and she will be a beautiful bride."

"Doyle has been coming to my office and coming to observe me in court. Now that they are engaged I will offer him a position in my firm."

"Pierre that is very nice of you. But it would make me happier if they lived in New Orleans rather than Miami."

"You don't have to thank me, Louis. I think he will make a very good trial attorney and an asset to my firm."

"For generations the Viverette family has succeeded no matter what catastrophes have occurred around us. We still managed to acquire wealth and power; but woe to anyone who tries to hurt anyone in our family. We will have our vengeance on them. If Doyle hurts Paris in any way we will avenge her suffering."

Sophia looked at the group who all nodded their assent, "Lady Madeline is right, we cannot let anyone hurt anyone of us. We must protect each other."

***

Doyle was aimlessly walking around the quarter for a couple of hours trying to sort out his feelings. He was not certain that he loved Paris, but he realized that this was his big chance to change his life and he had to seize this opportunity.

He realized that he was in the fringe area of the quarter where very few people ever visited. He was starved and looked around for a restaurant. He noticed a restaurant on the next block, The Sweet Potato.

He went in the restaurant and sat down. He noticed that he was one of the few white people in the restaurant.

A smiling young black man brought him the menu and said to him, "Welcome to the Sweet Potato. You are going to love our food man, I promise you."

Doyle laughed and looked at the menu, which was strictly soul food, so he ordered collard greens, cornbread and fried catfish with a cold beer.

The young waiter served him his food and said, "My name is Regis, enjoy your food, hear? When you want somethin' else just holler."

The food was good and he was thoroughly enjoying it when an attractive black woman. Briana, came to his table and asked if she could join him. He told her to sit down and asked if she wanted something to eat or drink. They drank and laughed until the place emptied and only the two of them were left sitting there.

Briana said, "I am going to have to shut the restaurant down and lock up now. I have some beer in my apartment. It's only a few blocks away. Would you like to come home with me?"

Doyle smiled and nodded, "Sure."

They walked the few blocks to her apartment, which was in a small building with a locked gate and large courtyard. She lived on the second floor and he followed her to into a small apartment with a diminutive kitchen, bedroom and living room. He sat on a faded couch in her tidy living room and Briana served them both another beer and sat beside him.

He looked at her and said, "Briana, why?"

She looked at him. "Because I want to fuck you. You're good looking, and I'm horny."

Briana stripped them both and led him to the small shower in her bathroom. She had a sponge and some soap in her hands and briskly washed him.

She threw him a towel and said in a sultry tone, "Get on the bed and I'll give you a massage.

"Oh, you're nice and big," she happily exclaimed as she rubbed the lotion on his throbbing member.

He took the lotion away from her and poured it on her breasts and thighs. He gently stroked her furry mound and she started to wriggle and become wet. He spread her legs apart with his hands and plunged into her hot pussy. She was so hot that he felt his cock was immersed in hot velvet. She moved him away from her and sat on top of him. He loved the feel of her strength; her body was hard with the exception of her full soft breasts. She was amazing. She turned him inside out and he just lay there and succumbed to her.

When she was finished with him, he put his clothes on and limped home. The following evening Doyle called Brandon and Annie and announced his engagement to Paris. They congratulated him and Annie wished him luck and excused herself from the conversation to grade her eighth-grade class's papers.

"Hey big bro, how are you doing? Do you like the firm you are working for?"

"Doyle, it's tough. I'm working in a firm with a hundred other attorneys. I am the low man on the totem pole. I have a lot of small cases like DWI, divorces, bankruptcies, real-estate closings, etc. I'm working my butt off and making very little money. It takes a couple of years to build a clientele. Thank God I have Annie, she's supporting the household."

"Patience. Rome wasn't built in a day. I know you're going to be a great attorney."

"Hey buddy, when do I get to meet Paris?"

"I am sure we will have an engagement party in New Orleans. She's a real beauty. You're going to like her."

"I'm really happy for you, Doyle. Congratulations again, little brother. And the best of luck to you."

Doyle dreaded calling his father and mother but he didn't want to procrastinate so he made the call and winced as he answered his father's obnoxious questions as to what Paris looked like and her bra size.

Alex arrived home just as he finished speaking to his parents. Alex had loaned Doyle the money for Paris' engagement ring. Doyle was planning to pay him back in installments when he started to work for Pierre.

Alex had met Paris several weeks before and pronounced her one of the most attractive women he had ever seen. It was his idea to have Doyle propose to Paris on the steps of the cathedral where they had first met.

"Alex, it is official, I am engaged to Paris. She loved it when I surprised her on the church steps and proposed to her. She is thrilled. We are meeting with her parents next Saturday night at their house."

"Are you happy amigo? How do you feel about getting married right after graduation?"

Doyle thought a moment before he answered. He hated to give up his freedom and marry, but he hated the idea of having no money and struggling to survive more than losing his freedom. He heard the dejected, scared tone in his brother's voice when he called to tell him of his impending marriage, and thought to himself, "I've been poor all my life; I don't want to ever struggle and worry about money again."

"Alex, I am a very happy man. I am excited about marrying Paris. We are going to have a happy life together. I want to thank you for all the help you've given me. You made this engagement happen; I'm buying you dinner at Mandinas!"

"Sounds great to me, I love their pepper turtle soup and fried soft shell crab. I'm ready to go."

*****

On Saturday night Norris picked Paris and Doyle up at Paris' apartment in the family Rolls Royce. Paris was wearing a green silk dress and matching short jacket, her dress was very short and Doyle had passing thoughts of running his hand up her skirt, but he was too intimidated by Norris to do more than think about it. He had no idea the Viverette family owned a Rolls Royce. Somehow the silver Rolls

Royce crystallized the wealth and status of his future wife, more than the mansion they lived in or the impressive artwork and antiques they possessed. He sat back in the thick leather seats, held hands with Paris and just relaxed as he savored the short ride in this bastion of luxury.

When they arrived at the manor they were welcomed in the house by Lady Madeline. She was wearing a silver-gray long jersey dress with a twisted silver and gold belt around her small waist. She wore her long white hair in a long braid twisted around her head. Her green eyes sparkled and the emeralds she wore in her ears and around her neck matched the color of her eyes.

"Congratulations to both of you," she said smiling as she hugged her granddaughter and Doyle.

They walked into the house and Lady Madeline led them to the living room where the family awaited them. Doyle looked at Lilly, Juliet and Sophia; all dressed in elegant dresses and fine jewelry. He appraised them as he had never done before.

Lilly looked stunning in a simple purple dress, which emphasized her slim figure and elegance. She had diamonds the size of marbles on her fingers, neck and ears. Juliet appeared in a low-cut navy blue dress, which tied at her hip. She was decked out in blue sapphires, which made her lightly tanned skin look golden. Sophia looked like a goddess in a white dress with a pleated skirt. Blood-red ruby earrings gleamed on her ears and matched an enormous red ruby on her finger.

He looked at Paris across the room and smiled. This was the life he had always dreamed about. All of his doubts about marrying Paris had been swept away.

Norris announced that dinner was served and everyone followed him to the dining room. Doyle realized he had never been in the dining room before. He walked into the room holding Paris' hand and saw a large room that looked like a replica of a medieval banquet room. A great round wooden table was in the center of the room. The red walls were covered by large tapestries and large ornamental mirrors. There were heraldic crests and coats of arms hung beside the French doors at the back of the room.

Doyle sat next to Paris on a huge poppy-red chair covered with gold trim and gold studs. A massive, circular, two-tiered chandelier hung above the table and there were two great free-standing candelabras near the table. A statue of a Viking stood on each side of the front entrance to the dining hall.

Paris turned to Doyle: "Papa decorates the rooms in the house like the displays in the museum. This is the most dramatic room in our home."

The painted china plates sat on larger gold plates and in front of each place setting there was a garland of sweet olive flowers. The crystal dishes and glassware refracted light and rainbows of color danced upon the table top.

"Oh Papa! Thank you for remembering how much I love the scent of sweet olive trees."

"It is my pleasure, Paris. Our chef has prepared a sensational dinner for us. I hope you all enjoy your dinner."

Norris filled the crystal champagne flutes with Roederer Cristal champagne. Everyone stood up and toasted Paris and Doyle, wishing them a happy life together.

When the remains of the dinner had been removed, Louis said, "Doyle, I want to welcome you to our family. I do not have a son; you will be like a son to me. I will help you in any way I can, I only ask this of you: treat my daughter with love and respect, keep her out of harm's way and be loyal to her. If you do hurt her I promise you, you will live to regret it."

"Papa, why must you say such ugly things to Doyle? He loves me, he would never think of harming me."

"Your mother's father—your grandfather—said the same to me."

Lady Madeline chimed in, "My husband was very protective of his wife and his daughters. He loved his family very much."

Doyle smiled and took Paris' hand in his, "I promise never to hurt or betray Paris in any way. I love her very much; she will be the mother of my children and the center of my universe."

Louis beamed, "That is what I wanted to hear."

Pierre said, "Doyle I would like to speak to you privately in the library."

Louis said, "Why don't the rest of us sit on the verandah; the weather is very pleasant tonight."

Pierre and Doyle joined them in the verandah an hour later. Doyle looked happy and so did Pierre.

Pierre said, "I have an announcement to make! Doyle will be working for me after he graduates and passes the bar exam. He has come to watch me in court on several occasions. He is in the top ten percentile in his class and I think he will be a good addition to our staff."

Paris stood up and kissed Doyle. "I am so happy for you! You will love working for Oncle Pierre."

"The next thing on our agenda is Juliet and I will be King and Queen of Rex this year. All of you will be riding in our court, including my mother and father who will be coming in from France."

Doyle was confused. He turned to Paris, "What's 'Rex'?" he whispered."

"It's a parade and a festival. A different king and queen is chosen every year. They are always prominent businessmen and-or philanthropists. It's a real honor to be chosen."

Doyle nodded, understanding the excitement of the family.

Juliet looked at Lilly. "I have to choose my gown this week. I want you to come with me. I want to look very regal," she said laughing. "After all, I'll be a queen for a day."

Lilly replied, laughing merrily, "Of course I will go shopping with my sister."

"Not to change the subject, but Paris do you have any idea where you would like your engagement party?"

"I'd like my engagement party and the wedding reception at the Monteleone Hotel. Doyle what do you think?"

"I'm going to leave all the planning to you. I am sure that we'll have a great engagement party and wedding. Planning weddings are for the bride. The groom usually just shows up."

"Very well put," agreed Pierre, laughing.

"I want to be married at St. Louis Cathedral," Paris continued. "I want to arrive with my groom in a carriage pulled by white horses with my parents and my maid of honor. I would like to have my reception at the grand ballroom at the Monteleone Hotel. I will be the third generation Viverette to have my reception there."

"Good choices," Louis agreed. "I know you love the cathedral, it is a beautiful church to be married in."

"June will be perfect. I graduate the beginning of May, and Paris and I would like to have a June wedding."

"Thank you Papa, and thank you Mama," she said hugging her parents. "I appreciate your help putting this all together. I know our wedding is going to be extraordinary."

Paris suddenly turned to Doyle and said, "You have not seen all of the rooms on the second floor of our house. I am going to take you on a guided tour." She dragged him out of the room with a wave to her laughing family.

"I am ready when you are."

They walked into the house arm in arm. As soon as they were away from the eyes of the family, Doyle kissed Paris passionately on the lips.

"Is there any place we can sneak away?"

"The house is pretty crowded with family and servants," Paris panted. "I know that they have you set up in the *garçonnière*, so I guess you are just going to have to behave yourself."

They walked in the library and Doyle embraced Paris with one hand and his other hand slid up her skirt.

"Doyle no, one of the maids could come in at any minute and we would be so embarrassed!"

She could feel herself getting wet and she could feel the hardness of Doyle throbbing through her skirt. She removed his hand from under her skirt and literally dragged him out of the library and into a long passageway covered by portraits of the Viverettes.

Doyle dutifully looked at two hundred years of portraits hanging on the wall before he saw Paris' portrait at the end of the corridor.

"You are beautiful. When was your portrait painted?"

"It was painted the month before I made my debut. I just turned sixteen," Paris smiled at the memory. "I posed in the gown I wore to my sweet sixteen parties."

Doyle stared at the cloud of blue-black hair framing her heart shape face. She was wearing an off-the-shoulder gown of deep purple that matched the color of her purple blue eyes and caused her creamy white complexion to glow. She was a magnificent-looking girl who had a rapturous aspect of enchantment on her face.

"Shirree's picture is at her house with her parents' and brother's portraits. Years ago the family portraits were divided up so everyone could have some portraits hanging in their house."

They walked back to the verandah and joined the family as they sat and planned for the all the festivities they would be involved in for the next six months. Doyle sat back in his comfortable chair, sipped a glass of wine and processed all he had learned about what it would be like marrying into the Viverette family. It was as if he had died and gone to heaven. He was not going to make any mistakes; this was his golden parachute. He was quite cognizant of the fact that he would not be dining at the Sweet Potato restaurant ever again.

Chapter 18

Sophia slept very well on the sleeper bed in Paris' room. She awakened when a nurse came in to check Paris' vitals.

Paris opened her eyes and confided in her godmother, "Maman Sophia, when I sleep I seem to have all these dreams of the past. I feel as if I am living in a time warp, it's all very confusing."

"It's normal Paris," Sophia assured her. "Your body has gone through a lot of changes. You have been suffering with a concussion. You were comatose. Confusion is normal in situations such as this. You are going to start physical therapy today. By next week you are going to feel great."

The nurse brought in two trays of breakfast food and two cups of coffee.

Paris took a sip of her coffee and laughed, "Maman, I can't believe the people in Miami like this coffee. It never ceases to amaze me. Where's the chicory?"

They finished their food and Maman Sophia prepared Paris for her shower and helped her wash her hair. She found a clean blue cotton pair of pajamas for her to wear, helped her put them on, and went to the other bedroom in the suite to take her shower and dress. Sophia took her own shower quickly, and when she returned to Paris' room only Christopher was there—Paris was in physical therapy.

Maman Sophia anxiously asked, "Does she remember what happened to her? Christopher, she never mentions what happened to her to cause her fall, but I don't want to upset her by quizzing her and asking too many questions." She sighed heavily, "How is Doyle?"

"He is fine. I'm discharging him this morning. All he needed was rest and food. I imagine he will be coming to see Paris shortly."

"I'll go to Paris' house and get the maids to move her clothing back. I don't want her to be upset when she comes home and realizes that her belongings are not in her room."

"I think that is a good idea. Her health is very fragile at this time. How long are you and the family going to stay in Miami?"

"I don't know. It depends upon what we find out about Doyle and how Paris feels."

Paris returned to her room with the physical therapist and gave

Christopher a big hug.

"I am so glad to see you Christopher. The therapist told me to walk around the halls and not stay in bed now that I'm feeling better. Where's Doyle?"

"He'll be here in about thirty minutes. In the meantime I just want to check your coordination and a few other things. Do you remember how you injured yourself?"

"All I remember is I went to bed and woke up here. I wish I could remember."

"You look great. Your bruises have faded and we will be removing the stitches from the side of your head in a couple of days."

Doyle walked in the room looking tired but much healthier than the day before.

He kissed Paris on the cheek and she said, "Doyle I am so sorry about your mother."

"Me too," he said sadly.

The Viverettes arrived looking relaxed and rested.

Lilly said, "Paris you look much better. I'm so happy."

Sophia said, "I have some things to take care of now that you are all here. I will see you later."

She rushed back to the house and the guards at the gate waved her through. She called the maids who were already in Palm Island cleaning another house. They promised to come to her house as soon as possible. Tou-Tou was thrilled to see her. He jumped all over and licked her fingers. She refilled his automatic feeder to the top and threw him some tiny dog biscuits.

It took the girls several hours to move Paris' clothes back to the bedroom she shared with Doyle. The Happy Maids agency sent another three girls to do the regular housework. Sophia helped restore Paris' clothes and belongings to her room. When everything was in its place, Paris would never realize her clothes had ever been moved.

Doyle stayed in the hospital with Paris until early afternoon. He sat at Paris' side and said a prayer of thanks that she did not remember their fight or what caused her concussion. He felt as if he was walking on egg shells. He did not know how she would react to what he had done to her.

At about two in the afternoon he was too tired to keep his eyes open. He made his apologies to Paris and her family and went home to sleep. He needed breathing room to think. He was not ready to deal with the Leon family or anyone else at this time. He just wanted to go to his bedroom and crash.

He saw Sophia's car in the driveway and the sight of it annoyed him. He couldn't even be alone in his own home?

He walked in the door and Tou-Tou feverishly began to bark at him. He walked to the kitchen to pour himself a cold drink of ice water and Tou-Tou followed him and proceeded to try to attack him by nipping at his heels. Doyle viciously kicked him in the side and the little dog collapsed to the floor like a broken doll.

Sophia woke up from a nap to the sound of the dog whimpering. She ran in the kitchen just in time to see Doyle kick Tou-Tou. She looked at Doyle, picked up the little dog and ran to her car without a word. She put Tou-Tou in her lap as she raced to the nearest vet. Tears were running down her face as she drove like a demon. She was in a fury and she needed her husband with her because her anger was so fierce she wanted to harm Doyle. She felt the essence of evil in his presence.

Doyle grabbed a bottle of Glenkinchie malt scotch, filled a silver bucket with ice, and quickly left the kitchen, escaping to the sanctity of his bedroom.

"My God," he thought. "This gets worse and worse. I am in a tight spot and whatever I do I seem to sink deeper and deeper into the abyss. I feel as if I am being sucked into quicksand."

He was sure he did not kick him very hard. The dog knew he did not like him and generally ignored him—that is, until the night that Doyle injured Paris. Ever since that night the dog hounded him whenever he walked in the house and tried to bite his ankles. He felt no remorse about hurting the dog.

He had more important things to worry about. He had to decide what he was going to do to stay alive. If he did not leave Paris, they would make sure Paris knew about his affair with Adriana. He would not be surprised if they sent out birth announcements to Paris and her family naming him the father of Adriana's child if he did not act quickly. He finally made a decision; he was going to have to get rid of his wife. He was going to have to do it in the next four weeks. He could then marry Adrianna four months later and no one would be suspicious. Then he remembered her pregnancy. People would be suspicious, but suspicion without proof meant nothing.

How was he going to murder Paris? He would have to do it

himself. If he paid someone to kill her they could blackmail him for the rest of his life. Or if they were caught, they could rat him out to get a lighter sentence He certainly didn't want to end up in jail. He thought of poison, but he knew nothing about poisons. Also with all the new medical knowledge available the forensic pathologists most certainly would determine that she had been poisoned. He could throw her down the stairs, but that would look suspicious.

Doyle took food and drink to the balcony off his bedroom and sat on a deck chair. It was a clear beautiful day. The water was calm and vividly blue. Fluffy white clouds floated in the blue sky and a pleasant breeze caused the palm trees to gently sway. He watched a flotilla of assorted boats peacefully parade in front of his dock.

He felt serene and relaxed, and then the idea came to him. He could take Paris on vacation to Nassau. They would stay at the Atlantis Hotel for a few days. Then he would charter a cabin cruiser, and they would visit some of the smaller islands around Nassau. Both he and Paris had licenses to pilot a boat. February would be a great time to be in the Bahamas. He would choose an area in the water where few boats traveled and sharks were known to patrol. It would be so easy for a strong wind storm to cause turbulence in the water and a swell of water could tip the boat causing Paris to fall over board. The seas between the islands were very choppy and strange things were known to happen in the vicinity of the Bermuda triangle. Many boats and airplanes had been mysteriously swallowed by the unpredictable sea in that region. Also the police in the Bahamas were known to be very lackadaisical in their investigations involving tourists.

Doyle suddenly felt very serene, content he had solved his problem. He would get some sleeping pills from a friend of his who was a doctor and drop them in her cocktail. It would be very easy to throw her inert body into the sea. There was no chance that her body would be recovered. He felt the sun warm his skin and he smelled the salt water. It was a glorious day. He decided to stay in the sun for another half hour before he forced himself to visit his sick wife in the hospital.

***

Papa Joe called Christopher, concerned for Paris' wellbeing after what his wife told him about Tou-Tou. Christopher had never liked

Doyle from the minute he met him.

Sophia met her husband at the Miami airport with her eyes swollen from crying and a big smile on her face. He dropped his carry-on so he could give her a big hug and kiss.

"Joseph, good news! Tou-Tou is out of shock and feeling better."

"Boo, I bet you have been hounding that vet to death?"

"You're so right. I went back to the animal hospital and asked the doctor if I could just sit and hold Tou-Tou until he closed his office. He was very understanding. I'm going to pick him up first thing in the morning."

They returned to the O'Connor house and went to Sophia's room so Papa Joe could unpack his clothes and take a shower. He then called Louis and made arrangements for the family to meet at a cocktail lounge near the house.

The investigator had sent Louis a preliminary report about Doyle. Louis wanted to discuss the strange situation they found Paris embroiled in. They did not want to meet in the house where Doyle could overhear their conversation.

As Joseph was dressing he looked at his wife and said tiredly, "Nothing makes sense. I know we discussed this on the phone before, but why would Doyle want to hurt Paris? The more I think about it, the less sense it makes. If he is not happy with Paris he could divorce her."

"He gains nothing by divorcing her," Lilly pointed out. "But he also has nothing to gain if Paris is hurt. The house, the cars, his office, even the furniture in the house and office do not belong to Paris. Everything is part of the Viverette family trust. If Paris died he would lose everything."

"It does not make sense to me either, but look what he did to Tou-Tou! He broke the poor dog's rib! Unfortunately Paris cannot, or does not, want to remember what happened. I have the feeling he might have abused her before and she is just blocking the pain from her memory."

"Sugar, if he did hurt Paris and left her alone in pain and bleeding, he can just as easily murder her in a fit of rage," Lilly said fearfully.

"I remember what I saw in my reverie the night of the blood moon," Maman Sophia added, "I saw Paris crying hysterically, bruised and covered with blood. If I did not come to Miami and find her battered on the floor, she could have died. It didn't look as if someone broke in and attacked her; nothing was stolen. And I cannot believe she just fell out of her bed and struck her head without being pushed."

Doyle went to the hospital around dinner time to visit Paris. The Viverette family was getting ready to go to the dining room for dinner. They stiffly invited Doyle to have dinner with them but he declined, saying that he had dinner before coming.

Doyle handed Paris a large bouquet and noticed that taped to the walls of her room were large colored flowers made of construction paper and a wide banner saying, "We miss you Mrs. O'Connor! Thank you for your gift of musical instruments for our band."

Doyle went to the wall and looked at the artwork posted there. "These are great, Paris. They worked very hard on making the flowers and banners for you. They even trimmed the flowers with glitter and sequins."

"I know! Most of my students are inner-city kids who have very few possessions. Whenever I give them something they are always very appreciative. Many of them are very talented and I try to encourage them so that hopefully in some small way I can encourage them to have a better life."

Doyle looked at Paris and said, "Honey, we haven't had a vacation together in over a year. I am going to take some time off of work and take you to Nassau. We can stay at the Atlantis for a few days. We can rent a cabin cruiser and go island hopping. We can relax and just hang out together and have fun."

"Oh Doyle," Paris gushed with excitement, "I am so glad you suggested it. You have been so busy working that we haven't spent much time together!" After her initial excitement, Paris slumped back in the hospital bed. "I've missed being with you, but I can't take a vacation right now. The band needs me. I can take a vacation at spring break. That's only six weeks away from now."

Doyle thought a moment. Perhaps six weeks would be better timing anyway. It would seem too suspicious having the accidents so close together.

He replied, "Six weeks will be perfect. I am afraid that I haven't been a very thoughtful husband in the past because I've been so obsessed with my career. But I am going to make that all up to you in the future."

They talked about their future plans and Paris glowed with happiness. "Doyle, I love you so much. I am so lucky to have a husband like you."

When the Viverettes returned from dinner Paris happily announced the vacation Doyle was planning for them. The family was stunned but didn't say anything except to comment on how nice Nassau is in the spring.

Doyle excused himself shortly after the Viverettes returned from dinner. He explained that his father was in very poor health and copiously pining away for his dead wife. Doyle felt he needed to be with him as much as possible.

Paris said, "Doyle that's one of the reasons why I love you so much; you are so dedicated to your parents."

In actuality, every time he wanted to go out to a bar by himself or had a date with another woman, he would tell Paris he was either working late or doing something for his parents. Once he reached his car he phoned Adriana and told her he was on his way to her apartment. He arrived at her high-rise building within fifteen minutes. The apartment complex was one of the highest buildings on Brickell Avenue. Adriana's apartment reminded him of an expensive concrete jungle. She greeted him with a big kiss and told him she had cooked seafood paella just for him. He winced as he kissed her in return.

Chapter 19

The family returned after dinner and said goodnight to Paris.

Louis hired a private registered nurse to spend the night with Paris. He wanted to make sure that she was never alone when she was in the hospital.

Paris watched television for a little while after her family left and she quickly fell into a deep sleep. Within minutes her thoughts floated back to one of the happiest days in her life: her engagement party. Every time Paris stepped into one of Yvonne La Fleur's gowns she felt she was transformed into a goddess encased in soft silk and clingy satin. Daisy regretfully pulled herself away from the beautiful hats and joined Shirree who was trying on clothing from the beautiful array of silk and chiffon dresses that Yvonne ordered from France for the opulent Mardi Gras balls, weddings and other formal events. The profusion of beautiful gowns and cocktail dresses were a clothes horse's delight.

Daisy was thinking she could spend hours examining all of the beautiful creations when Shirree interrupted her reverie by saying, "Daisy, I can hardly wait to see Paris' engagement gown."

"I imagine it is a work of art," Daisy replied wistfully.

Paris was in a dressing room with Missy, who had assisted her for many years at Yvonne's. Missy was meticulous in making sure that each and every dress sold at Yvonne La Fleur's fit perfectly.

Missy helped Paris put on her gown and said, "Paris this is a very sexy, but elegant gown, perfect for your engagement party. You look gorgeous in it."

"Thank you Missy. I love the feel of this dress. Let's see what Shirree and Daisy say about it."

Paris walked to the dais and modeled her dress to Shirree and Daisy. The dress was made of champagne colored satin with a sweet heart neckline, spaghetti straps and a large diagonal bow which cut across the bodice of her dress, accentuating her bust line. The satin dress clung to her bodice and hips; then it flared to her ankles. She then pirouetted around and modeled the champagne colored sheer lace jacket which swirled around the bow and fastened at her waist.

"Paris," Shirree said, "you look amazing! The color of your dress glows and emphasizes the darkness of your hair and your eyes."

"I agree with Shirree," said Daisy. "Your dress is outstanding, and you wear it well. No one will be able to take their eyes off of you."

"I thank you ladies," Paris beamed as she did a mock curtsy for them. Missy walked in and announced, "Ladies I have three rooms set up for your gowns for the Rex Ball. Mandy and I will help you put them on."

She directed them to their dressing rooms and carefully helped Paris remove her gown. The three girls walked to the dais to model their gowns.

Missy said, "We have to make sure the gowns are floor length; those are the rules of all the Mardi Gras balls. If your gown does not fall to the floor, you will not be admitted to the ball. I know you have heard this a hundred times before, but I just want to remind you again."

Each girl tried her gown on. Mardi Gras dresses were flamboyant and had a lot of beads and sequins on them. The colors favored were Mardi Gras colors, gold, purple, and green. The gowns were wild and fanciful. They represented the unique vibrancy of Mardi Gras. The girls looked at themselves in the mirrors surrounding the dais, admiring their Mardi Gras gowns and expressing pleasure with the tight bodices and full skirts of their fanciful and ornate gowns.

They went back to their individual dressing rooms where Missy and Mandy carefully helped them remove their dresses, so they could try on their gowns for Paris' engagement party. Shirree chose a ruby red gown with a halter neck, and a slit up one side for the party. Daisy chose a strapless black chiffon gown with a long flowing black skirt.

As soon as they were outside Paris said, "Lunch time, where do want to eat?"

Trying on clothes had stimulated their appetites.

Daisy replied, "How about O'Henry's?"

Shirree and Paris quickly agreed.

O'Henry's was a few blocks away from Yvonne La Fleur's and the girls walked quickly to get there. O'Henry's specialized in great burgers. The girls walked into the crowded restaurant and finally found a table in the back of the room. The tables were covered with red-and-white-checkered colored oil cloth table cloths. The floors were covered with peanut shells. Each table had a wood bucket of unshelled peanuts on top of the table. The three of them found a table in the back of the room and sat down.

They did not have to open the menu to order. The waitress came to the table and took their order for three medium rare bacon cheese burgers with fries and sweet tea. Their tea was served immediately and they dug into the peanuts. Daisy cracked open a peanut, removed the outer shell and threw it on the floor.

"I love throwing the shells on the floor. It gives me a feeling of being primordial."

They sat around munching their peanuts when Daisy said, "Something has been puzzling me for a long time. Is Sophia part of the Viverette family?"

Shirree answered, "That is an interesting question. Remember we talked about our great, great, great-grandfather Jon Charles Viverette who was an artist who studied in Paris? Well, he's Sophia's grandfather too. I believe she is a first cousin, many, many times removed."

Paris picked up the story. "Grandfather Jon's wife, Mary Louise, died in childbirth having their third child. He was about forty at the time and he was very lonely. The family cook Mimi married a Creole man who was very light skinned and they had a daughter named Angeline. Angeline was beautiful and looked white. She was about seventeen. She could not participate in the quadroon ball because her mother was not a Creole and was very dark. This was very disappointing to her and her family because they wanted her to find a good man to take care of her.

"Angeline's father, Charles, wanted his daughter to have a protector and make her debut at a ball but the Creole matrons would not accept her in their society because of her lack of education and the fact that her mother was too dark skinned.

"After Grandmother Mary Louise died, Grandfather Jon became obsessed with seventeen-year-old Angeline. Jon expressed interest in painting Angeline in the nude. Charles refused without Jon first making a *plaçage* to seal their relationship.

"Jon was so smitten with Angeline's beauty that he built a Victorian mansion for her. He then called in a notary to have a legal deed issued to her as well as a document stating that the children he sired with her would share all of his assets jointly with his other children."

Daisy sighed, "Actually that is a very romantic story. Did he paint any pictures of Angeline?"

Paris replied, "Yes he painted dozens of them. Some of them are in museums, some of them Sophia has, and some of them are hidden on our estate. Grandfather was senile before he died and hid much of his later work."

"What did Angeline look like? Was she really beautiful?"

Shirree answered Daisy's question with a smile. "In the portraits our grandfather painted of her she was beautiful. She had curly thick dark brown hair, almond shaped dark eyes, and honey colored skin."

Paris said, "Enough of family, why don't we go to Saks? I need some gloves and shoes."

Doyle's family was expected to arrive four days before Paris' engagement party, which was on a Saturday night. Norris rented a black stretch limousine so all the O'Connor's and Viverettes could ride together. When he rented the limousine he also rented a police escort. In Louisiana it was very common to hire a police escort when you hired a limousine. It made people feel that they were very special. The Viverettes had planned a sightseeing tour of the city, a tour of the plantations, and a boat ride down the Mississippi.

Paris was very nervous about meeting Doyle's family. He had told her very little about them; actually he rarely spoke about them. Their plane was expected about eleven in the morning. Norris picked up Paris and Doyle from her apartment at ten-thirty and they were on their way to the airport. Doyle was very apprehensive of Paris meeting his family. He was even more apprehensive of the Viverette family meeting his family. He had no idea what his unpredictable father might do. He knew Paris would excuse his father's ill behavior, but he had no idea what her parents would think of his rather lackluster family.

Norris heard them before he saw them. Doyle was walking next to an older man with a loud raucous voice. The older Mr. O'Connor had black hair spattered with a lot of gray. His face was red and weathered and he had the red bulbous nose of a drinker. His deep purple blue eyes were bloodshot. Paris was walking with a thin petite gray haired woman who reminded Norris of a little sparrow. Behind them he could see a man who resembled Doyle, but taller and heavier. Walking next to him was a tall woman, on the heavy side, with a deep tan and a big smile on her face.

Norris opened the door of the limousine and said, "Welcome to New Orleans."

Once their luggage was in the limousine and everyone was seated,

Norris began to drive to the Viverette plantation.

Daniel O'Connor loudly asked his son, "What is going on, are we being arrested?"

"No, Pop, we have a police escort so we can avoid the traffic and arrive at Paris' house sooner."

"This is really something," Daniel muttered. "I have never had a police escort in my whole life, except when they arrested me. Whew, this is fun!"

They arrived at the Viverette manse in record time. Norris drove to a guest house about a mile from the main house.

Dina, who occasionally worked for the Viverettes when they had guests staying in the guest quarters, welcomed the O'Connor's.

Paris said, "We will be having lunch around twelve. Norris will pick you up and bring you to the house. If you need anything just tell Dina and she will get it for you."

Doyle stayed to visit with his family and Paris drove back to her house with Norris.

"Doyle, you lucky son of a bitch, you found a gold mine! I hope you ain't going to forget your old man!" was the first thing Daniel O'Connor said to his son when they were alone.

"Dad, please I beg of you, don't get drunk and please act like a gentlemen."

"Don't take me for a fool. I'll be on my best behavior. I will take care of you, and you will take care of me."

Norris arrived promptly at twelve and the O'Connor's were driven to Bayou House. When they arrived at the mansion, Annie exclaimed with excitement in her voice, "What a beautiful house!"

Paris greeted everyone and introduced the O'Connors to her family. They were seated in the verandah and Annie was fascinated with the manse and furnishings.

Daniel O'Connor was happily inhaling a large glass of aged scotch. He was oblivious to his surroundings and totally enamored with the taste of his drink. Daniel downed his scotch and quickly looked around for someone to refill his glass. He noticed Sophia sitting at the other side of the room; he pointed to her held up his glass and said, "Girly I need a refill."

Papa Joe, infuriated at the way Daniel spoke to his wife, walked up to Daniel and grabbed the glass out of his hand.

"This time make it a double," said Daniel insensitively.

Papa Joe looked at him and flippantly said, "Yes Master."

The Viverette family ignored Daniel's rudeness and gave all their attention to the other members of the O'Connor family. Lunch was served on the verandah. The menu was composed of everyone's favorite Louisiana dishes; Jambalaya, red rice and beans, gumbo and fried shrimp.

When everyone had finished eating Lady Madeline smiled at Christine O'Connor and said graciously, "I would like to show you the French quarter. I am sure you will enjoy seeing St. Louis Cathedral and some of the other interesting sites."

Norris brought the Rolls Royce around and helped Lady Madeline and Cristina into the back seat. They arrived at the quarter and Lady Madeline asked Norris to drop them off at Jackson square and return in an hour.

Cristina enjoyed seeing the cathedral and all the interesting people and sights in the square, the hour of sightseeing passed rapidly. When Norris returned to the square Lady Madeline requested he take them to Yvonne La Fleur's.

As they reached the shop Lady Madeline said, "They are having a clearance sale at the shop I thought perhaps you would enjoy buying some things."

Cristina's eyes widened in surprise, "I would love to buy some new things but I don't know if I can afford to buy anything. I did not bring much money with me."

"Leave everything to me. I'll be able to get you some good bargains."

They walked into the shop and Yvonne was behind the counter stitching a beautiful white gown.

Lady Madeline said, "Yvonne, this is Cristina, Paris' future mother-in-law."

Cristina smiled and said, "Hello." She looked around the store and exclaimed, "Everything is so beautiful! I've never been to a store as beautiful as this."

Missy led Cristina to a large fitting room and said, "Relax in this chair and I will be back with some nice dresses for you."

An hour later, Cristina had purchased a navy blue silk long gown, a beige suit and several casual outfits. She paid her bill and profusely thanked Yvonne and Missy for their help.

The group went to a tea shop where they were served an exotic-tasting tea poured from a silver pot which they sipped from small china cups. In the middle of the table there were dishes of small pastries and finger sandwiches. Cristina sipped her tea daintily and nibbled on the finger sandwiches.

She looked at Lady Madeline, her plain face glowing with pleasure and said, "This is one of the nicest days I have had in my life. I feel like queen for the day. Thank you so much."

Lady Madeline smiled back at her and said, "I have enjoyed the day as much as you have. You are marvelous company. I hope we will have many opportunities in the future to go shopping together."

Norris drove the Viverette and O'Connor families to the Monteleone Hotel for Paris' engagement party. He was wearing his best tux and feeling very grand as he sailed through traffic with police sirens blasting through the still night. The ladies and the gentlemen were all dressed in their finery. Several beauticians were at the house in the afternoon to give the ladies facials and do their hair and nails. The men weren't left out as they all got manicures, including Norris.

The family went to the rooftop of the hotel in the Riverview Room where the engagement party was going to take place. The Riverview Room showcased the city of New Orleans and the Mississippi River from its windows. The lights of the city below sparkled like stars and the view from the top of the roof was spectacular. The ornate room had high, beautifully decorated ceilings with huge crystal chandeliers and posh furniture. There were carving and serving stations set up all around the room for meat, shellfish and pasta. There was a fountain of pink champagne flowing majestically on the buffet table next to the ice carvings of graceful dolphins.

Shirree arrived with David and his brother Christopher, who had come home for the weekend so he could attend Paris' engagement party. They were the first guests to arrive. Shirree's parents had ridden to the party in the limo. Paris came to greet them and gave David and Christopher a big kiss.

Christopher looked at Paris, paused and stuttered, "Paris you look gorgeous."

Paris gave him a warm hug and another kiss with her thank you.

The musicians arrived and started to practice their music. Three bars opened in different sections of the room and the guests started to wander in. Paris' family and the O'Connor's were at the doorway in a receiving line so every guest would be introduced to Paris' parents and grandmother as well as Doyle and his parents. All the ladies and men of the Viverette family wore gloves and shook hands with the guests. The O'Connor families were also in the receiving line, which stayed in place for about an hour to give every guest the opportunity to be introduced to Paris' fiancé and his family. Lady Madeline stood next to Cristina O'Connor knowing that the timid woman needed moral support.

"Cristina," she said quietly, "you look absolutely marvelous. The navy blue lace dress is very flattering to your complexion and I like your new hair style."

Cristina blushed with pleasure and thanked Lady Madeline.

When the receiving line was finished, the family had a table reserved for them close to the band and everyone helped themselves to the abundant buffet table and side stations. The music was loud and hot. They played all of Paris' favorite jazz music. She and Doyle danced the first dance together. Everyone exclaimed what a beautiful couple they made. They were young and beautiful, not to mention beaming with happiness.

The night flew by. At midnight the desert tables were covered with fresh fruit, homemade ice cream and French pastries. The successful engagement party broke up around one o'clock in the morning. The next afternoon Norris took the O'Connor family to the airport. The O'Connor's had a wonderful visit and they were excited about coming back for the wedding of Doyle and Paris.

Chapter 20

The family and Christopher were waiting at the appointed neighborhood bar near Palm Island when Sophia and Papa Joe arrived. They joined two tables at the back of the bar to accommodate everyone. The jovial tone of the meeting would change with Louis's news.

"I have the investigators report," Louis said softly to the group. "Doyle is very careful. Miranda, his private secretary, is the only one in the office who can answer his private phone. He owes no large amounts of money to anyone. He has few personal friends and he never flirts with the secretaries in his office or invites them out to lunch."

"He sounds like a saint," Papa Joe commented gravely.

Louis continued, "The detective tailed him earlier this evening and followed him to an expensive Brickell Avenue apartment complex. It took a lot of perseverance and a five hundred dollar bribe to the head of security to find out who Doyle was visiting. It is someone we know and you are not going to believe who."

At that point Louis paused, and Lilly chided, "Please do not play games."

"He visits Adriana Franco, Alberto Leon's niece. And he frequently takes her out for the evening. I could not believe it when he told me."

"My God," Lilly exclaimed. "He must be crazy!" The more the knowledge settled in, the more heated Lilly became. "The nerve of them! To brazenly sit at our table as if they were our friends while Adriana is sleeping with Paris' husband!"

Pierre replied, "Doyle is far from crazy. He is a shrewd, calculating man. I've had an opportunity to see how he reacted to various situations. He was very taken aback; perhaps shocked when he saw the Leons sitting at our table. There is something happening we are not aware of."

Louis nodded slowly: "I agree, Pierre, that's why I am having Adriana Franco followed also. I am very worried about her being a part of the notorious Leon family and I do not want Paris dragged into the dangerous web of the Colombian drug cartel."

"Oh come on," Lilly said sardonically. "He is not running to her apartment and taking her out because she is his client. It is clear that he is sleeping with that wretched girl."

"My dear wife, I have the same opinion as you, however my instinct tells me that there is more to this story than just their affair. Our agency will gather all the facts for us. It is a waste of time to speculate about what is happening without having all the facts."

Juliet, who was listening intently, finally jumped in. "We don't know what we are dealing with. Doyle is a dangerous man, the Leon family is dangerous; why don't we give Doyle the house and whatever money he wants and just walk away?"

Pierre looked at his wife and said, "There are very good reasons why we cannot do this. First, we really do not know what is happening, or what Doyle is up to. Second, if we pay off Doyle, he will never stop demanding money from us."

"Unfortunately, my brother, you are right," Louis agreed regretfully. "We will find out the truth. We will hire as many detectives as it takes to get to the bottom of this. We have the advantage; Doyle does not realize that we are watching him. We have a detective observing everyone who enters or leaves his office. We mustn't challenge him in any way; we must treat him with friendliness and affability so he does not think we suspect him of anything."

Christopher sat quietly, processing all of this information.

Sophia said, "What about the trip to the Bahamas that Doyle is planning? We cannot let Paris go to the Bahamas alone with Doyle."

Lilly shook her head emphatically, "There is no way my daughter is going alone anywhere with that lunatic. When she is discharged from the hospital she can never be alone with him; one of us has to be with her at all times."

"You are absolutely correct, Paris cannot be left alone," Christopher said. "I'll come up with some sort of plausible medical reason so that she is protected."

There was a serious tone to his voice as Pierre said, "That is a good idea. However I feel that it would be dangerous at this time to let Doyle think that we would interfere with his Bahamian trip. One of us will have to be with them."

"Louis, Pierre, I agree with you but I have some ideas about distracting Doyle."

"Joe, if he takes Paris to the Bahamas, she will be in a very vulnerable position. I know he plans to hurt her in some way."

"Yes, Louis, she would be in a very vulnerable position. I don't intend for him to take her on that trip. I have a contingency plan to offer to him that I think he will find more desirable than the trip to the Bahamas…when the right time comes."

"I suppose you are going to keep me in suspense, Joe, and not tell what you have in mind."

"When the time is right Louis I will tell you what I have in mind. Please let me take care of this problem. I promise you will not be disappointed." Joe said, chuckling.

The family left the bar and returned to the O'Connor home around midnight. Everyone went up to their rooms except Papa Joe who sat in the living room sipping scotch and reading the newspaper.

Doyle walked in the house a short time later and was very surprised to see Papa Joe sitting in his living room. Papa Joe greeted him warmly and apologized to him for not attending his mother's funeral.

"Doyle, I am sorry about your mother."

"Thank you for your condolences. It's been a very difficult time."

"Well, son, I can imagine how upsetting this is for you. If I can do anything for you please let me know. Tou-Tou was injured today. Sophia spent most of the day with him at the vet's. I know you have a lot of things on your mind but I would appreciate it if you could watch out for him when Sophia brings him home. I know he is so little it would be very easy to accidentally step on him."

Doyle looked carefully at Papa Joe sitting on his chair, his face calm and expressionless; his shrewd dark brown eyes staring into Doyle's eyes. He felt that Papa Joe's eyes were piercing his soul.

Papa Joe continued to speak, "We all have accountability to protect children, women and the elderly. The stronger we are, the bigger our responsibility is to save the small and weak from harm."

He felt exposed. "Papa Joe, I am very tired. Good night."

"Good night, Doyle. I hope you sleep well."

Doyle quickly went to his room. He lay clothed on his bed, shivering. He was transparent to Papa Joe. He pondered how a man who had made no threat to him could scare him so much. Papa Joe emanated power and he had no idea where that power came from.

Suddenly Doyle thought he heard the muted sounds of drums and chanting. He went to the bathroom to take a shower; however the drums and chanting followed him. He covered his head with a pillow after he showered and returned to his bed. The pillow did not mask the sound of the drums and chanting.

"I'm going mad," he muttered to himself. "I'm hallucinating."

He tossed and turned until at long last he fell asleep.

When Doyle woke up the next morning he chided himself about his fear of Papa Joe. The drums and chanting were probably a figment of his imagination. He was exhausted last night and he probably had too much to drink. He laughed at himself for thinking that someone could just look into his eyes and read his mind. He decided to stop drinking for a while. It was making him paranoid.

Chapter 21

Paris was discharged from the hospital with the caveat that she limit her activities and not return to her volunteer work until Christopher felt that she was absolutely well. He also made an appointment for her to see a psychiatrist the next week.

Paris opened the door to her house and Tou-Tou barked in delight at her return. Sophia had warned her that he had bumped into something and hurt his ribs so she gently lifted him and cradled him in her arms as he happily licked her face.

Lilly, Juliet and Sophia decided to stay with Paris until she was in perfect health and the danger in her life was removed. She still tired easily and slept more than she normally did.

Papa Joe had to leave for New York to attend another seminar. Louis and Pierre had business obligations in New Orleans, so all the menfolk left.

Paris went up to her bedroom when she arrived home and made no comment about her clothes in the closet. Doyle was loving and affectionate to his wife. He made no comment about her family staying at the house. He made a point of being pleasant and charming to everyone.

The ladies were breakfasting on the patio when Sophia received a surprise phone call from her husband who was speaking at a botany seminar in New York. Sophia clicked her cellphone off and quickly rushed out to the patio to share her news with the others.

"Joe just told me that Sotheby's auctioned off one of Jon Charles Viverette's pictures of my great, great, great-grandmother for two million dollars! The art community is finally acknowledging what a great artist he was!"

"I am happy that the world is finally recognizing his talent," said Lilly.

"I especially like the painting with Angeline in the nude rising from a giant white rose," Sophia added, laughing. Then she gasped, "There are supposed to be dozens of his pictures hidden around our home and plantation! If they're each worth two million..."

"We've found some around our home and land also," Juliet chimed in. "We are lucky that people did not appreciate his artistic talents before and buy up all of his work.

Lilly went upstairs to Paris' room, where Paris had fallen asleep with her clothes on. Lilly found a blanket and covered her. *She looks so beautiful and so young,* Lilly mused as she gazed upon her sleeping daughter.

***

Paris was reliving her first Mardi Gras with Doyle as she lay in a deep sleep. It was Lundi Gras, the day before Mardi Gras. Paris, Doyle, Shirree and David had just returned from the all-day party staged by the Zulu Social Aid & Pleasure Club and the Krewe of Rex.

The party began at the foot of Canal Street and the Mississippi River. The music was wonderful, the dancing was wild and the liquor flowed. The food was delicious and abundant as were the luscious King cakes—large cakes filled with cream cheese or fruit, custard, chocolate etc., and cut into slices. The cakes were covered with icing in the Mardi Gras colors of gold, purple and green. Each cake contained a small plastic baby in it. Traditionally, whoever finds the baby in their slice of cake has to buy the next King cake or throw the next party.

They were sated with food and drink when they arrived at the girls' apartment. The first thing everyone did was to take off their shoes and sprawl on a chair or couch. Paris went into the kitchen to brew a pot of coffee. Shirree placed the cups, saucers and napkins on the table and told everyone to help themselves.

Doyle sipped his coffee: "I've been in New Orleans for seven years and I still don't understand Mardi Gras."

David replied, "Mardi Gras is the heart of New Orleans and separates this city from all the other cities in America. The whole city is involved with the holiday. Even the school children have their own Mardi Gras parades and parties. There's also a parade for dogs call Barkus."

"When does Mardi Gras actually start? I mean what is the actual day it begins?"

"Mardi Gras kicks off January sixth, the twelfth day after Christmas; it begins the day of Epiphany. That is the first day we eat King Cakes and when the first Mardi Gras Balls are launched."

"David, how did the tradition of Mardi Gras originate? Until I moved to New Orleans I heard very little about it."

"In the middle of the second century some pope decreed that there would be forty days of sacrifice before Easter Sunday. They referred to those forty days as 'Lent.' The people were supposed to eat little food, practice abstinence and consume no meat or alcohol until Easter. Lent started on Wednesday and that day, as you know, is called Ash Wednesday. The day before lent is called 'Fat Tuesday,' or in French, 'Mardi Gras.'"

"Hey, David," Doyle said laughing, "that's very interesting but, what does that have to do with New Orleans?"

"The first recorded Mardi Gras was celebrated by French settlers in Louisiana was in 1699," Paris said as she took over the tale. "In 1743 processions and masking in the street was recorded in New Orleans as well as carnival balls. Rex stages the largest pageant on Mardi Gras day. Rex was started by a group of New Orleans businessmen partially to honor the visit of Grand Duke Alexis of Russia to participate in the 1872 Carnival season. The second reason was to draw tourists to the city to stimulate the economy which was in bad shape after the Civil War. The gentlemen felt that the splendor and pageantry would lure tourists to the city in the future."

"Enough history," Shirree moaned dramatically. Turning the conversation to the present, she said, "Remember, we are marching in the Rex Parade tomorrow afternoon after Zulu. No one on the float is allowed to take their masks off when we are in costume."

"I love the theme and the costumes," Paris remarked. "We're going to be on the Queen's float. You guys will get to see them tomorrow."

David said, "Guys we have a big day tomorrow and then we have the Rex Ball tomorrow night which will usually last until morning. I have got to get some sleep."

"I'm dead tired too. I am leaving with you David," Doyle said.

Paris and Shirree walked their men out the door and quickly kissed them goodnight.

"Paris, the pagans might have been satiated with sex before Lent but with all the alcohol, parties and balls during Mardi Gras, it's awfully difficult for this girl to move, let alone have sex."

"Amen, sister." The evening parades were over, there were hundreds of people milling around the streets. The streetcars had stopped running and it was impossible to get a cab, so Doyle was forced to walk home. Doyle found the devotion to Mardi Gras amazing. People were camping out along the street for a good spot for the parade. They were friendly and jovial to everyone who passed by. There were old people, young people and babies camping out. They never fought with each other; they all had one thing in common: their love of Mardi Gras and catching throws.

He finally arrived home, dead tired. He went to his bed and fell asleep with his clothes on.

He woke up to the sound of the television. Doyle grabbed something to eat, showered and grabbed his costume for the parade, and his tuxedo. He said goodbye to Alex and ran out of the house .He managed to catch a cab, that could only take him halfway to Paris' apartment because of the swarms of people on the street patiently waiting for the Zulu parade. Doyle had seen the Zulu parade many times. It was an enormous, very popular large parade, famous for tossing painted coconuts, and having wild painted faces which matched their feral costumes.

Doyle finally arrived at Paris' apartment. He rang the security bell and David came down the stairs in his Egyptian rower costume. Doyle looked at David and snickered as he studied his costume.

"You look really fine David; you would have made a first-class Egyptian."

"Hey, sport, you're not going to look any better after Shirree puts on your eye makeup and you squeeze into your flesh-colored tights and black wig."

Fifteen minutes later Doyle was wearing flesh-colored tights under a white short belted tunic and leather sandals. His eyelids were embossed in black kohl which gave them a slanted appearance. A coal-black Egyptian wig with long bangs hovered on his head, completing his Mardi Gras slave costume. David looked at him and started to laugh.

Shirree and Paris walked out of the bathroom wearing duplicate long gold strapless dresses with the same style wigs the men wore, only longer. They had slathered black kohl around their eyes. The girls strutted and pirouetted around the room proudly displaying their Egyptian finery. They had full-body flesh-colored leotards under their skirts and under their strapless dresses so their shoulders and arms would not be cold—February in New Orleans was very nippy. They wore large gold cat masks which totally disguised their faces.

David put on his gold tiger mask and Doyle put on his gold elephant mask.

David groaned, "I hope we don't suffocate in our masks."

Doyle said, "I don't understand why we have to wear junk all over our eyes when we are wearing masks over our faces."

Paris replied patiently, "The kohl on our eyes sets the theme of that period. It gives the aura of authenticity to our costumes. And when we leave the floats we can remove our masks."

Norris called to let them know he was downstairs waiting for them. They arrived at the lot where the floats were parked and when Norris walked out of the car they saw he was dressed as an Egyptian also. He held his wig and mask in his hand when he opened the door for them and went back in the car to put his wig and mask on.

The chariots were magic. Some had pyramids on them, others were made to look like the large rowboats of the golden age of the pharaohs, and others looked like the insides of tombs. There were large mummies in some of the floats and a few were replicas of the Nile. There were huge masked animal figures to represent the Egyptian gods and beautiful small animals made to look as if they were carved in gold as well as inlaid canopic coffinettes which were originally made to hold organs. The four of them went from float to float absorbing the beauty and vividness of the faux-Egyptian antiquities.

Doyle and David went back to their float as Paris and Shirree went to the Queen's float, which was a sumptuous chariot. On the Queen's float there were only Paris, Shirree, Sophia, Lady Madeline, Lilly and Juliet. Juliet, the queen of Rex, was Queen Nefertiti. She was wearing a fitted purple gown dripping with faux gold jewelry. Around her head was a high curved cervical crown. The crown made her neck appear long and slender. Lady Madeline wore a wine-colored velvet toga which made her appear very regal. Sophia and Lilly wore light-green togas decorated with layers of faux gold. All the ladies of her court wore gold cat masks. Queen Nefertiti sat on a gold throne. Paris and Shirree were on either side, fanning her with large purple feathers. The rest of the ladies sat on smaller thrones around the float organizing their throws. Colorful silk pillows were scattered all over the chariot, along with enormous half-man, half-animal stone cats, monkeys and lions.

Doyle and David were slaving away on their large ship float. There were hundreds of bead necklaces to be hung up. The doubloons were packed in tall boxes as were the cups, stuffed animals and small faux-gold tombs. The ship float had sixty people on it and everyone on board was working hard to arrange their throws. The outside of the ship was gray with brightly colored hieroglyphics. The King's chariot was the first float to move. Pierre was dressed in white robes wearing a gold mask of a pharaoh with a beard. On his head was a high-curved circular crown. He sat upon a tall gold throne with one man on each side fanning him with vivid green-colored feathers.

The large pageant of Rex marched down south Claiborne Street; crowds of people lined the streets yelling, "Throw me something, mister!"

After tossing their trinkets for a while, Doyle was becoming visibly less enthusiastic about the constant throwing.

David leaned forward and said, "Doyle, one of the rules of Rex is we have to keep tossing throws wherever we march."

"No problem," replied Doyle, feeling as if his arms were about to fall off.

The screams of the crowd became a strange hiss-like sound. Everyone was wildly waving their arms in the air hoping to catch beads.

When they hit Rampart Street the crowd changed and suddenly women of all colors, shapes and ages began to lift their shirts and show their breasts as they screamed for beads. Men were freely wagging their willies for beads.

Doyle felt like a nobleman tossing throws to the thousands of mendicants reaching for them. He was amazed at the feeling of power it aroused in him. He wondered how many pounds of beads, doubloons, cups, candy and stuffed animals his aching arms had thrown. He stared at the crowd for a moment and felt the masses of people on the street screaming, stripping and begging for throws. It was wild. It was thrilling. It was Marti Gras, the last night of Carnival. Tomorrow would be Ash Wednesday, the first day of Lent, and the city would be amazingly cleansed of the festival during the night.

The spectacle took four long hours. Doyle and David felt like they had been run over by a truck when it was over.

Doyle exclaimed, "What a great day. I am exhausted but I had a real good time."

David said, "Remember, save some of your energy. We have the big Rex Ball tonight."

"Oh my god, my feet are killing me! Do you think anyone would mind if I came to the ball barefoot?"

151

"No, I don't think they would mind, provided you paint your toe-nails purple, green and gold."

At six-thirty Paris and Shirree came out of their rooms dressed for the ball.

Shirree said, "Paris, you look fabulous. I love your embroidered emerald-green halter gown. Turn around so I can see the back of your dress."

Paris twirled to show Shirree the low cut back of the dress and how the full skirt swirled when she moved.

"Your dress is magnificent, Shirree. I love the beaded décolleté of your dress and the tiered skirt. Mauve is your color. Yvonne La Fleur has fabulous creations."

Doyle heard the girls' voices, opened his eyes and said, "You both look very delicious. You girls will be the belles of the ball."

Shirree woke David up and at seven they were all dressed, their masks in place, promptly standing outside of their apartment waiting for Norris to pick them up.

The limousine arrived and the four entered the limousine, greeting the family who were already seated in the vehicle sipping champagne. The family walked into the auditorium together. They were seated at the front table in the auditorium. This was the head table for Rex and his court. Pierre Viverette was King Rex, the King of Carnival. Juliet was the Queen of Carnival.

Doyle sat back in his custom-made tux—a gift from his almost uncle-in-law, "King Rex"—and observed Paris' family. The women were all beautiful, gracious and dripping with expensive jewelry. The men were well groomed, friendly, well-mannered and much respected in the community.

The music started to play and Doyle asked Paris to dance with him. She was an amazing dancer, so light on her feet and she could waltz as well as tango. She looked like an angel in her beautiful emerald green dress.

He was very proud of her. He pulled her closer to him; just the feel of her body thrilled him. That's what perplexed him, he loved Paris and she excited him. Why then did Beverly's breasts seem to haunt him? He couldn't erase the glory of making love to Beverly and the feel of her lush breasts pressing against his chest as Paris wrapped her body against his.

They arrived home from the ball in the wee hours of the morning.

They walked hand-in-hand up the stairs into Paris bedroom.

Doyle softly whispered to Paris, "I want to undress you."

Paris remained motionless as Doyle unzipped her dress and it fell to the ground. He slowly removed her black lacy underpants. He picked her up and placed her on the bed. She watched him as he rapidly removed his clothes and leaned over her prone body. He ran his tongue up and down her thighs, carefully avoiding the dark mound between her thighs. He then slowly ran his tongue over her breasts and sucked her nipples until she whimpered in desire. He kissed her hot, moist mouth as he lightly ran his fingers on her thighs and then began caressing the silky flesh between the lips of her dark mound. She was so hot, so wet; he could feel her rapid heartbeat and her gasp of pleasure. His fingers explored inside her pulsating center before he placed his tongue deep inside of her. She screamed in pleasure and she became as hot as molten lava. He picked her up and put her on top of him. She wriggled so she was sitting on his hot engorged penis and it was deep inside of her. He moved within her as he roughly clasped her round firm bottom and they both tore at each other in wild pleasure.

Chapter 22

Paris woke up to the smell of delicious cooking. She walked down to the kitchen where the ladies in her family were putting the final touches on dinner. Tou-Tou was hungrily sniffing around the floor hoping to find a few tidbits for his dinner, but he dropped everything and immediately ran to Paris when she came down the stairs.

"I won't forget you, Tou-Tou. You'll share our dinner. I still love you even though you sleep in Sophia's bedroom now rather than mine." Paris happily picked him up and hugged him. "What smells so good?" Paris asked as she sat down and stroked Tou-Tou's fluffy white fur.

Lilly replied, "Your Aunt Juliet grilled hamburgers and chicken. I made potato salad and fruit salad, Sophia made cornbread and roasted corn on the grill."

"It smells heavenly. Where's Doyle?"

"He called a few minutes ago. He has a meeting and he won't be home until late. Will you please put the plates and glasses on the patio table?"

"Of course Maman," Paris said a little sadly. "Did Doyle say how late he was going to be?"

"No, honey, he didn't give me a specific time." Lilly then changed the subject by saying, "It is a beautiful evening; there is a refreshing breeze and the roses and honeysuckles are in full bloom. We thought it would be nice to eat on the patio."

The ladies sat down on the patio and ate their pleasant dinner. They drank some wine with their cheese and crackers and watched the sunset streaking the sky in colors of orange, pink and gold.

Juliet said, "This is a magnificent sunset, the ocean water looks emerald green and there is a feeling of tranquility around us."

"I love having dinner on the patio and watching the sunset. It's my favorite time of day. I usually sit here with Tou-Tou because Doyle is rarely home this early in the evening."

Sophia cleared the patio table and Juliet put the leftover food in the refrigerator. It only took a short time to clean the kitchen. Tou-Tou remained close to Sophia following her around the kitchen as she cleaned.

The women walked upstairs together, said goodnight, and walked to their separate rooms. Tou-Tou was right behind Sophia and followed her into her bedroom and he made himself comfortable on her bed.

*****

Long after everyone in the house was asleep, Doyle crept in as silently as he could. He removed his shoes in his car and carried them into the house. He quietly opened the door of his bedroom, tip-toed into the bathroom and removed all his clothes with the exception of his boxer shorts. He inched his way into bed and breathed a sigh of relief—everyone in the house was asleep; no one had heard him come home.

He tried to fall sleep, but he was too wired to relax. He was living two lives. He was a pawn and an android. Carmen Franco had called him the week before and announced she was having an engagement party for him and Adriana.

Doyle had promptly arrived at Adriana's building at six.

"Oh Poppy, I'm so excited," she said, her face beaming with pleasure. She was wearing a short black dress with tomato red shoes and her short red hair was smoothed with gel and pulled away from her moon-shaped face.

Adriana directed him to her family house on Lady Island, which was an island connected to the mainland by a causeway. When they exited the causeway they drove through a jungle of large trees and shrubbery. They came to a high gate where a guard recognized Adriana and opened the gate for them. He drove through the gate and down a road until he saw a humongous Pepto Bismol-colored pink stucco house and realized it was the only house on the island. They continued down the road until they reached a moat that separated the road from the house. He stopped the car and an attendant appeared immediately to take their car. They exited and walked over a small foot bridge which led to the front of the house, where a uniformed houseman ushered them in. Doyle realized the house was built like a medieval fortress. There was only one footbridge that led to the house.

Once inside they were ushered into a room that reminded him very much of a hotel ballroom. The room had large crystal chandeliers decorated with colored crystal flowers. The floors were black and white marble. Oval tables with white lace tablecloths were set for dinner. There was a stage in the front of the room where a band of six Latin musicians dressed in powder blue tuxedos and black sombreros were energetically singing and playing their instruments. The tables were filled by a large collection of well-dressed people chattering and drinking cocktails.

Everyone clapped and toasts were made to the new couple's happiness. Adriana was aflutter with joy. Doyle was numb with despair. The whole evening became one large blur to him. He pasted a big smile on his face and pretended to be having a marvelous time. He was not hungry; but he forced himself to eat whatever food was set before him. He was very careful to take only sips of the champagne and wine offered him. He knew the Leon family was watching him. He and Adriana were expected to dance together and appear intoxicated by each other's presence. He forced himself to embrace her and touch her lovingly for effect; they danced for most of the evening. He found dancing preferable to being quizzed by her family, who repeatedly asked him when he would be divorced from his wife.

He drove Adriana home as rapidly as possible. She was so busy chattering that she failed to notice Doyle's abject misery. As Doyle lay in his comfortable bed after sneaking in, he chastised himself for making the biggest mistake of his life: bedding Adriana Franco. He knew he was going to pay dearly for his mistake for the rest of his life. He was so involved in his problems that he didn't even realize Paris was not in bed with him.

*****

The next morning Juliet and Sophia took separate cars to school so that after their volunteering Sophia could visit Little Havana and Juliet could meet Lilly and Paris at the spa. Paris and Lilly had an appointment to see Dr. Julian Wolf, the psychiatrist Christopher had recommended.

Dr. Wolf's office was comfortable but understated. The whole office was beige: he had beige carpeting, beige leather furniture and a beige wood desk in his waiting room. The few pictures on the walls were of squares, triangles, and circles in muted colors framed in beige.

Lilly looked around the room and quietly said in French so the other people in the waiting room wouldn't hear her, "*I guess he wants his patients to be in a non-threatening environment."*

Paris giggled and replied in kind, *"This is certainly not The Louvre."*

Finally Paris' name was called and she entered the innards of the office leaving Lilly thoughtlessly reading a magazine. She was ushered into another room by the receptionist.

Dr. Wolf greeted her with a big smile and ushered her into his office. They shook hands and Paris felt tremendous strength in his grip. Paris sat on a dark-brown leather chair across from a matching brown-leather couch. The wood floor in his office was covered with a faded, well-worn Persian carpet. To the side of the leather couch was a huge aquarium built into the wall, filled with vividly colored salt water fish and graceful flower-like sea anemone which daintily swayed in the water.

The doctor sat across from her on the couch and smiled. She liked him immediately. He reminded her of a red fox. He had reddish brown hair, a large reddish brown mustache and a trim reddish brown pointed beard. His eyes were bright green and he was slightly tanned. He wore a short-sleeve T-shirt which showed his well-muscled arms. She had to keep from laughing as she mused over the fact that his name was Wolf, but he looked like a big fox.

He started by asking a few questions and all of her doubts, her pain and her fears came quickly tumbling out of her mouth. Time seemed to fly by and she was amazed when he told her their hour was up. They decided that she would see him daily for two hours for the next two weeks.

They drove to PF Changs to meet Christopher for lunch. Christopher arrived within minutes of their being seated. Over crab wantons, sweet-sour soup, orange peel shrimp, and Mongolian beef, Paris extolled the wisdom of Julian Wolf. She signed three release forms—for Christopher, her mother and her father—so they could call Dr. Wolf and discuss her progress with him at any time.

Paris looked at Christopher and her mother and in a very forceful voice said, "The family can know about my sessions with Dr. Wolf, but I don't want Doyle to know."

Lilly deliberately avoided looking at Christopher and restrained herself from asking. She noted that Paris was devouring her food. She had been barely eating since her accident. She was amazed at the immediate change in Paris that Dr. Wolf had evoked in only one hour.

She seemed to be re-energized and even cheerful. She laughed at a few things Christopher said and Lilly realized that it was a long time since she had heard Paris laugh.

When Paris excused herself to go to the ladies room Lilly looked at Christopher and asked, "Who is this man? Svengali?"

Christopher laughed and replied, "Julian Wolf has written three best-sellers on his methods of helping people cope with problems. He also teaches people how to identify the stress in their lives and remove it. He is a genius in the field of psychology. He actually sees very few patients. He spends most of his time on all sorts of experiments relating to the destruction of our health caused by the stress in our lives."

"I am so glad that Paris was able to see him. Thank you for making it possible for Paris to see Dr. Wolf, Christopher."

Lilly leaned over and kissed Christopher on his cheek. "You are a beautiful man."

***

Sophia decided to spend the afternoon in Little Havana. She thought of it as an adventure because when you entered Little Havana you were symbolically entering another country.

Little Havana was the area settled by the first wave of Cuban refugees who settled In Miami. Over the years many other Spanish-speaking people arrived and moved there. However, it was still a Cuban stronghold. Spanish was the only language spoken in this area and Castro was a hot topic for the people who resided here. Many Cuban people had been living in this country for over forty years and never learned one word of English. Many of them considered themselves exiles, not citizens. They planned to return to Cuba when Castro died and reclaim their property.

Sophia parked her car in a guarded lot a short distance from Little Havana and walked several blocks to the colorful area. The streets were filled with people who were laughing, eating, drinking and talking to one another. Most of the men were wearing pastel-colored Guayabera shirts, khaki pants and sandals. The women were wearing vividly colored dresses or flowered shorts and blouses. They were friendly and waved to Sophia as she walked by.

Sophia went to a small Cuban café where she indulged in a

medianoche sandwich with an order of fried plantains. She relished the unique taste of the well-seasoned food, and finished her lunch with a small Cuban coffee.

She left the café and went to her favorite *botanica*. The botanica carried a multitude of candles, some of them were shaped as a man or woman in colors of red, black and green. There were other candles in glass cylinders in an array of colors or layers of candles. Oils, herbs, potions and all sorts of tools for the making of spells connected with the Santeria religion were displayed on shelves in the store. Statues of beautifully decorated saints in all sizes and colors were abundant and sat next to skillfully carved wood statues of African deities. In the corner of the room was a large triangular altar where statues of saints, African deities, carved and painted American Indian heads with feathered headdresses, and an array of dolls were positioned with offerings of apples and honey in front of them. There were glasses of water and jars of coins on the altar. The food and the money were placed on the altar to please the gods so the gods would bless all the people who entered the botanica with good luck.

The manager of the shop, Maria, greeted Sophia warmly. She was a middle-aged plump Hispanic woman with long braided hair wearing a red-flowered cotton dress. They exchanged pleasantries and Sophia reached in her purse and handed a shopping list for Maria to fill.

The shop was filled with a number of shoppers. In southwest Miami there were hundreds of botanicas. There were also hundreds of businesses owned by Hispanics that contained small altars in their place of business. The altars were put in auspicious places to bring prosperity and luck to the business.

"Maria, how is your church in Hialeah doing?" Sophia asked politely.

"The city of Hialeah say no can sacrifice chickens and goats to our gods in church. We sued the city. This is the way we do our religion and the United States give us freedom of religion. The case goes to the big court. They say because to sacrifice animals is part of our religion and we no torture the animals and we eat them after the service it is okay. So now we have mucho, mucho members."

Sophia said, "I am glad you are doing so well. I am sorry I cannot wait to see Julio. Please tell him I wish him well." She handed Maria some money "This is to cover my supplies and also my donation to your church. I would appreciate it if you would mail my supplies to me in Louisiana."

"Julio feel bad he no see you. I wish you good luck. I send everything on your list to Louisiana. Soon I hope you come back to see us."

As Sophia drove back to Palm Island she truly felt as if she had taken a trip to a foreign city. She looked back at the streets of Hialeah, where people shopped at sidewalk vendors and gathered on the streets to visit with one another. They played dominos and cards in the parks together and sometimes danced in the streets.

A few minutes later she was in Miami profuse with chain stores and giant cement high-rises that blocked the view of most of the beautiful beaches and ocean. Sophia drove by areas of picturesque mansions surrounded by palm trees and lush gardens. The intercoastal waterways were crowded with giant yachts majestically sailing on the emerald green sea.

She walked in the house and heard Paris' voice filled with energy and laughter. Paris greeted her with a warm hug and big kiss.

Lilly was sitting with a big smile on her face and she said to Sophia, "The spa was great. You have to come with us next time."

Juliet said, "I had a great day too. I not only went to the spa, I bought a magnificent handbag and a great pair of shoes, on sale."

The phone rang and Paris answered it. She came back in the room and said, "That was Doyle, he wants to take me to dinner. Would I offend you if I went to dinner alone with him?"

After a long pause the words "absolutely not" seemed to tumble out of Lilly's mouth. "We will be fine; the three of us will go out to dinner."

*****

The ladies went to Houston's restaurant and had an early dinner so they could get back to the house and speak to Louis while Paris and Doyle were not around. Lilly called Louis as soon as they arrived at the house. She was very unhappy when she hung up the phone.

"My dear sister, what did he say? You look like you have seen a ghost. Your face is so pale. What's wrong?"

"Louis says that our investigators followed Doyle and watched as he picked up Adriana Franco and they drove to a private island. The investigators surveyed the island from across the causeway and saw a lot of cars and activity going on. They assumed that they were having a party on the Island.

"One of our undercover people has been working in Adriana's apartment building as a parking attendant. Apparently Adriana told the concierge she was getting married and she was waiting in the lobby for her fiancé to pick her up and take her to their engagement party."

"The most horrible and upsetting thing is the party at the Franco house was supposedly an engagement party for Adriana and Doyle!" Lilly shouted, crying hysterically. Sobbing and shaking, she looked at the others. "I am so afraid he is going to do something horrible to Paris. I am so frightened for her."

Juliet looked at her sister and shook her head in anger. "I don't know what to think. This is cruel and horrible. Doyle is a monster. Do you think he invited Paris out to dinner to tell her he is leaving her to marry another woman?"

Sophia felt sick to her stomach. She never really liked Doyle, but to be engaged to another woman and celebrate his engagement with his fiancé's family when he was married to Paris was obscene and vicious.

She thought a few moments and said, "I don't think he can afford to divorce Paris. If he does that he will leave his marriage with very little money and that's not Doyle's style."

Lilly replied: "Sophia, we have to save Paris from harm. We must wait up until they come back from dinner. I am going with Paris to Dr. Wolf tomorrow morning. After that I will take her to the school so she can resume her voluntary teaching again. You and Juliet will be here to let the detectives in to search Doyle's safe." Lilly stopped crying angrily adding, "We must find out what Doyle is planning. We don't want him to know we are suspicious and we cannot let Paris go out alone with him again."

"Lilly, what excuse are our sleuths going to have for being in the house?"

"To avoid any curiosity from the guards or the neighbors they will be in a repair truck that belongs to a legitimate company that repairs washing machines and dryers. Apparently they have used this ruse before."

"I just realized the paradox of the situation is that we do not have to feel guilty or uncomfortable about having the house searched. We do not need permission to have the house searched or bugged. We can have the detectives or anyone else legally search the house as everything was purchased by the Viverette trust, so everything is strictly legal, because we own the trust."

"We have to wait and see what is going to happen with this situation. I pray he does not keep breaking my daughter's heart, or harm my daughter physically again. The worst problem of all is that Paris seems to still love him. She would be devastated if she found out the truth about him. How are we going to be able to protect her? That is the most important thing. In addition to everything else Doyle has done, he has managed to entangle us with a drug cartel."

*****

About two hours later Paris and Doyle arrived home. They were holding hands and Paris seemed very happy.

Chapter 23

Paris was fast asleep. Since her accident she constantly dreamed of her past in New Orleans.

Again, she was dreaming of the days before her wedding. The main house and the guesthouse were overflowing with her family and Doyle's family. Grand Mere Simone and Grand Pere, her father's parents who currently lived in the south of France, were staying in the main house. Doyle's family was staying in guest-house one and the rest of her family from France were staying in guest-house two.

Two days before the wedding Paris hosted a party for the ladies at Windsor Court, where they would partake of a high tea. Norris helped the ladies into the black stretch limo and they sped through the city to the posh Windsor Court Hotel. They entered the hotel and went to Le Salon where a large oval antique table had been reserved for their party. Le Salon was tastefully furnished with distinctive antiques, a richly colored gold-and-beige carpet, a fireplace and a grand piano.

The ladies were offered tea poured from a silver teapot into thin hand-painted bone china cups and or if they preferred a "Mar-tea-ni." Most of the ladies accepted both. The first course was tiny tea sandwiches made of caviar and salmon as well as the typical English cucumber and curried turkey. They were placed on a three-tier silver tray in the center of the table and served by waiters wearing white gloves. The next course was scones of all variety accompanied by whipped cream, lemon curd, raspberry preserves and Devonshire cream. The third course was chocolate dipped fruits, chocolate truffles, petit fours, and tartlets.

The O'Connor ladies admired the finery of the dishes and the cutlery as they enjoyed their tasty finger sandwiches and tea. The Viverettes had opened a new world for them. They had never been exposed to limousines, fine dining, posh furnishings and glamorous clothing. They felt as if they had been transported to an exciting new planet. They were very happy Doyle was marrying Paris, and they were able to experience a way of life beyond their wildest dreams. Paris was going to have her bachelorette party tonight and Doyle would be having his bachelor party. They would both be celebrating the last days of their freedom.

Andre accompanied Doyle, Alex and a group of Doyle's other friends to a discreet gentleman's club in the Quarter where they ate and drank to oblivion. Alex had his first lap dance and decided it would not be his last. Doyle could not keep his eyes off a very tall dark-skinned lady of the night who had hair and eyes the color of midnight; she had the largest boobs and smallest waist he had ever seen.

Andre watched Doyle fixate on her all evening. When Doyle went to the men's room Andre went up to the lady and slipped her a hundred-dollar bill to come on to Doyle. When Doyle returned from the men's room Allie came over and invited him to dance with her. They went out on the crowded dance floor where there was so many couples dancing together that everyone seemed to be glued together.

Doyle cupped her buns and pulled her body close to him. He told her she was beautiful and he wanted her. She rubbed herself into him and teased him into distraction. He could not believe gyrations on the dance floor could cause him to pant. He begged her to walk outside with him and she nodded her assent. He had to have her; he was very drunk and very turned on. He ran his hand up her leg and put his fingers into her pants and sought her center. But, low-and-behold, he found a hard cock. The "girl" was a transvestite. He/she quickly turned and disappeared into the crowd. Doyle decided it was time for him to go home.

That same night Paris met with her cousins and her bridesmaids in the Courtyard restaurant at Pat O'Brien's. They sat close to the Flaming Fountain and ordered Hurricanes to drink. They laughed and teased Paris, telling her this would be her last night as a free woman. After their second round and some food they were ready to go across the street to the Cat's Meow—a famous karaoke bar. By two in the morning they were all wiped out and went back to Paris and Shirree's apartment to call cabs. Marisol spent the night.

The wedding rehearsal started at the church after mass, but the family arrived early to attend the mass. After the rehearsal everyone was invited to dinner at Emeril's Restaurant on Tchoupitoulas Street. Norris had hired another limousine and driver so that all the people in the wedding party would have a ride to the rehearsal dinner. The rehearsal dinner was a great success. Marvelous food, fine wines and happy people looking forward to Paris and Doyle's wedding the following evening.

Promptly at noon on June the fifth, all the bridesmaids in Paris' wedding party were picked up at her apartment by Norris and taken to

Enchante Day Spa on Magazine Street where they would be treated to an afternoon of massage, pedicures, facials, manicures, and hair styling. Norris had already taken the Viverette mothers and grandmothers along with Doyle's mother and sister-in-law. All the ladies had whatever type of massage they wished followed by a Cleopatra milk bath and whatever type of facial they desired. Between treatments the spa served the ladies assorted sandwiches and iced tea. At four o'clock the ladies of the wedding party were all buffed and polished. Their hair was artfully styled and there makeup was flawlessly applied to their faces.

Norris delivered the ladies to the Monteleone Hotel where several adjoining suites of rooms had been reserved for the Viverette-O'Connor wedding. Paris dressed in a suite with only her immediate family present. Lady Madeline had loaned Paris her diamond necklace as something old. Her other grandmother Simone had given her a diamond bracelet as something new, and her mother had purchased a blue-lace garter for her as something blue. Sophia helped her put on her wedding gown which was a white satin and chiffon strapless gown with a dropped waistline and a chapel train. She then put on an embroidered lace long sleeve jacket with trumpet sleeves covered with crystal beading and sequins which matched the bodice of the dress. She wore white satin heels and white hose to complete her ensemble. In true French tradition she was having an all-white wedding. She wore a cornet of sweet olive flowers on a white tiara with a white veil attached to it. Once her dress, jewels, and tiara were in place she twirled around in a circle showing the back of her dress which was covered by the embroidered lace jacket.

Lilly looked at her daughter with tears rolling down her cheeks, "You look magnificent Paris. You are the most beautiful bride I have ever seen."

Paris laughed. "Mother I believe you are biased."

In French tradition the bridegroom meets his bride at her house and escorts her to the church. The ladies accompanied Paris to the elevator and they rode down to the lobby where Doyle stood in front of a black carriage pulled by two snow white horses. Doyle helped Paris into the carriage and away they sped to St. Louis Cathedral.

As soon as Paris and Doyle rode off in their wedding coach Lilly turned to the ladies of the Viverette family and said, "It would be perfect if only Suzette were with us to watch Paris getting married. She would be so proud of her. I wish she had lived long enough to be able to see what a beautiful bride, and what a wonderful woman Paris has become."

Sophia said, "Suzette is with us in spirit. I am sure she is rejoicing with us that Paris who is part of her is so happy, and such a beautiful person as well as a beautiful bride."

At seven-thirty in the evening the wedding processional began. Doyle and his best man Alex entered from the side of the church. Elizabeth, the young flower girl, walked slowly and proudly down the aisle scattering fragrant white rose petals from a white basket, creating a carpet of flowers. The bridesmaids wore light champagne silk gowns with a sweet heart neckline, fitted bodice, long full skirt and matching silk gloves that came up to their forearms.

After the processional, the mass began with the singing of a number of hymns. After the traditional prayers, blessings and hymns, the vows and ring ceremony began. Paris and Doyle exchanged vows and the priest blessed their rings as symbols of their love and fidelity. After a passionate kiss Paris Viverette was officially Paris O'Connor.

The bride and groom walked out of the church onto a bridal path of laurel leaves which were placed in the path of the new couple to bring them happiness. The procession left the church and the bridesmaids gathered around Paris as she tossed her bouquet. Daisy joyfully caught the bouquet and would not let go of it for love or money.

Mr. and Mrs. Doyle O'Connor's carriage came for them and they were taken back to the hotel. They walked to the Royal Anne Ballroom where their reception was to be held. Within minutes the ballroom filled up with guests.

Paris and Doyle looked around and saw ice sculptors of mermaids on every serving table. There were serving stations for shrimp, clams on the half shell, roast beef, pasta, and ham. There were tables over flowing with salads, salmon, caviar, smoked trout and a variety of cheeses and fruit. Every table had an enormous centerpiece of white roses, carnations, and moth orchids. All the decorations on the table were snowy white.

Doyle looked at Paris, took her in his arms, and embraced her saying, "Paris Marie O'Connor, I will love you until death do us part."

"Oh Doyle I love you so much. I am honored to be Mrs. Doyle O'Connor."

The newly blessed and married couple kissed deeply and shamelessly.

Louis went to one of the bars and beckoned Doyle and Paris to join him. He handed Doyle a large silver toasting cup which he had crafted for them. It had both their names engraved on the cup.

"Doyle, Paris this cup is called a *coupe de marriage*," Louis explained. "This cup is to guarantee you both a healthy life. I have another surprise for you," he said as he moved to the back of the bar and removed a strange looking sword.

"This is a sabre," Louis said simply, and without warning, he took a bottle of champagne and beheaded it with the blade. The top and cork popped off the bottle and the champagne cascaded to the floor. Louis smiled with pride. "The Hussards under Napoleons command would ride up on their horses and behead the champagne with their sabres." He chuckled merrily, "It took me a case of champagne, but I finally got the knack of it."

Lilly looked at her husband laughingly, "Louis this is why I love you so much, you always surprise me."

Louis poured the beheaded champagne into the *coupe de marriage* which he handed to Doyle. He told the bartenders to fill the flutes of everyone around the bar with champagne opened the ordinary way and toasted the bride and groom, "May your lives be filled with health, love, and joy."

Doyle and Paris both took turns drinking from the cup, which was kept filled to the brim as new people steadily came to the bar to make toasts to them. The dinner was served buffet style and waiters circulated with trays of hot and cold canapés.

There were ten musicians on the stage in the ballroom playing their musical repertoire. After most of the people had finished their dinner, the emcee on the stage called the bride and groom to the dance floor to dance their first dance together as man and wife. All the guests stopped speaking so they could admire the beautiful newly married couple dance. Everyone commented on what a handsome couple they were.

The pastry tables were set up, there was a wedding cake made of cream puffs piled together in the design of a pyramid with caramel sauce drizzled over them. It was surrounded by petits fours. On another table there was the traditional many tiered white wedding cake with a picture of a miniature bride and groom on the top. Yet another table held an enormous chocolate groom's cake in the shape of a law book in honor of the groom's profession.

After the emcee entertained the guests with his marriage jokes, the musicians began to play music for dancing. The emcee called the bride and her father up to dance and also the groom and his mother. The protocol for the next dance was for the groom to dance with his new mother-in-law and vice versa. Daniel staggered up to the dance floor and with great relish grabbed Paris tightly and began dancing with her. He was all over her like gravy on rice and she felt her face turn beet red as he dragged her around the dance floor.

He squeezed her as close as he possibly could and said loudly, "I bet you are sweet and wet like a Georgia peach."

Paris recoiled, pushed him away and walked off.

Sophia, following the scene on the dance floor, took Paris' hand in comfort. "I could not see Papa Joe and I did not know what to do to help you."

"Thank God he lives in Miami and I will not be seeing him very often. I'm not going to mention this to Doyle. He would be so humiliated. I was just so shocked at his behavior."

Sophia hugged Paris and said, "Let's go back to your room and freshen your makeup and return to your wedding party."

The reception lasted until two in the morning. Every guest left with a large package of wedding cake in a silver ice bucket. Each bridesmaid received a gold bracelet with a large golden heart attached to it engraved with Paris and Doyle's initials and the date.

After the last guest departed and the family went to their rooms in the hotel, Paris and Doyle limped up to the bridal suite where they were staying for the night. Doyle locked the door and they both immediately began to take their shoes off and undress. Doyle cautiously helped Paris remove her veil and wedding gown and carefully handed the clothes to her and she gently hung her delicate garments on padded hangers. Doyle filled flutes of champagne and handed one of the flutes to Paris.

Paris held up her champagne flute and said, "Let us drink to Mr. and Mrs. Doyle O'Connor, may we always be as happy as we are tonight."

"I will certainly drink to that," Doyle agreed as he quickly emptied his champagne glass with one hand and grabbed Paris with the other.

He put his glass down and picked Paris up and carried her to the balcony where he gently placed her on the chaise lounge.

Paris whispered, "Doyle we're naked. Someone will see us."

"No one will see us. Our balcony faces the pool and courtyard and there is no one out there. I checked."

Doyle slowly began to kiss and stroke Paris' breasts and arms. He sucked her nipples and then pulled her on his lap where he slowly stroked her back. He began kissing her warm sweet mouth as his fingers strayed to her behind and then he lifted her and put his fingers deep inside her mound.

"Paris you are so hot, and so wet. I love it when you are like this."

Paris was panting and couldn't form the words to respond.

Doyle whispered in her ear, "This is our wedding night I want to make this special for you."

Paris could feel his hard hot cock pushing against her stomach; she was so excited her whole body was quivering with desire. He pulled her legs around him and slowly put himself inside of her as he pulled her ass into his body. He moved very slowly inside of her.

"Doyle!" she screamed, "you're driving me crazy!"

Her arms were wrapped around his neck and she started to move her body as quickly as she could. She could feel her body sucking the sweetness from his cock until she felt him erupt inside of her and then she began to scream and dig her fingernails in his back until she was satiated. She couldn't move. They fell asleep in each other's arms on the balcony and the next day they started their three week honeymoon to France and Ireland.

Chapter 24

A few moments after Paris and Lilly left the house, security called; there was an appliance company wanting to deliver something. Within minutes a white minivan appeared with the name Gomez Dryer and Appliance Company printed in bold black lettering on the side.

Sophia opened the door and six middle aged men dressed as workmen came in the house with tools and gadgets. Each man showed Sophia their picture identification which identified them as working for the detective agency Louis had hired. Sophia introduced Juliet and herself to the man named Dave, who was in charge of the crew. He explained that the first thing they were going to do was take pictures of the contents of Doyle's safe.

Sophia led them upstairs to Paris and Doyle's bedroom. She took them into Doyle's closet and showed them his wall safe.

"Louis told me his daughter fell and badly injured herself. I would appreciate it if you would show me where you found her and acquaint me with the rooms of the house."

Sophia replied, "I will be happy to show you everything, but what do you expect to find?"

"We have Luminol with us which will allow us to trace the blood spatter patterns and hopefully allow us to figure out how she was injured."

Sophia looked at David quizzically and said, "I have heard of Luminol but I really do not understand how it works."

"It is a chemical that we mix with an oxidizing agent. We spray it in a darkened room and wherever it comes in contact with blood it turns a bright luminescent blue."

"David, you mean that the blood cannot be washed away?"

"No, Mrs. Moses, traces of blood remain in the floor or furniture no matter how many times they are washed. Also the blood can't be bleached out of material and DNA can be extracted from the blood spatters."

"That's amazing," Sophia remarked as she watched in fascination as Tony fiddled with the dial of the safe, poking it, prodding it and spinning it. Just like magic, the door of the safe opened up. When they finished Doyle's closet they darkened the bedroom and sprayed

Luminol on the furniture, the bed and the floors of the bedroom.

While Sophia showed Dave where she found Paris unconscious in the nursery next to the bedroom, Juliet showed the other men the rest of the house.

Juliet and Sophia watched one crew as they sprayed Luminol on the floor and furniture, and photographed every inch of every room. Then they quickly photographed the areas of the room which glowed with illumination. The marble end table next to Doyle and Paris' bed immediately glowed blue when the Luminol was sprayed on it.

Sophia pointed to the table, "This is where Paris first injured herself. I'm so glad we are finally going to find out the truth about her injuries."

The crew finished in about four hours. Dave told Sophia and Juliet that he would be developing the photographs and then sending the blood-spatter patterns to the forensic lab he worked with. He told the ladies that Louis would have the results in about two days. Juliet and Sophia thanked the crew and the men left leaving nary a clue behind them.

Sophia retrieved a miffed Tou-Tou from the backyard and opened his doggy door so he had his freedom returned to him. She gave him some doggy treats to make up for the isolation he had endured and cradled him in her arms.

"Lordy," Sophia exclaimed, "I feel as if I was part of a detective show."

Juliet replied, "I feel as if I were part of a forensic team. Doyle's behavior has caused us to explore a whole new world."

"Paris and Lilly are seeing Dr. Wolf and then they are going to Paris' school to work with the children. What would you like to do today?" Sophia asked.

"I would like to go to the day spa down the street, have a massage, a pedicure and a fabulous new hairstyle. That's what I feel like doing."

"Sounds heavenly to me, now that my hair has gotten longer I need a new color and style. I will drive. It'll be a nice relaxing normal day."

*****

Sophia and Juliet returned home hours later feeling pampered and relaxed. They sat on the patio drinking tall gin and tonics feeling very mellow and peaceful. Paris and Lilly arrived home a short time after them and the first thing they noticed was Sophia's new hair color was golden, styled in a short pageboy.

"Your hair looks fabulous, Sophia. I love you as a blonde," said Paris."

"I also think you look stunning as a blonde" Lilly acknowledged. "Juliette, you look fabulous also. I am glad you both enjoyed your day. I must tell you ladies Paris' students were thrilled to see her. They said they enjoyed having both of you teaching them, but they were overjoyed to see Paris."

"Maman, I enjoy being with them. It is so wonderful to be able to bring music into their lives."

The phone rang and Paris went to answer it. The ladies listened closely to her entire conversation.

"You're working late again? I suppose you don't know what time you will be home. I am getting rather tired of this. I really don't want to put up with this anymore!"

Lilly, Sophia and Juliet stared at each other with surprise and pride. To their knowledge she had always acquiesced to Doyle. She never questioned him about his activities or criticized him. Paris quickly hung up on him and returned to the patio.

"Well, family, once again Doyle will not be joining us for dinner. Why don't we go out? We have to celebrate Sophia's new look."

Everyone agreed. Sophia suggested a Cuban restaurant in Little Havana.

As the Viverette ladies were having a lovely dinner, Doyle was having a stressful one. Adriana had demanded Doyle take her to dinner so she could discuss details of their wedding with him. He told her he would take her to dinner another evening, but she pressured him.

When he called Paris and told her he wasn't planning to be home for dinner, he was amazed at her response. She had never showed any anger toward him whenever he told her he was going away for business or wouldn't be home for dinner. He was not happy about leading two lives. He could not concentrate on his law practice. The thought of being the husband of Adriana and a member of the Leon family sent shivers down his spine.

Adriana and Doyle went to a large seafood restaurant in Coconut Grove. Doyle made sure they were seated in an inconspicuous booth at the back of the restaurant. As soon as Doyle's cocktail arrived and they ordered dinner, Adriana opened a sample book filled with different colored paper invitations in a zillion styles and types of writing. At the end of their dinner they had chosen the correct invitations for their imperious wedding.

*****

Paris waited up for Doyle. He arrived home around midnight. She quietly but firmly read him the riot act. He was amazed at how poised and determined she was. Doyle realized that Paris was changing; she was not going to put up with his abuse or bullying. He wondered if she remembered him slapping her. He knew that it was imperative that he appease her or she wouldn't go with him to the Bahamas. Doyle knew he would have to humble himself in order to mollify Paris.

"I'm sorry, Paris. Forgive me for being so selfish. I have been engrossed in my work. I wanted to finish all of my work before we leave for the Bahamas so we could have three beautiful weeks together. I have had an epiphany and I realize you are the most important person in the world to me."

Paris' face remained impassive. Doyle continued, "This will be our second honeymoon. We will start fresh and new. Please, baby, I love you so much, I know I have been an inconsiderate jerk, but I'm changing. I am going to love you and worship you the way you deserve." Doyle studied Paris' face—she was showing no emotion whatsoever.

"Doyle, I will go the Bahamas with you and I will hope we can salvage our marriage. I'm trying to repair our marriage for my own reasons."

"What do you mean?"

"I will explain everything to you when we're there. We both have our secrets. I am going to sleep in a different bedroom. I will see you in the morning."

*****

The next morning Paris went with Lilly to Dr. Wolf's office. Dr. Wolf started the session by telling Paris how pleased he was with her progress. They had discussed her childhood and the death of her sister, Suzette, which had caused her to go into a paralyzing depression. She could now discuss the loss of Suzette without crying and she could remember her sister in love without the horrible feeling of loss whenever she thought about her.

"Paris, I would like you to tell me about your relationship with Doyle. Please start from the beginning of your marriage."

"Our wedding gift from my grandparents was a honeymoon trip to England, France and Ireland. We had a wonderful honeymoon. Doyle was very excited about our trip. We stayed at my grandparent's villa in Cannes and in the Ritz in Paris and London. We stayed in the Dromoland Castle in Ireland and did nothing but sightsee and make love for six weeks.

"He enjoyed the museums, the art galleries and the antiquity of Europe. He was fascinated by the beauty of Ireland and overwhelmed by Dromoland Castle. Naturally he loved the Irish; he loved the stories the people told in the local pubs and we explored the history of Ireland. I loved the music of Ireland, the bands were great and I enjoyed watching the harp being played. We enjoyed seeing the Stone Age monuments and all of the beautiful castles.

"After our honeymoon we decided to continue to live in our family apartment at the Pontalba building. My cousin Shirree lived there too, but the apartment was so spacious that we never crowded each other. We put our wedding gifts in storage until we decided where we were going to live permanently."

"Did he enjoy working for your Uncle?"

"Yes, he did at the beginning. He kept telling me how clever my uncle was and how much he was learning from him. He worked long hours and he said he loved every minute of being an attorney."

"What were you doing at this time?"

"I was attending Tulane University—I was in my senior year of college. Shirree was also attending Tulane and in her senior year. We graduated from Tulane in May. My degree was in music education and Shirree's degree was in interior design. After graduation Shirree decided to move to New York with our friend Daisy Parker, who was originally from New York. Shirree thought it would be exciting live in New York and to begin her career as an interior designer in New York City."

"What did you do after graduation?"

"I didn't need to make money. I had enough money to live on from my trust, so I started volunteering in the public schools as a music teacher. As well as teaching music, I held charity events to raise money for music books and musical instruments for the schools that could not afford to buy them for the children."

"How did Doyle feel about you doing volunteer work rather than getting a job?"

"We never discussed money, Dr. Wolf. We were living rent-free in my family's apartment. My family rented cars for us. Daddy grew up with Burt Le Beofe, the owner of the local Jaguar agency, so everyone in the family drove a new Jaguar every year. Doyle was delighted with the situation."

"Paris, did you and Doyle have a lot of discord in your marriage?"

"The only discord in our marriage now and when we were first married is he wanted a baby from the minute we were married and I wanted to wait a couple of years before I became pregnant. He kept pressuring me and finally I became pregnant."

"How did he respond?"

"Doyle was elated. He couldn't do enough for me. He directed all of his energy to pleasing me and making sure I was taking care of myself. Doyle and I were so happy and we were so carefree, so much in love; we were always together, and we could not get enough of one another."

"Paris, please tell me how and when the change in your relationship occurred?"

"One Sunday afternoon Doyle and I were sitting on the patio and we heard the loud sound of a trumpet and the thump of a tuba coming from Canal Street. A jazz funeral for a local musician. I wanted to go join the parade, but Doyle didn't want me to go. He was afraid that I would get hurt in the crowd of people.

"I told him that I'd been to a lot of jazz funerals so he grudgingly went with me to the procession. It was enormous. Traditionally the people who are hosting the organization are the first line of the parade and those following the march are the second line. When we reached the procession the street was filled with the vibrant music of a New Orleans-style brass band. The men and the woman were dressed in vivid clothing. They wore sashes, wild hats and bonnets and carried brilliant parasols and banners. Everyone was dancing, singing and strutting to the fabulous jazz music.

"I followed the parade for a block and Doyle chased after me. I was laughing, dancing and sashaying down the street with all the exciting people around me. It was such an exciting happy day.

"Doyle grabbed my arm and began to pull me off of the street away from the crowd and the intoxicating music. I lost my balance and fell to the ground. I painfully stood up and realized that I had injured my leg and my back, I could hardly walk.

"We did not speak until we reached our apartment. Once we were in the apartment Doyle began to scream at me. He told me that I could have fallen and lost our baby. I told him that he caused me to fall. Doyle proceeded to yell at me and tell me I was dancing around like all those street people and I had no dignity.

"We did not speak at all that evening. The next day I went to the doctor because I had torn a ligament in my leg and my back hurt so much I was crying. While I was at the doctor's office I had horrible stomach cramps and pain. I ended up having a miscarriage. The doctor's office called my mother and she picked me up and took me home to Bayou House."

"Paris you must have been devastated."

"Yes I was, doctor, and I blamed myself, even though if Doyle had not dragged me off the street I would not have fallen and hurt myself."

"What happened after you went home Paris?"

"Dr. Wolf, I went into a terrible depression. Doyle came to visit me at Bayou House and told me I lifted my skirts and acted like a whore, not a decent white Christian married woman. I couldn't stop crying. When Christopher's father came over to check on me he prescribed anti-depressants for me.

"I stayed with my parents until I could walk again without limping. I was uncertain about whether or not I wanted to go back to Doyle. He changed his attitude and apologized for the horrible things he had said to me. He kept coming over and begging my forgiveness. He kept promising me that he would treat me differently. He claimed he had learned his lesson. He repeatedly told me that he could not live without me. He told me that he acted like a lunatic that day because he loved me, and was so fearful of my falling and injuring myself. He wore me down and I finally returned to New Orleans with him."

"Paris, why did you decide to return home to Doyle?"

"As I just told you, he wore me down. But primarily, I think it was because I wanted to believe him. I was very much in love with Doyle. I kept remembering the good times we had together. I felt I would never love another man the way I loved him and, sadly, I thought that no man except Doyle would ever love me. I was truly convinced that he was the only man in the world for me."

"Paris, tell me when did Doyle become abusive?"

"My marriage became a disaster after I had my first miscarriage. He began to verbally abuse me and to criticize every little thing I did. It started with stupid little things…not organizing the kitchen properly, I was a bad cook, I used too many spoons."

"What did you do?"

"I told him to reorganize the kitchen the way he wanted it to be, and he did. However he kept chipping away at me and I began to doubt myself. I tried to do everything perfectly so he wouldn't complain."

"Did that appease him?"

"Not really, Doctor. Then he complained about my hair, the way I dressed, and my friends. He frequently criticized the way I smiled, the way I spoke—in other words, everything I did was wrong."

"Was he ever happy with you?"

"Yes, he was happy when I became pregnant again."

"How did he treat you when you were pregnant again?"

"He was loving, concerned, and seemed to worship me."

"How long did his loving behavior last?"

"Unfortunately not that long."

"Paris what caused your fall from grace this time?"

"Doyle came home in a bad mood. He told me my uncle had treated him unfairly and had chastised him for not giving his client adequate representation."

"He screamed at me and told me he hated my uncle, and my uncle treated him as a lackey and looked down on him and his family. His eyes became large and crazed; his voice was shrill and penetrating.

"I had to get away from him. I could not stand the sound of his voice so I dressed and ran down the stairs to escape from him. He bolted after me and my heel caught on a stair and I fell down the stairway."

"Paris, did you lose the baby then?"

"No, strangely I was fine directly after the fall. I lost the baby two weeks later. The doctor told me it was a spontaneous abortion; probably the result of a chromosomal or developmental abnormality."

"Paris, we are doing great. I'm very proud of you. You seemed to recall everything that has occurred between you and Doyle. We are going to continue with your relationship with Doyle tomorrow."

"Thank you, Doctor Wolf. I am beginning to see my relationship with Doyle in a new light. I see how weak and needy I have been in this relationship. Everything is suddenly starting to make sense."

Lilly was sitting patiently in the waiting room doing needlepoint as she waited for Paris. Paris gave her mother a big smile as she walked out of Dr. Wolf's office.

"Maman," she said, as they reached the car, "I am a very lucky lady. I have a wonderful family who loves me and stands by me."

"Paris, there is nothing as important as family. No one in our family is ever alone. Being part of a loving family is the most precious gift a person can have."

They went to Houston's for lunch before they went to work at Paris' school.

At lunch Paris said, "I would like to invite Christopher to dinner tonight at my house. Today, when I recalled some unpleasant times in my life I remembered that Dr. Charles, Christopher's father, was always ready to help me."

"I agree, Paris. When you were in the hospital Christopher watched over you very closely. He made sure that you were well taken care of. I believe your complete recovery is partly due to his finding the right doctors to supervise your condition. I have noticed, for instance, that you seem much happier since you have been having sessions with Dr. Wolf."

"Why don't you call and invite him to join us for dinner now?" Paris said.

"I will call Sophia and Juliet to pick up something fabulous for our dinner tonight."

Over lunch Paris was quiet and contemplative. Looking up at her mother she stated out of the blue, "I'm no longer blaming myself for being a bad wife; and most importantly, I am no longer blaming myself for the miscarriages I have suffered."

"I'm so happy to hear you speak these words!" her mother cried. "You are a wonderful person and you have been a loving and kind wife. I have never criticized your husband before because of your love for him. Everyone has to make their own choices about who they love. I'm so glad you are finally seeing Doyle in a different light."

That night Paris went to the bedroom she was temporarily using because she had no desire to share a bed with Doyle at this time. She lay awake and thought of all the decisions she was going to make for her future.

Chapter 25

The next evening Doyle took Paris to dinner.

As soon as they left, Lilly called Louis from the study of the O'Connor house where there was a speaker phone. Juliet, Lilly and Sophia were expectantly waiting to hear what Louis was going to say. Sophia had a feeling of dread the moment she heard the somber tone of his voice.

"Ladies, Joseph and Pierre are here with me and I am going to explain what our detectives have found. Doyle has set a wedding date to marry Adriana Franco three months from now. They have already selected the wedding invitations." Louis paused before continuing. "In the safe they found some cash, but most importantly they found two life insurance policies. One policy is for two million dollars and it is on Paris' life, and the beneficiary is Doyle. Another is a two million dollar policy on Doyle's life and Paris is the beneficiary.

"Christopher turned over all of Paris' pictures and hospital records so the forensic doctor could study her injuries and be as precise as possible in his diagnosis of what happened to Paris. Based on the blood splatter and Paris' injuries, the forensic doctor concludes that Paris was slapped across her face, then fell and hit her head on the marble end table in her room. She was carried bleeding into the bedroom at the end of the hall after she was injured. The next day she walked to the kitchen, to her bedroom, and finally passed out in the nursery next to the master bedroom."

"I am in a state of shock, Louis. Why is this happening?"

"Sophia, we have found out that supposedly Adriana Franco is pregnant and Doyle is the father of her baby. The Leon family is forcing him to marry their niece as quickly as possible."

Lilly and Juliet had been mute during this exchange. Finally Lilly said, "Louis, what are we going to do? I firmly believe Doyle is planning to kill Paris for the insurance money in the Bahamas."

"Lilly, the three of us, Joseph, Pierre and I, concur with you. In fact he has already chartered a cruise boat which will be waiting for them when they arrive in Nassau. We have come up with a plan. Please try not to worry. I will explain everything to you when we are together and we have all the details."

"What kind of plan do you have, Louis? Our daughter's life is riding on your plan. In fact she's having dinner with Doyle tonight! I hope she is in no danger!"

"Lilly, he's not going to hurt her, it would be too suspicious if Paris had two accidents in a month. Doyle is not stupid."

"Please tell us what you are planning; I have a right to know."

"All right, Lilly. We are going to have a treasure hunt of our grandfather Jon Charles paintings. I believe that Joseph told you they were recently auctioned in New York for over two million dollars apiece. Anyone in our family who finds the paintings will be allowed to keep them, and of course sell them if they choose. Doyle is aware that there are dozens of the paintings on our properties. He will not turn down an invitation to visit Bayou House and try his luck at the treasure hunt.

"Lilly, I want you invite Doyle to the treasure hunt. It will take place weekend after next. Juliet and Sophia, I will need your help with all the details so will you please make arrangements to return to Louisiana tomorrow. I also want you to bring Tou-Tou with you."

"We will leave Miami tomorrow," Juliet replied. "But who's going to protect my sister and Paris when we leave?"

"All of the phones are bugged so our investigators will know what Doyle is planning. Also our cousin Adrian Jantot will be arriving from France tonight and staying at the house with you."

"Louis," Lilly said emphatically, "have you gone mad? We don't have a cousin Adrian."

"We do now. He will be your protector and bodyguard. Also there will be discreet security guards watching you, Paris and Doyle at all times. You will tell everyone that he is Lady Madeline's second cousin. He is an un-assuming man, so Doyle will not feel threatened by him. He also is very skilled in the martial arts. I will speak to you tomorrow ladies. Love you, Lilly."

Juliet said, "I will get the cards. We might as well play Bourre while we wait for our new cousin Adrian Jantot to arrive."

The ladies played Bourre, a bridge-like card game from Louisiana's Acadiana region, and spoke among themselves.

"I won't be able to look Doyle in the eye after hearing about this," Juliet said. "He sat at her bedside and pretended to care for her. He is disgusting as well as treacherous."

Security called, announcing a visitor had arrived, by the name of

Adrian Jantot. The three women laughed over the fact that suddenly a new cousin was appearing from nowhere. The doorbell rang and a tall distinguished man was at their house. He was wearing a well-cut navy blue suit and carried an expensive-looking suitcase. He had an aristocratic face, dark brown hair peppered with silver, and steel gray eyes.

Later that night, when Paris arrived home from dinner with Doyle, she was surprised that the ladies of her family were still up, feverishly playing Bourre with a strange man.

Lilly looked at Paris with a big smile on her face, "I don't believe you have met your cousin Adrian Jantot. He was born in Louisiana, but now he works for the Bank of England. I hope you don't mind if he stays with us for a couple days?"

Adrian greeted Paris with a big hug saying, "The last time I saw you, you had pigtails and played with dolls. You have grown into a beautiful woman."

Paris politely thanked him and introduced him to Doyle, who shook Adrian's hand with a scowl on his face.

Lilly said, "Everyone please sit down. I have a big surprise for y'all. We're having a treasure hunt at Bayou House and the surrounding buildings. We are going to be looking for Jon Charles paintings! Now that the prices have gone up and his work is finally causing a sensation in the art world, he should be enjoying his well-earned fame—even if he is dead. It is ridiculous for his work to be hidden in the old church or the attic of one of our properties."

Paris said, "That is the week Doyle and I were going to vacation in Nassau."

"My dear daughter this was the only week we get all of the family together. I am sure Doyle will take you another week."

Excitement could be heard in Doyle's voice as he replied, "Paris we can always go to Nassau another time. I love treasure hunts! Will we be able to keep the paintings we find?"

"Absolutely Doyle! If you find a painting, it belongs to you and you are free to do whatever you wish with it."

Doyle's face lit up in pleasure, "I certainly will be there."

Sophia, Lilly and Juliet looked at each other with smiles of satisfaction on their faces.

Chapter 26

Sophia somberly looked at Lilly and Paris as she kissed them and bid them goodbye. Paris handed Tou-Tou's traveling case to Sophia after she had hugged and kissed her little dog promising him that she would be seeing him the following week. Juliet cried as she kissed Paris and Lilly goodbye at the front door.

"Aunt Juliet, we will be seeing you next week. Why are you so sad?"

"I don't know why I am crying. I guess it is because I am so happy you have recovered so quickly and so well."

They all walked to the front door while Sophia drove her rented gray Mercedes out of the garage and everyone helped load the car with their luggage. Juliet and Sophia waved gaily to Paris and Lilly as they drove out of the driveway. Once they were out of Palm Island and on the expressway, all of their pent-up anxiety and fear was released and Juliet and Sophia were both nervously crying.

"I am so glad Adrian is staying at the house."

Sophia took Juliet's hand and said, "Everything is going to be fine. Doyle O'Connor is no match for the Viverette family."

"Of course Doyle O'Connor is no match for our husbands. Did you see the look of ecstasy on Doyle's face when Lilly mentioned the treasure hunt?"

"Doyle will not be a threat to Paris in the very near future."

As soon as Juliet and Sophia left, the Happy Maids came to clean the house. Paris had an appointment with Dr. Wolf and Lilly asked Paris if they were meeting for lunch after her appointment.

"Maman I have some other appointments today so I will not be able to have lunch with you."

"That's fine, Paris, I am going to spend the rest of the day at the spa. I need to be pampered today."

Lilly's mind was at ease because she knew the men from the agency would be following and protecting Paris. She blessed her husband for having the foresight to arrange security for their daughter at all times. Paris hurried to Dr. Wolf's office and was quickly ushered into his office. She sat in a comfortable chair watching Dr. Wolf's brightly colored fish gliding in their enticing clear water as the doctor began their session.

"Paris, why are you in Miami?"

"Doyle worked at my uncle's law firm for two years. I thought he was happy working for my uncle, but apparently he wasn't. He came home one evening and said he wanted to move to Miami and go into a practice with his brother Brandon. He wanted to do nothing but criminal cases and Miami had more of those types of cases than New Orleans. He felt he could make a lot more money in Miami and he felt suffocated by the small-town attitude of New Orleans."

"How did the idea of moving to Miami make you feel, Paris?"

"The idea was very upsetting to me. I love Louisiana. I enjoy the city of New Orleans. I love living close to my family and my friends. I had been to Miami several times and I really didn't like the city at all. It's so big. I feel lost in it. If I have to move, I would prefer to move to New York. I love the theater, the museums and the excitement of New York."

"How did Doyle convince you to move?"

"Doyle charmed me, begged me and then threatened to divorce me if I refused to move to Miami with him. Only then did I sit down with my parents and tell them I wanted to move to Miami.

"God bless my parents. They are the kindest people in the world. They bought a fashionable commercial building in the downtown area of Miami. My father loaned him money for advertising and start-up fees for his practice at a very low rate of interest.

"My family bought us our enormous house on Palm Island and gave us *carte blanche* in re-doing the whole house. My uncle Pierre even referred clients to Doyle."

"Doyle is a very lucky man. Did he appreciate what your family did for him?"

"No he did not! He did not understand how my family did business. Everything we buy is purchased by the Viverette trust, which is an investment trust for all of our family. Everyone receives interest from the trust and everyone in the family has a monetary interest in our vast holdings. My family has done business in this manner for generations."

"So if Doyle were to divorce you..."

"He would get nothing from your trust. I pay for the upkeep of the house, the food, and the dues on all the private clubs we belong to. All the money that Doyle earns as an attorney is his money to keep. If we divorced I would make no claims on any of his earnings."

"If you had a child, Paris, would that child have a financial interest in the Viverette family trust?"

Paris appeared deep in thought for a moment before she quickly said, "Yes, of course my child would have a financial interest in the family trust."

Dr. Wolf stroked his thick red-brown beard as he listened to what Paris was telling him. "Paris, when did you become pregnant again?" "I became pregnant after we lived in Miami for about six months. Once again," Paris recounted with tears running down her cheeks, "I lost our baby in the first trimester of my pregnancy. The gynecologist explained to Doyle that the miscarriage was the result of a chromosomal abnormality. After the miscarriage Doyle was irate and made my life hell."

"How?"

"He started to work late at his office several nights a week. He was irritable and complained about everything. I could do nothing right. He told me I looked horrible, I was not gracious. He told me people disliked me. He threw things at me. He told me I was his curse and he was stuck with me."

"Did you become pregnant again?"

"Yes two years ago. This time I fell down the stairs."

"What caused you to fall down the stairs?"

"Doyle and I were in our bedroom and he was looking for a particular white dress shirt to wear to a meeting. I looked all over for the shirt but I couldn't find it. He started to scream all sorts of horrible obscenities at me. I was scared of him, he acted like a crazed animal and when he came storming after me, I tripped and fell down the stairs. I lost the baby and broke two ribs."

"You had four miscarriages in six years of marriage. Your husband verbally abused you and did everything he could do to demean you. Why do you stay with him?"

"I was too ashamed to tell my family," Paris said sobbing. "If my father knew what Doyle did to me, he would have killed him. I became too depressed to make any decisions. I became a zombie. I went to the school where I volunteered three times a week. I then went grocery shopping and came home. I didn't make any friends as I was fearful to bring them to the house, I never knew what Doyle might do or say. There was no one to confide in, I tried to pretend that I was happy and my husband adored me."

"Paris, I can't tell you what to do. I can't make any decisions for you. But I want you to think about your situation. I want to give you food for thought: You are a beautiful, talented woman. You have a caring family. You are kind and loving. You deserve someone who can appreciate you and treat you with respect. You are not alone. You are very important to many people. You have a wonderful future ahead of you. I want you to erase any feelings of guilt you may have about your marriage. You are blameless. Your husband has deliberately tried to make you feel a sense of guilt for your miscarriages and everything that has gone wrong in your marriage.

"I am sorry our session is over now, but I want you to think about your life and your future. I want you to look ahead ten years from now. Think about the way you want to live, and what would make you happy and we will discuss it tomorrow."

Paris left the doctor's office and fled to the bathroom so she could calm herself and prepare for her next doctor's appointment, which was on the other side of town. As soon as Paris left his office, Julian Wolf called Christopher.

Christopher picked up the phone and Julian said, "Christopher, I have a moral and a legal issue with our patient Paris O'Connor, I need to meet with you as soon as possible."

Christopher made an appointment to see Julian later that afternoon. Paris arrived home late in the day. She was horribly upset but she was determined not to allow her mother to see her unhappiness. She remembered Doyle telling her that he had a business engagement for this evening and would be home very late. She was very relieved that she would not have to face him. Paris was suddenly revolted at the idea of ever sharing a bed with Doyle again. She decided to make her temporary move a permanent one. She moved all of her toiletries and clothes to the bedroom she was temporarily using, which was closest to her mother's room. She quickly organized the toiletries and clothes she had moved with her and fell asleep. She was so exhausted and overwhelmed by her day that she fell asleep on her bed fully clothed.

***

Norris was waiting at the Delta luggage carousel of Louis Armstrong Airport for Sophia and Juliet. The ladies happily greeted him and Tou-Tou barked his welcome to Norris. Within a short time, Norris gathered their luggage and placed it in the trunk of the beautifully detailed, and lovingly maintained, family Rolls Royce.

It felt good to Sophia to be home. Everything in her home was clean and orderly. She unpacked her clothes and went outside to check her garden. The three-story pristine white Victorian house that she and Joe lived in had a large gray turret on the roof which could be seen from quite a distance. The wide white-pillared verandah, which encircled the first floor of the house, was filled with comfortable lounge chairs, tables and potted green foliage.

The house was built in the late 1800's by her great, great, great-grandfather Jon Charles for her great, great, great-grandmother Angelina. He wanted to make sure his beloved Angelina had a fine house; a house that could rival any mansion in the Garden District of New Orleans.

The house had been preserved over the years in its original integrity. Nothing was replaced or changed except the wallpaper, curtains and the modernization of the kitchen and bathrooms. The floors were made of the finest mahogany and the furniture was made in France by the finest artisan who shipped the furniture piece by piece to Louisiana.

The package of supplies that she had bought in Little Havana had arrived. She opened the box of provisions and stored them in her pantry. Sometime later, they dressed and walked over to Bayou House where Louis was entertaining Juliet, Pierre, Sophia and Joseph.

Louis greeted them warmly with an iced bottle of Cristal and six champagne flutes. Juliet and Pierre arrived seconds after Sophia and Joseph. Everyone helped themselves to the food on the buffet table.

After they finished eating Louis told them he was flying to Tampa to speak to Dr. Wolf about Paris' condition. He was eager to hear the assessment Dr. Wolf had made about Doyle, predicated on what Paris and Christopher had told him. Paris had signed a HIPPA agreement giving Dr. Wolf permission to discuss her case with her parents.

"I would have spoken to him on the phone," Louis explained, "but after what I've learned from our sleuths, I am going to be very cautious about what I say on the telephone to anyone in the future."

Sophia and Juliet told the men how excited Doyle was when Lilly invited him to the treasure hunt. Joseph laughed heartily when he heard Juliet and Sophia exclaim over Doyle's greed.

"I have found over twenty pictures in the attic of our house and three in the old church. Now we just have to plan how we are going to arrange our treasure hunt."

Chapter 27

Queen Seri and Mr. Charles sat on the grass and admired the golden sun setting over the bayou.

The beautiful oak trees were draped with moss and gently swayed with the breeze. It was the night of the full moon. It was not a dramatic blood moon, but it was a full moon worthy of being celebrated.

At the stroke of midnight Sophia, in her long white robe, set up the altar with brightly decorated saints and an Indian chief wearing his elaborate feather headdress. She added coconut shells, white candles, and scattered white rose pedals over the snow-white cloth covering the altar. The pungent odor of incense pervaded through the crowd of worshippers. Papa Joe began playing his trumpet and groups of people all dressed in white wandered in playing their musical instruments. The crowd thickened and the chanting started out softly and then gradually it became louder as it accompanied the snare drums, the banjo, the guitar and the cornucopia of other musical instruments that accompanied a Voodoo ceremony. Queen Seri, wearing her white turban and long white robe, danced around shaking her tambourines. Mr. Charles sat on the grassy knoll playing his flute.

Papa Joe raised his hand and the crowd instantaneously quieted. "I welcome you to our Voodoo ritual and our Voodoo Society. We welcome you here tonight to contact and honor the spirits of our dead, our Loas and the spirits of the universe. We are not separate, we are all joined together. Remember our credo 'treat others the way you wish to be treated.' We are mirrors of each other's souls."

Papa Joe stopped speaking and began playing the trumpet. Others played the drums and the sound of cymbals grew louder.

Sophia stepped forward and raised her arms to the sky. "Our Loas and the spirits around us are very hungry. We must feed them so they will shower us with blessings."

Papa Joe opened the cage and removed an enormous black rooster. He held the rooster over the altar and said, "We are as one. God is manifest through the spirits of our ancestors. We must make sacrifices and feed our gods."

He pulled out a machete from the back of the altar and slit the neck of a large black rooster. He then sprinkled the rooster's blood over the

Saints and gods on the altar. The supplicants chanted as they individually made their way to the altar. Their arms overflowed with offerings of mangos, peaches, rice, black beans and honey. They carefully place their offerings around the blood spattered saints on the altar.

Sophia lavishly poured the thick sweet rum on the saints as all chanted and sang to them. She continued her singing as she placed a thick black cigar next to each one of them. She then lit a cigar and smoked it, blowing the smoke directly on the saints and the altar.

The worshippers approached the altar. Sophia, Mr. Charles and Queen Seri gave each worshipper a cigar and a large bottle of rum. Papa Joe lustily resumed playing his trumpet. The music was loud and haunting. The flock was wildly drinking and chanting. They were clapping their hands, stamping their feet and laughing joyfully. They drank the strong syrupy mixture and smoked their huge cigars. The more they drank, the more spirited they became. They started to bathe each other with the sweet alcohol and some fell to the ground in ecstasy.

Papa Joe went and fetched a large thick black snake which he held up in the air saying, "This is *Bon Dieu* under whose auspices we gather with all who share our faith."

He draped the snake around his body and walked amongst the crowd, draping the snake on each of the worshipper's bodies. The worshippers placed the snake around their bodies and their bodies began to tremble. Suddenly the sky was illuminated with flashes of jagged golden light. The spellbinding sound of cymbals became louder and louder. When they reached a crescendo, a tall slender woman with velvety golden skin, long dark curly hair and large black eyes swirled through the golden mist. She was barefoot wearing a long blood-red diaphanous gown. Around her neck were several long narrow coral snakes with thin red, black and yellow stripes ringing their bodies. She began quickly dancing, and caressing the snakes. The snakes curled round her neck and arms as she became a whirling dervish in the bright moonlight. Her body scintillated in rhythm to the sound of the crashing cymbals.

The flock was mesmerized by the lady in red. They frenetically shouted, "Santa Barbara, Santa Barbara!" as she quickly moved and darted in all directions.

The congregation joined the lady in red. They wrapped her in a circle and wildly started dancing around her and stomping their feet. They moved with tremendous fervor and passion until exhaustion overcame them and they fell to the ground in a state of rapture, still wildly chanting, "Santa Barbara! Santa Barbara!"

Many of the worshippers were already being ridden by their Laos. They were shaking and speaking in the tongues of their spirits. Some swooned and fell to the ground while others frothed at the mouth and crawled on their hands and knees, their bodies gyrating as their ancestors and gods took possession of their bodies and the Loas rode them. The night was hot; the air was thick and charged with energy.

Sophia fell to the ground and her spirit guide lifted her to another dimension where Suzette was waiting for her.

Suzette welcomed her warmly as she hugged and kissed her. "Sophia thanks you for watching over Paris. I want you to know Paris is pregnant and she will give birth to a healthy baby girl. Rejoice you are going to have a new godchild to love."

A white mist gradually appeared and engulfed Suzette. There were so many things Sophia wanted to ask her and tell her, but Suzette vanished in the mist and Sophia fell into a deep sleep.

*****

Sophia woke up late the next morning with Suzette's words reverberating in her head. It was a beautiful bright sunny day morning and her aunt had a fresh pot of chicory coffee simmering on the stove.

Sophia greeted her aunt cordially. "Tante," she said hesitating, "I spoke to Suzette last night. She was as close and real to me as you are this morning. She looked so beautiful and glowing she astounded me. She told me that I was going to have a new godchild very soon, a beautiful baby girl. And then she disappeared."

"Cher, I do not know why you seem so surprised. You had a vision of Paris bleeding and confused in Miami on the night of the blood moon. You went to Miami and Paris was bleeding and in a state of fear."

"No I don't doubt my own faith, I have waited so many years for Suzette to contact me that when she finally did I was overcome with joy. She was so beautiful and so serene that I almost felt as if she were still alive. I guess I was overcome with her telling me Paris was pregnant. I still miss her so much. I wish she was alive."

*****

Later that day, Sophia found herself at Bayou House. She wanted to visit Suzette's old room. At the house she found Maryanne, the cook, in the kitchen eating breakfast.

"Welcome back! It is so good to see you Miss Sophia. I hope you enjoyed your trip to Miami?"

"It turned out to be a fruitful trip, Maryanne, but I am very happy to be home. I woke up this morning thinking of Suzette. I am going to freshen up her room. I have not visited her room for a long time."

"I have someone clean her room all the time, but I know what you mean. No one from the family has been in her room for a long time."

Sophia walked upstairs to Suzette's room, marveling that the light airy bedroom was still filled with Suzette's scent. In a moment of reverie she pictured Suzette as a child sitting on a large chair in her room gazing out of her window daydreaming. Sophia lay down on the bed wearily. Soon she was fast asleep, dreaming of her.

Suzette was sitting next to Sophia on the bed; her face was glowing with pleasure. "Sophia, please don't cry for me. I am very happy here. At last, I am at peace. I am watching over my family and protecting them."

She gently kissed Sophia on the cheek and disappeared. Sophia had no idea how long she had been sleeping, but when she awoke she felt happier than she had felt in a long time.

Chapter 28

Doyle was so involved with his own problems that he never wondered or cared that his wife had moved to another bedroom. He was deep in thought about José Leon. The treasure hunt might be his key to freedom. If he found enough paintings he would flee the country with them. He could change his identity and have enough money to be free. *Freedom!* what a sweet thought.

Meanwhile, Paris sat in Dr. Wolf's office and said, "I have been thinking about what you said and everything that has happened between Doyle and me. My memory has come back. I remember waking up after I had a nightmare and crying. He started to shake me by the shoulders saying I had ruined his sleep. He ordered me out of my own bedroom and grabbed me. And I fell, hitting my head on the corner of the end table. Doyle picked me up and dumped me on the floor of a bedroom down the hall.

"The next morning he called and told me to move my clothes and belongings to another bedroom. My face and hair were covered with blood."

Dr. Wolf was surprised at how relatively calm she was at this new revelation. "What are you going to do with this knowledge?"

"I am going to tell my family what occurred. I have already moved out of the bedroom I shared with Doyle. I have one more session with you and then I will return to Louisiana with my mother. Oh, and I'm pregnant. I believe this will complicate my decisions.

"Paris thought for a few moments and then she started smiling, "I am not in love with Doyle anymore. I owe him nothing. I am not going to live with a man who has beaten me physically and mentally. I am deserving of a man who will love me and treat me with respect. Thank you, doctor."

Lilly met Paris for lunch and they went to small Thai restaurant a few blocks from the doctor's office. After they finished their lunch, Paris looked at her mother and said, "Maman, you are going to be a grand mere."

"Paris, *Ma Petite*, are you going to be alright?"

"Yes, mother. The doctor ran all types of tests. The baby is fine."

"Paris I am very happy for you. I know how much this means to you."

"Mother, I am going to divorce Doyle. I thought that we could leave for Louisiana tomorrow after I have my last session with Dr. Wolf. I'm going to my school today and say goodbye to my students. I'll send them money for more band instruments and set up some music scholarships."

"You have everything so well planned. I'm glad you are taking charge of your life, my beautiful daughter." Lilly said as she blotted the tears falling down her cheeks.

"Maman, I am not telling Papa until we go home."

"That is a very good idea."

Cousin Adrian arrived at the house the same time as Paris and Lilly. Lilly opened the door and welcomed him.

"Do you ladies have a lot of things to pack?"

"We have a tremendous amount of things to take and we are leaving in the early afternoon," Paris replied.

"I have an idea. One of my business associates lives in Miami and owns a moving company. Show me what you cannot take with you and I will have them move your belongings."

"You are a blessing, Adrian! That will make it much easier for Paris and me. We will be able to take everything we want back to Louisiana and not have to come back to get the rest of Paris' belongings."

*****

Paris and Lilly packed that night and the next morning the movers showed up with a stockpile of boxes in every size.

Paris heard Doyle come in very late that night and leave very early the next morning. Paris left him a curt note telling him she was going to Bayou House.

Norris picked up the ladies and ten suitcases at the airport. Lilly had warned him ahead of time to not say anything to Louis about Paris moving her belongings home.

Later that evening the family joined at Bayou House to welcome Paris home and have dinner. Maryanne made all of Paris' favorite dishes for dinner.

After dinner was finished, and the last piece of strawberry pie had been devoured, Paris said, "I have two announcements to make. I'm pregnant with a baby girl. And I am going to divorce Doyle."

There was total shock and silence at the table when she finished speaking. Her father came up and hugged her. He had tears in his eyes as he kissed her and congratulated her.

"Paris I am so happy about both your announcements. I am thrilled."

Juliet and Pierre kissed her and congratulated her as did Sophia and Papa Joe.

Juliet said, "We are all thrilled for you. Have you told Doyle about this?"

"No, I prefer to tell him with my family around me in Louisiana rather than in Miami."

"I think that is a very good plan Paris. Have your family back you up."

"Thank you, Papa. I knew you would understand. I don't want to discuss my relationship with Doyle or explain any of the reasons I want a divorce. I just want my freedom."

Lilly looked at her daughter and smiled. "Paris you owe us no explanations. You owe Doyle no explanations. You have to do what makes you happy. We want you to be happy."

Sophia hugged Paris and said, "I am so happy for you. You are going to be a very good mother."

Paris looked at her family and she could see their love and affection on their faces. "I am so lucky to have such a wonderful family. Very few people have the privilege of being surrounded by people who love them."

Paris was exhausted and said goodnight to her family. She kissed everyone and hugged them affectionately as she cheerfully went upstairs to her childhood bedroom to sleep.

After Paris had gone to her room, Louis looked at his family a big smile on his face, beaming with pride. "I am very happy, I am thrilled. Doyle can no longer hurt Paris. Better yet, she's not heartbroken."

"You are right Louis. We have Dr. Wolf to thank for this epiphany."

"Lilly, do you think she will be able to carry the baby full term without having another miscarriage?"

"The doctor seems to think that she will be able to. He tested Paris and the baby for everything imaginable and the baby appears to be perfectly normal. You're going to be a grandfather!"

Pierre looked at his brother thoughtfully, "Everything is going to work out well Louis. We are going to use his greed against him. We'll coax Doyle into signing a contract stating that he forgoes all parental rights to his child. In addition, he will sign the petition agreeing to his divorce from Paris. Nor will he make any claim for compensation from Paris or the Viverette estate. In return he will have legal ownership to the paintings he acquires during the treasure hunt."

Louis laughed "Very good thinking brother. I would not want him taking my grandchild to a Leon family picnic. But truly, he deserves nothing after almost killing my daughter and becoming engaged to another woman while still married!"

"What if my daughter wishes to share parental rights with Doyle?"

"We will have to cross that bridge when we come to it, Lilly. But in the meantime we have a plan in place to protect our daughter and granddaughter.

"I have just about completed the details for the treasure hunt. I know the family will be pleased by the results. Remember it is much better to feed an enemy than to starve him. People think twice before biting the hand that feeds them."

Everyone said goodnight and walked to their homes.

Paris could not fall asleep in her room. She walked across the hall to Suzette's room, removed the sapphire blue silk bedspread and curled up in Suzette's blue silk sheets. The aroma of Suzette's perfume pervaded the room and lulled Paris to sleep.

Some hours later Paris felt Suzette's presence next to her.

"Paris, I am so glad you came home. You are on a path filled with love and a wondrous future. Sleep well my beautiful girl."

Paris fell into a comfortable peaceful sleep. When she awoke, she felt energized and filled with confidence. A sense of peace and resolution pervaded the air.

Chapter 29

Doyle woke up to an empty house. He had been so enmeshed with Adriana and the Leons he had not given any thought to Paris or her family.

He went to the closet and realized all of Paris' personal belongings were gone. He looked all over the house for a clue to her whereabouts. The icy fingers of reality jolted him into motion and he re-aligned his priorities.

Doyle called Paris on her cellphone. No answer. He called Bayou House. Norris answered the phone and told him Paris had gone somewhere with her mother for the day. Doyle called the Moses residence and Sophia answered the phone. He tried using his most cordial voice with Sophia as he asked about the treasure hunt. Sophia was polite and friendly. She assured him they were expecting him to participate in the treasure hunt and she looked forward seeing him in two days. He noted that her voice was polite but not overly friendly. He breathed a sigh of relief. He was safe for the time being. He fervently said a Hail Mary and then thanked the Blessed Mother for sparing him from ruination. He went to his office and had his secretary send Paris a large flower bouquet and gift package of sweets with a lovely note.

While he was contemplating how to save his marriage, Doyle's cellphone rang. It was Adriana with her whiny voice telling him, once again, that he had to take her to dinner. He had a fantasy of putting his fingers around her plump neck and strangling her.

*****

Two days later Doyle was in Louisiana and Norris picked him up from the airport. Paris never returned his phone calls and the fact that she didn't even meet him at the airport led him to believe that he was going to have quite a challenge to win his wife back. Norris drove him to the guest cottages down the road from the main house. Apparently everyone was aware of the fact that Doyle and Paris were sharing separate quarters.

Norris opened the cottage for Doyle, told him cocktails would be served at the main house at six and rapidly left the cottage. Doyle noticed that Norris seemed anxious to get away from him.

He was at the main house at six. Cocktails were being served in the Pavilion. Everyone was already there with the exception of Paris. He greeted the family warmly and when Louis offered him a martini he readily accepted.

"Where's Paris?" Doyle asked casually.

Lilly replied, "Paris has a terrible headache, so she's dining in her room."

He was surprised to see that Sophia's Aunt Seri and Mr. Charles were dining with the family. He hoped that they were not going to be participating in the treasure hunt as well as the other members of the family. He managed to smile as he endeavored to emanate friendliness. Everyone was polite and friendly to him but all of the family appeared to wear a guarded expression.

Louis was grilling steaks and corn on the grill. Conversation changed to the details of the treasure hunt the following morning.

Joseph explained the ground rules to Doyle. "We want to get an early start tomorrow morning so we will meet on the verandah for breakfast at seven. We will have a drawing. Each person will draw two slips of paper which will give them the right to search two areas on the plantation where Jon Charles may have hidden his paintings. We will all have a lot of fun and hopefully become a little richer in the next two days."

After dinner coffee was served with cognac and everyone left directly afterward so they would be fresh for the next day's activities.

Doyle went to his room in the guest cottage and called Paris on her cellphone. His call went directly to voicemail. It was going to be difficult to charm his wife if she refused to see him or talk to him.

The next morning Doyle met with the other four treasure hunters on the verandah of Bayou House. Norris had set up a simple buffet breakfast on the verandah and everyone helped themselves. Doyle found himself spoiled whenever he stayed with the Viverettes in Louisiana. He could always count on freshly squeezed orange juice, chicory coffee, freshly baked bread and cinnamon rolls for breakfast.

After breakfast Joseph handed Doyle a crystal bowl to choose two folded pieces of paper, which would determine his fate. He said a Hail Mary and with baited breath put his hand in the bowl and pulled out his choices. Joseph passed the bowl to Louis so he could remove his two entries and then the bowl was passed to Pierre. Joseph reached in the bowl and took the remaining entries.

Joseph opened his slips of paper and read them out loud. "I will be visiting the old company store and the old school house."

Louis read his two slips of paper. "I have the pleasure of ransacking the old kitchen and the hospital."

Pierre flipped open his slips of paper, "Looks like I will be searching the blacksmith's and the slaughterhouse."

Doyle read his out loud, "I have the sugar mill and the old church. That's strange I've never noticed a sugar mill on the property before."

Norris replied, "That's because it is on the other side of the plantation; so are the other buildings. I have packed picnic boxes and cold drinks for all of you gentlemen and I will drop you off at your destinations and pick you up at five p.m."

Doyle was panting to arrive at his destination. He could hardly wait to start searching for Jon Charles' art work.

Doyle chose the old mill as his first selection to seek his fortune. From the outside, the old mill looked like a small white wooden building with a large chimney and a large wind mill adjacent to it. The exterior of the mill was kept in its original state, as were the other buildings on the plantation.

Doyle looked at the building and thought to himself, "this is going to be a cinch to search." Then he walked in the door and realized that apparently over the years the old mill had become a storage room for junk. The mill was covered with wall-to-wall stuff. He realized he was going to have to clear everything out of the mill before he could find anything. The first thing he removed was a butter churn, and then he waded through the rest of the junk around him. Doyle moved rubber tubes, scales, all types of sticky rollers, air pumps, circular knifes, sticky perforated boxes, masses of fertilizer, large glass bottles, boards and all sorts of metal objects that he could not identify.

By the time he stopped for lunch and looked at his watch, he could not believe it was two o'clock in the afternoon. With everything cleared out he searched every inch of the sugar mill and found absolutely no art work. He managed to climb up an old rickety ladder to search the inside of the chimney. Then he climbed to the top of the ladder and used an ancient broom to dislodge all the cob webs above him. Pounds of dirt and soot fell all over him. He persevered to the very top of the chimney but there was no art work to be found. When five o'clock rolled around he was dirty, defeated and depressed.

Norris arrived in his clean Rolls Royce and looked at the filthy, red-eyed Doyle. The other three men were already in the car. Norris opened the trunk of his car and pulled out a blanket which he handed to Doyle to wrap himself in. They dropped a pitiful looking Doyle off at his cottage and told him dinner would be served at eight. He ripped his clothes off and ran to the shower where he steamed himself in rapturous clean water and Hermes soap. He then fell into a deep sleep, waking only when Norris called him and told that the family was waiting for him to join them for dinner. He quickly threw on clean clothes and walked to the verandah.

The first thing Doyle noticed was Paris was seated at the dinner table. She was wearing a violet dress, which brought out the purple of her eyes and the creaminess of her white skin. He thought she looked radiant. She was absolutely beautiful. He could not take his eyes off of her.

The next thing he noticed was an oil painting sitting on a large easel. He stared at the large painting of a blacksmith shoeing a sorrel mare with eyes of shining gold in front of the blacksmith's cottage. The painting was remarkably colorful; he was mesmerized by it. Pierre saw Doyle staring in awe at the painting.

"This is one of the best examples of Jon Charles' work that I have ever seen. I was very lucky that I found it at the blacksmith's shop. Tomorrow is another day I am sure you to will find some paintings."

Doyle, trying to distract himself from his anger, sat down at the dinner table next to Paris, saying, "Paris you look absolutely breathtaking."

Paris smiled, looked at Doyle and said impassively, "Thank you for the lovely compliment."

Norris served wine to everyone at the table as everyone discussed the happenings of the day. Louis looked at Doyle shaking his head in bewilderment, "You surely looked like you had a horrible day when we picked you up at the sugar mill."

"I moved dozens of boxes and objects and climbed a chimney!"

"I am sure you will have a better day tomorrow," Louis replied.

"I'm sure you are right." Doyle turned to Paris and asked her how she spent her day.

She was polite but distant to him as they spoke of commonplace things while they ate their dinner.

After dinner Doyle asked Paris to take a walk with him around the garden. She acquiesced and they walked out of the house together. As they were walking down the path away from the house Doyle tried to put his arm around Paris and she removed it.

She stopped walking. Looking at Doyle, she said in a clear calm voice, "Doyle I am divorcing you. My memory returned. You dragged me out of our bedroom giving no thought to the fact that my head was covered with blood!" The more she spoke, the more heated she became. "To add insult to injury, you called me the next day told me you were going out of town for the weekend then demanded I move my belongings out of our bedroom. Ironically you forgot that the house and everything in it belonged to me and my family!"

Doyle was speechless; he hadn't prepared himself for the possibility that Paris would regain her memory. He had been so caught up in the tangled web he wove for himself with the Leon family.

He finally replied, "I'm sorry Paris. You are right, I have abused you. I have been a horrible husband to you. Please give me another chance! I will make it up to you. I love you. I want to take you to the Bahamas where we can have a second honeymoon together. I'm a changed man."

Paris quietly listened to him. When he finished speaking she said, "Goodnight Doyle. I will not degrade myself by listening to anything else you have to say." She then turned her back on him and walked away.

He realized he could not run after her in front of her family so he walked down the path to his cottage. He went to his guestroom and helped himself to a double scotch from the wet bar in his room. It was good scotch. Before he was even aware of it he consumed the whole bottle of Glenfiddich.

He imagined Paris' family was aware that he had abused her. He felt exposed and humiliated. There would be no trip to the Bahamas. There would be no millions of dollars in life insurance. He was penniless. Doyle fell asleep fully dressed sitting on a chair in his guestroom. He awakened about an hour later. He was a man with a mission. His only salvation was to go to the old church and search for Jon Charles' paintings.

He changed into a pair of jeans, T-shirt and tennis shoes and then began to search for a flashlight. He remembered exactly where the old church was. It was only a short distance from the guest cottage. In fact all he had to do was follow the path in front of the cottage and it would lead him to the church.

Within minutes he was at the old white wooden church with the large white cross on the roof. He walked in the church and was amazed to find it freshly painted and immaculately clean. He turned on the lights and the inside of the church dazzled with light. On the side of the wall close to the door was a container with holy water which he ran his fingers through as he made the sign of the cross. There was a statue of Mary with the babe Jesus in her arms and statues of St. Barbara, St. Anthony, St. Lazarus and Our Lady of Charity. The sweet smell of incense scented the church. Masses of fresh flowers covered the altar. Scented votive candles in holders sat on a table across from the altar. The long moveable wooden benches were old and scarred, but the statues of the saints were new and marvelously decorated. He looked beyond the altar and saw fine-looking stained glass adorning the windows of the church.

He felt uneasy as he walked around the church. He sensed there was a presence around him, watching his every movement. He decided to immediately search for the paintings and leave the church as soon as possible.

The first place he decided to look for the paintings was under the long wooden moveable benches. He turned over three benches before he found a wooden casing which slid away and revealed an oil painting on canvas. He smelled the wooden casing and realized it was made of cedar wood which protected the paintings over the decades. He held up the painting which was an exact miniature image of the inside of the church. He kept looking under the benches and found another casing which slid away showing another oil picture, which he held up to the light. This picture portrayed a beautiful woman cradling a small babe in her arms. He studied it carefully and realized the magnificent image was the copy of the statue of Mary holding baby Jesus at the front of the church.

He could not find any more pictures under the benches so he began looking in different places. He looked under the altar and found another painting. It was protected by a casing like the others. He slid the painting away from the casing and anxiously looked at his third oil painting. An exotic woman dressed in a long red gown and wearing a vivid red coral necklace was dancing on the bayou. She had velvety-gold skin, long dark curly hair, and almond-shaped black eyes. Doyle had never seen an oil painting so alive. He could almost feel the heat of her skin through the canvas. He carefully carried his canvases out of the church, shutting the lights off as he walked out.

He had the strangest feeling he was being followed but he knew that was impossible. He was exalted with happiness. He had won. He had six million dollars-worth of paintings in his arms. He would get the pedigrees of the paintings from the family, sign divorce papers for Paris, put the paintings up for auction anonymously, and be in Switzerland in two weeks. He thought about Rio but that was too close to Colombia.

Doyle thought he heard a strange hum coming from the surrounding trees; he looked around but saw nothing except gray moss hanging over the twisted limbs of the ancient oak trees. Suddenly the forest was charged with electricity and the beautiful lady in red, the one adorning the painting he held in his hand, was dancing wildly around him. He was stunned. How could the lady in a picture painted almost two centuries ago come alive and dance in the bayou before his very eyes? She beckoned him to dance with her.

"My God," he thought, "I've never seen a woman as stunning as she."

He carefully rested his paintings on the roots of a large oak tree and ran towards the dazzling dancing lady. He thought he heard the sounds of drums and chanting in the distance. His first thought was that he was so fatigued and hallucinating. Doyle tried to embrace her as she swirled around him. Her loveliness captivated him. She ran away from him and when he caught up with her she danced away from him once more. The sound of the jungle drums and the chanting increased. He was crazed with desire for her. Even from a distance, he could feel heat emanating from her body and her exotic scent. The closer he was to her the more excited he became. His body ached with desire for her. She moved away from him again and he raced after her. The sound of the drums and chanting thundered through the woods. He heard the wind rustling through the oak trees. He was stupefied as he watched the trees bend and sway in all directions.

He finally caught up with his magical wood-nymph clothed in red silk. He put his arms around her and she seemed to evaporate into the mist. She reappeared once more and he embraced her, this time the temperature of her body was so sweltering that she singed his arms. He clung to her despite the intense high temperature of her body. He hypnotically watched as her small long red, yellow and black coral necklaces slid off of her neck and climbed all over his body. Once again she swirled away. Only when he felt dozens of sharp little fangs puncturing his body did he realize he was being attacked by snakes. He tried to move his hands to pull them off of his neck but paralysis had already set in his body and he was unable to move as the coral snakes injected their venom into him. He felt the burning venom flow through his veins as he lay on the ground helpless, but conscious of what was happening.

He suddenly remembered what Louis had said to him after he and Paris announced their engagement. "Doyle you will be like a son to me. Treat my daughter with love and respect, keep her out of harm's way and be loyal to her. If you hurt her or do bodily harm to her you will live to regret it."

The last thing he heard before he sank into oblivion was the sound of Tou-Tou howling at the beginning of daybreak.

Chapter 30

Sophia watched as Shirree and Paris walked up the garden path to her house pushing their identical baby carriages. They both waved to her and Tou-Tou saluted her with a loud bark as he chased after the carriages. It seemed like only yesterday that Shirree and Paris were little girls walking down the very same path wheeling their dolls in identical carriages. They came in the house to visit her and enjoy her freshly squeezed lemonade and homemade chocolate chip cookies. Sophia held the babies and commented on how quickly they were growing.

Angeline Marie Viverette O'Connor was born October 1, 1997. She weighed only four pounds and had to be in an incubator until she gained more weight. Other than being premature she was perfectly healthy. Only after Angeline's birth did Paris allow anyone in her family to buy any baby clothes. Paris was thrilled with her little girl.

Shirree gave birth to Jon Pierre Charles Viverette on November 3, 1997. She never mentioned who fathered Jon Pierre, and no one ever discussed the baby's paternal roots.

Little Angeline O'Connor was only five months old but she already had a full head of golden brown hair and amazing blue purple eyes and a happy disposition. Jon Pierre, who was only seven weeks old, had a few strands of blonde hair on his round head and big brown eyes. Shirree and Paris amassed a library of books devoted to raising happy, healthy babies.

Paris, being the benefactor of Doyle's insurance policy, became instantly two million dollars richer upon his death. She reveled in her good fortune—getting a large sum of money that was not expected is a marvelous experience; like winning the lottery. Paris donated a large portion of it to the school where she volunteered in Miami and attempted to share her happiness by helping other worthy causes.

Louis and Pierre, both proud grandfathers, were obsessed with taking pictures of their grandchildren at all times—when they were sleeping, eating or just being. Lilly, Juliet and Sophia were fixated with shopping for baby clothes and toys for the infants.

Being surrounded by loving friends and family made life easier and livelier for Paris and Angeline. After much heartache and tragedy,

Paris was happy, healthy and living in the city they loved: New Orleans.

Doyle's mysterious death by coral snake bites—a snake not native to the area—remained a mystery, although Sophia had some suspicions about the painting of Angeline that he had found on the night of his death.

The coral snake is a reluctant killer of mankind. It prefers small frogs. A person must almost invite the slow, calm and painless death its toxic bite provides and since the creation of an anti-venom in the 1960s there have been no human deaths in the U.S. attributed to this placid reptile which rarely grows more than two feet in length.

Lilly, Juliet and Sophia were fixated with shopping for baby clothes and toys for the infants. Sophia gave both mothers identical brightly colored musical animal mobiles she had bought for the infant's cribs. Shirree and Paris were enchanted by the colorful happy little animals that would rotate above their babies' cribs and play, "Mary had a little lamb." They could not thank Sophia enough for her gift.

The girls stayed a couple of hours and then packed up their babies, diaper bags and new mobiles and started to walk home. It was almost Christmas time and Sophia could not believe all the changes that occurred in 1997. Shirree's divorce from Mark was finalized in three weeks and he was totally out of their lives.

After weeks of being crucified by the press Louis hired a public relations firm to clear Paris' name. Paris was so involved with motherhood that she neither read nor watched anything that did not have anything to do with babies. She was amazed when her father told her about the smear campaign that the Franco-Leon family had launched against her. Louis told her about the public relations firm he was hiring and the subtle tactics they would be using to gradually counteract the negative publicity that had been circulated about her.

Paris seemed perplexed about the venomous things that had been printed about her. She did not want to think about the ugly accusations that had been made. She was more than happy to have her father solve the problem of her character assignation.

The first action taken by the firm was to explain Doyle's death on a reality show that re-enacted unique deaths. The sheriff's department happily appeared on the show; in fact they were thrilled to be on television. They were proud of their police department and all the modern equipment their Parish owned. The lead detective Sam Durand was about thirty-five; had light brown hair cut very short, and a stocky build. His smiling tanned face was covered with freckles, and his kind big blue eyes dominated his face. He had a master's degree in criminology from a local college.

He went over the details of the case starting with the call they received at seven in the morning from Joseph Moses. He began his dissertation with "We arrived at seven-fifteen and found the body near a large wild oak tree. It rained in the early hours of the morning and the ground was still muddy. The only foot prints going in the direction of the Oak tree from the guest house were the decedents, and they were dry.

"The rain had stopped about six in the morning. Mr. Moses found the body about seven in the morning and called us immediately from his cell phone. His footprints originated at his house and ended at the body under the oak tree, and the surrounding area. His three dogs' footprints were over the area also. All of their foot prints were still wet. He stayed with the body until we arrived.

"An ambulance arrived a few minutes after my officers arrived and took the body to the coroner's office. My men and I took pictures of the area where the decedent was found. We photographed the foot prints and searched for anything else that could be important to our investigation."

The coroner, Mason Deveroux, was the next to speak. He explained the details of the autopsy he conducted. "The decedent had a blood alcohol level of .29. Legally if your blood alcohol is .08 you are considered intoxicated. The decedent's blood level was so high that he was in a stupor; he could not properly understand anything and had impaired sensations. Mr. O'Conner was bitten by Arizona coral snakes which are more dangerous than the snakes indigenous to our area.

"We put out a reward for information leading to the owner of the Arizona Coral snakes. A student from the local college studying herpetology came forth and told us he brought a few Coral snakes from Arizona to compare their size and venom with the other two types of Coral snakes found in the United Sates. Somehow they crawled out of their cages and disappeared. He apologized for not reporting the loss of the snakes to the sheriff's department."

Sam and the coroner brought a cage of snakes with them to the television show. They held each snake up and explained which were poisonous, and which were harmless. There were a lot of snakes to see. The bayou literally crawled with poisonous and non-poisonous snakes. The most attractive of all the snakes were the brilliantly colored Coral snakes.

The television show was received very well by the public and was replayed several times. The next thing the public relations firm did was to keep distributing information to the press about the volunteer work Paris did as a music teacher in inner city schools in Miami and New Orleans. The articles also mentioned that she donated musical instruments to schools that could not afford to buy instruments. She also set up music scholarships in Miami and Louisiana. Newspapers and magazines also carried stories about the philanthropic Viverette family. Lists of the charities they supported all over the world became public knowledge.

The gossip about Paris and the Viverette family became yesterday's news and Paris ceased being a negative target for the press. Papa Joseph returned the three paintings Jon Charles painted to their resting places in the old church. The family decided that the paintings were part of the church and not meant to reside anywhere else.

Sophia was mystified about the coincidence that befell Paris. Out of all the men in the world why did she end up marrying the man who was the son of Daniel O'Connor who raped her mother, and was her father. Paris' tragic marriage was to her half-brother. Daniel O'Connor was also the grandfather of her daughter. It was incongruous that two generations of O'Connor men damaged two generations of Viverette woman. She had never showed the diary to her husband or anyone else but she decided to share it with him today. Perhaps he could explain the tangled web of destiny that hovered over her loved ones.

About the Author

Charlene Touby is a former Miami and New Orleans resident who is both fascinated with and deeply appreciative of local history and customs. She is currently a resident of Winston Salem, N.C. This is her first novel and has been abridged in this edition because a great deal of the historical facts she accumulated are incidental to the telling of the compelling story she has written.

Charlene is mother of a daughter, Laurel (resident of NYC), a son, Michael (resident of Winston Salem) and grandmother of Hannah, Harrison and Rebecca Touby.